ALL'S FAIR IN LOVE AND LEADERBOARDS

ALINA LANE

ISBN: 978-1-7368977-6-8 (ebook)

ISBN: 978-1-7368977-7-5 (paperback)

Cover Design by: Najla Qamber, Najla Qamber Designs

Edited by: Jessica Snyder Edits and Happily Editing Anns

Printed in United States of America

https://alinalane.com

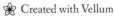 Created with Vellum

JOIN ALINA LANE'S NEWSLETTER

Want to receive exclusive news, content, specials and giveaways!

Subscribers are always the first to hear about Alina's new books and projects.

See the back of the book for details on how to sign up.

To Claire and Breanna
For all the things.
Love you.

1

MEADOW

THERE ARE THREE THINGS IN THE WORLD I CAN'T stand. The obscene cost of nut butter, EagleEyeBeastPI, and Griffin Gallagher.

Now those might seem like weird things to hate. But I promise they all make sense.

Let's talk about nut butter. The deliciously smooth and never ever crunchy—because that's a travesty—peanut butter is pennies on the dollar in comparison to the cost of the specialty nut butters my palate prefers. Almond, cashew, hazelnut...the list of deliciousness goes on and on.

I can pick up a tub o' peanut butter for under ten bucks at my local chain grocery store, but try that with Nutella or pistachio butter? Not possible. Even walnut butter is massively more expensive than plain-Jane, stick it between two pieces of bread and go about your day peanut butter.

One might call me a snobby nut butter consumer, but I've been known to get down with a solid peanut spread when I have to. It all depends on the day of the week and how I'm feeling. Let's face it. Some butters are just made better than others. My pantry holds more than enough options on the worst of days to keep my addiction to high protein, high fat, high calorie options alive and thriving.

Finding the jar of my go-to almond butter depleted is enough to blip my heart rate—but this morning the scrape of my butter knife along the plastic container of deliciousness causes irritation to slice along my shoulders. Which means a trip to the warehouse style bulk grocery store is in my future —because it's the only place I can get the best almond butter in existence. I'm an amazing neighbor, so I'll check with the other people on my floor of the apartment complex to see what they need.

I already have the membership card, so they might as well benefit from it, right?

I snag a pad of paper and head down the hallway, starting at the farthest apartment from my own. Owen Garcia answers his door. Shouts of laughter echo behind him from his kids and husband, Miguel. They've lived in the building for about three years, the longest out of everyone, and their daughters are the cutest kids I've ever seen in my life.

"Hey, Meadow, how's it going?"

I hold up my notepad. "You guys need anything?" Owen's an editor for the valley newspaper, and Miguel is a public defense attorney, so they usually have a list for me since they're both busy and I'm happy to help.

"Oh my God, yes. Thank you. One second. Let me get you our list."

When I first started offering to grab them anything they needed while I was out, they didn't want to take advantage of me. But after Maddy, their six-year-old, came down with a stomach bug when Miguel was in court, a panicked Owen asked me to run to the store for them. Now? They have a standing invite to the block parties my parents throw.

"How was the ride this morning?" Owen asks as he hands me the list.

I scoff. "Second place—again."

"You'll catch him eventually." There's a crashing sound in the background, and Owen spins to find the damage, his door shutting behind him.

Tanking my ride this morning brings us to the number two thing I can't stand. It used to be I could strap on my riding shoes and clip in to my favorite heavy metal, EDM, or groove rides and sweat myself into my happy place for the day.

Now, I wake up and sign in to my favorite classes and trail behind EagleEyeBeastPI. Every. Single. Day. When I first got the follow request I approved it because I'm always down to make a new friend, and one that's in the same line of business as I am was welcome.

What I wasn't ready for was him skunking me every morning and leaving me in the dust on the leaderboards. I'm used to being the top dog on those leaderboards. But no longer. Now I have him to contend with.

I tuck their list in my pocket and knock on Mr. Hadid's door, though he almost never answers. He's lived here for about a year, but I haven't been able to make a lot of progress with him.

Mrs. Nelson is my last stop, and I inch my way to her door like a ninja on a stealth mission.

Which brings us to hate number three. I hate that I can't ask my eighty-year-old neighbor, Mrs. Nelson, diagonally across the hall if she needs a jumbo pack of toilet paper or incontinence underwear without *him* hearing.

Griffin Samson Gallagher. The bane of my existence.

He moved in six months ago, and it's been hell ever since.

As a private investigator, I see some of the worst people humanity has to offer, and yet Gallagher still managed to hit my "irks me beyond imagination" list. And he ends up on the "can't kill him because I look terrible in orange" list at least weekly.

Last month I was prepping for the store run, and there he was, leaning against the wall, hipshot, arrogant, and the ultimate pain in my ass. I passed him with the intention of ignoring him when he requested I pick up a jumbo pack of magnum-size condoms.

Did I buy them? You bet. I didn't even charge him. If his mission in life is to annoy me with his very existence, then mine is to ensure he doesn't reproduce himself. Really —it's my duty to humanity. Some people volunteer at charities; some build houses in countries that lack running water or food. I make sure my neighbor has more than enough birth control to survive a nuclear war.

As of right now, I'm out of almond butter, tanked my ride, and am actively avoiding the bane of my existence.

My hand is poised to knock when the door at my back opens, and I kiss any hope of this day being okayish goodbye.

"Well, lookee what we have here. If it isn't Flower Power herself."

Goddammit.

Twisting, I take in the most evil being in creation. Trademark smirk in place, there he is, leaning in his damn doorway, and I clinically absorb his appearance. Gallagher's not handsome in a traditional sense. It's almost as if his features formed in a "this is what you get" way and his genetics said "challenge accepted" on making them work. The hawkish nose, the most stubborn jaw line, and a mouth so lush it's in direct contradiction to his arresting features shouldn't work, but they do.

Another thing, he's not tall. I'm five six, but if I wore heels, I'd likely match him in height. Whipcord lean, he looks skinny, but he's not. That's a red herring for fools who underestimate him—like I did.

The first time I came across my neighbor wasn't in the apartment building. Oh no. It was at the end of a twenty-minute skip chase where Gallagher jumped out from around a corner and clotheslined the perp. Then he had the audacity to challenge me for the contract completion. I ended up claiming the bounty, but ultimately he got the last laugh when I came home from work to find him moving in next door to me. In the six short months since he's moved in, we've gone head-to-head on a number of jobs, so I see more than my fair share of his face. The case leaderboard my sisters and I use to track our case completion and compete in a fun family manner in the office is a visual list of my losses right along with my losing streak on the bike every morning. It's starting to sting. I used to run both boards and now I can barely keep up on either.

"What do you want, Gallagher?"

"You shopping again?"

Is it possible to roll my eyes so hard I give myself a concussion? Asking for myself.

"Yes," I say. I'm so going to regret this. I know that I'm going to. "Did you need anything?"

A sinister twinkle brightens his cognac-colored eyes, and today is going to be the worst Thursday in existence.

"Now that you mention it, I could use some more condoms, but also some lube."

"Lube?" I sputter. Also, how in the hell was he able to

go through a mega pack of prophylactics in less than a month?

You know what? Never mind. I don't want to know.

"Yeah. The one with the industrial-sized bottle and pump lever. I'd go myself, but I have an appointment with a beautiful woman this morning."

Oh. My. God. He cannot be for real. Ew.

Wait a second. I smirk. "I didn't know that you had that much trouble arousing your partners, Gallagher."

"Oh, it's not for me, Flower Power."

I ignore the juvenile nickname he thinks is hilarious or cute. As if I haven't heard it all before. "Then who's it for?"

"You, of course."

"What do you mean, it's for me?" I haven't dated in who knows how long, and that's not something that I have the time or the willingness to change in the near future. And I buy my own lubrication, thank you very much.

He opens the door at his back and fires his parting shot. "I figure it'd be easier to remove the perpetual stick shoved up your ass if you had a little gliding help. See ya later, Flower Power." He shoots me a smug grin and jaunty salute. Before I can flay the skin from his bones with a scathing retort, he turns back into his apartment and closes the door.

Motherfucker.

I hate Griffin Gallagher.

PHOENICIAN INVESTIGATIONS HAS BEEN HOUSED in the same small house-turned-office in downtown Phoenix since my mom announced she was pregnant with triplets and my dad realized more than just their one-bedroom apartment was about to change.

My sisters and I basically grew up here. As kids, we cleaned, filed, and probably made more work for our dad than we cleared, but we eventually moved to our own cases and have leaned into our individual strengths.

The slate-blue front door slams behind me as I snarl and stomp my way back to the converted kitchen we use as a breakroom.

I yell, "I'm going to go to jail for murder. Don't post my bail because I will be guilty."

"I'll grab my shovel," Willow calls.

"I've got the hydrofluoric acid," Fawn says.

I slide the coffees I picked up on the way onto the counter with more force than is necessary and drop into the chair next to Willow.

Fawn and Willow share a speaking glance. Fawn asks, "Gallagher or EagleEye morning?"

I jerk my shoulders and try to shake my head at the same time, trying to fidget my way out of murder plans. Fawn cocks an eyebrow, her eyes laughing at me.

Willow also finds my aggravation funny and smirks at me. "Do you ever think that they're the same person?"

"No, because I haven't pissed off the karma gods that much in any of my lifetimes."

They both laugh at the surly tone.

My sisters suck.

"So which was it?" Willow asks.

"This morning? Both of them. But rounded out with the trifecta of being out of almond butter."

I nod and grab the coffee cup marked with an *M* and take a sip. The sweet taste of coffee hits my tastebuds, and it's not a Nutella and banana sandwich, but it goes a long way in cooling my ire with this morning.

"Why don't you block him?" Willow asks.

I rear back. "And let him think he won? No."

"Meadow. You don't actually know this guy. Who the hell cares if he thinks he won? The sooner you oust him from your morning, the better off you'll be. Mark my words."

"What'd Griff do?" Fawn asks with a familiarity I don't appreciate.

"Griff? Since when are we using his first name *and* shortening it?" I squawk.

"Come on. It's kinda funny. He's an ass because he knows it bothers you. If we were in elementary school, I'd say he liked you. Maybe this is his adult way of pulling your pigtails."

Ew. No.

"Willow. He doesn't like me. We can barely live in the same building without toppling it. Don't get me started on the stupid shit he asked me to pick him up from Costco this morning."

Both of them grab their coffees and settle in, eagerly awaiting the next episode in the saga of weird shit Gallagher makes me buy.

Willow asks, "Was it another bearskin rug?"

"Or a smart toilet?" Fawn jumps in.

"More condoms, despite buying him a hundred-pack last month, and then he asked for the jumbo bottle of lube apparently sold there."

I didn't know lube came in that size, or that it was available to purchase anywhere outside of shady Internet sites where your whole identity is confidential.

"He did not. Costco sells that?"

I'm nodding before Fawn finishes her question. If I had to be traumatized by my neurotic neighbor, I'm sharing that experience with the both of them.

"They sure do, and based on the reviews, it puts all the other lubes to shame in the back-door-assistance department."

Willow's smirk morphs into a grimace of disgust and she stands, grabbing her coffee before saying, "Well, I'm off to meet with a client. Dinner at Fawn's tonight?"

Fawn nods and says, "Yep! We're having lasagna."

"Damn it, Fawn. I didn't sweat through a sixty-minute climb ride this morning to eat both pasta and cheese this evening."

"Sorry, not sorry! See you at six. Loves." She grabs her coffee and heads upstairs to her office.

"Loves," I respond.

Dad sticks his head around the corner of the kitchen and asks, "Who are we killing this morning, Sweet Pea?"

I'm surprised to see him this early. He's been toying with the idea of retiring—again—and usually comes in later. He's been mentioning retirement every six months or so for a couple of years now, but nothing ever comes from it. Especially considering we all get our competitive spirit from him. He's just lying in wait to take the top spot on the firm's case board. But we keep him on his toes.

Fawn, Willie, and I have a pool going on his actual retirement. Whoever gets within a month of the date of his last case gets all the moola. Routinely, we add ten dollars here and there, and it's up to a nice chunk of change after the number of times he's claimed he's going to start "scaling back."

"Nobody, Dad. Just bitching. What are you doing here so early?"

"Uh. Wanted to talk to you about something."

"Sure, what's up?"

Dad opens his mouth to say something and my phone

buzzes in my pocket. My best friend's name flashes across the screen.

I hold up my finger to Dad and say, "One second."

I swipe to accept the call. "Hey, Jenn."

"Meadow." My scalp prickles and gooseflesh runs down my arms because she sounds terrified.

Please don't let this be what I think it is. Please.

"What happened?"

"I just got a breather call. A bench warrant was issued for him this morning."

Fuck. Fuck. Fuck.

I take a deep breath. Nothing good comes from an investigator losing her shit and panicking. Sweat beads on my hairline, and my heart thumps painfully against my sternum.

"Lock your doors. I'm on my way. I'll be there in ten minutes. Do not open the door for anyone, and I mean anyone."

I hang up the phone and Dad says, "Bobby called. One of your perps skipped bail. Martin—"

"Martin Hernandez. Jenn's ex," I interrupt.

"Shit."

I grab my car keys off the table and shove my phone in my pocket. "Yep. The idiot had court this morning and didn't show. Why did they let him out on bail in the first place?"

"I don't know, Sweet Pea. You want me to call Bobby and say you're taking the trace?"

I head toward the front door, Dad keeping pace with me. "I don't know, probably. But he'll run fast and far if he sees me."

"That's why we chase him down."

"Jennifer's safety comes first here. I think he called her

this morning. I'll be back later and we can figure it out, but I have to go get her now."

I let the door slam behind me and run for my car.

Jennifer's house is in Glendale, a suburb west of Phoenix. After breaking a few land-speed records, I pull into the driveway and park. There's an older model Ford parked along the street, but otherwise no other cars. Dense black security screens cover her windows, and if you look closely enough, you can make out the security lights on the front corners of the roof with the cameras attached to them.

I know all about her security system. I helped her install it after all.

The flagstone path mostly muffles my footsteps as I walk up. Just as I cross into the shadowed cover of the porch, the door opens.

I pull Jenn in for a hug. Hard. We dealt with Martin being granted bail, knowing that he would eventually have to pay for his assault. Her security system wasn't the first part of us planning for him getting out of jail. Since he was arrested, she's moved from Phoenix to Glendale and not shared her new address with many people.

I'm grateful she's in a new place that he knows nothing about.

"Hey. It's okay. We'll figure it out. Let's go inside," I say, while rubbing her back.

We break apart and head inside. I kick off my shoes and set them in the little tray she has beside the door.

"I'm making some tea. You want?"

"Sure." I follow her into the kitchen.

Her movements are jerky as she fills the kettle. I hate feeling like this. My shoulders twitch with the need to get out there and look for him. To investigate and track this bastard down.

The slight tremor in Jenn's hand as she scoops out loose tea leaves is enough to get me moving. I step around the island and bump her hip with mine. "Here, let me. Tell me about the call."

The fear in her blue eyes pisses me off and weighs my shoulders down with guilt.

If I had seen the signs sooner, maybe we wouldn't be here.

No. I can't think like that. I'm better off focusing on what I can do.

There's nothing in the world that I wouldn't do for my family. And Jenn is definitely family at this point.

She sucks in a lungful of air and starts. "I was just getting logged into work for the day. I'd planned to work from home for the first part of the day since I have therapy this morning. My phone rang and it was an unknown number, but I answered it anyway. No one said anything, but then heavy breathing came through the line. I think I said something sarcastic like 'real mature, asshole' and I was about to hang up when there was a muffled pop in the background. It wasn't loud, but it startled me, so I hung up."

"Okay, what happened after you hung up?"

"The more that I sat there thinking about it, the more my gut started pinging. So I looked and saw the bench warrant was issued, then I called you."

After another breath I say, "We don't know a lot at this point, but Bobby called Dad—"

"Are you going to trace him?"

"Yes, even though if he saw me looking for him, he'd run far in the other direction. I still have to talk to Dad about the logistics, but"—I make eye contact and hold it—"you're going to be covered every single step of the way. You got me?"

Jenn's chin wobbles and a single tear escapes and runs down her cheek. "I got you."

Fucking abusers.

She's my best friend. The next thing to family and I couldn't protect her from one asshole.

"I think that you should come stay with me or my parents for a little bit. If that was Martin who called, then he managed to get his hands on your new number, and it's a safe bet that he might know where you live now. Let's operate with caution in regard to your personal information. Plus, there's safety in numbers. If you're not at Dad's, then you're at the office with us. If you can't get into the office, you can still work remotely, right?"

A small curl to her lips accompanies her reply. "I don't know—what do you think Andrew will say?"

I smile at that. Jenn had been a fraud analyst for a large bank, but after everything with Martin, Dad offered her a job at Phoenician as our office manager.

"I think there's not really a safer place for you than work right now and Dad would agree."

And there's not. Between Fawn, Willow, Dad, and me, there's almost always someone in the office. The security system is top of the line, something that Fawn—the overprotective one of us—designed.

I have a spare room and a pullout sofa. It's not much, but we can make it work if she decides to stay with me at night instead of my parents.

This might seem over the top. An abusive boyfriend getting out of jail is one thing, but after failing my friend the last time, I won't let her down again.

"Okay, I'll stay with you."

I bump my shoulder next to hers and say, "It'll be like college all over again."

Jenn smiles lightly. "Hopefully much cleaner this time."

I smile and pull my phone out to send a family group message.

Me: Change of plans. Dinner at 7 at my place tonight. Martin's skipped bail and Jenn got a breather call.

I silence my phone and tuck it in my pocket. I can answer their questions later, but for right now I'm going to shove the worry down and help my friend pack.

2

GRIFFIN

HEAT BEATS DOWN ON MY SHOULDERS IN A FIERY WAVE of misery. May in Phoenix, Arizona, is no joke. It's not even nine in the morning yet. After moving down from Flagstaff six months ago, I thought I'd be okay once the temps started rising, but this is worse than I thought.

Automatic doors whoosh open, and a wave of cool air blows over me as I walk into the assisted living facility.

Amy, one of the day managers, has her head buried in a desk drawer as she digs for something.

"Hey, Amy. How's it going?"

Her cap of salt-and-pepper hair pops up. "Hi Griff. No complaints, how about you?"

"Still upright and breathing." I scrawl my name on the visitors' form and jot down the time.

"I can see that. You got a minute?" She's careful to keep her face neutral.

Fuck. "Sure."

"Come on, let's talk in the office. You want a bottle of water?"

"Nah, thanks though."

I dutifully follow until I'm seated in front of a desk, and Amy taps away on her keyboard.

"Griffin,"—a small smile curls her lips—"we love Celia, and we're happy to have her here, but the last two months your payment has been paid late, and we haven't gotten this month's yet. So I have to have this conversation with you. That's all this is at this point—a conversation. Now tell me, is everything okay?"

Amy was the one who helped me get Mom transferred here. She walked me through the steps and stages of everything, and I'm grateful to her, but I'm still gonna lie my ass off. "Yeah, everything's fine. Work was just a little slow, but it's starting to pick up."

Everything is far from fine. Work isn't slow—there's tons of work. But no matter how many jobs I pick up, I never seem to get ahead.

I'm the new guy in town. Trying to establish my reputation among the other private investigators means I'm picking up a lot of jobs and working like two dogs.

I thought moving us down here would be the best option. Mom needs the resources that are more readily available. But those resources and this care facility aren't cheap.

But it's what she needs.

Amy sighs, and I know she knows I'm lying.

The truth is I'm fucking tired. I'm running on fumes, and there's no end in sight for the foreseeable future, but I can't stop now. I love my job. Outwitting criminals is a fun game of cat and mouse, and I love to win. But even that isn't enough to help with the never-ending exhaustion that comes with working eighty hours a week.

"Okay, Griff. I'll hold off sending out a formal notice for

a week or two. You let me know if you need anything, you hear?"

"Yes, ma'am." I stand, not able to handle another ounce of the pity weighing the room down.

I'll just have to work harder. Earn more money, take more cases. I can sleep when I'm dead, right?

Amy doesn't have to give me more time to pay. According to the contract I signed when moving Mom in, if payment isn't made by the fifth of each month, fees start to incur, and eviction proceedings can start.

I'm just very lucky that I know and have charmed most of the staff who work here. Helps that Mom isn't harmful or aggressive.

I walk down the green hallway before turning on to the yellow. The colored walls help the residents stay oriented. With every step nearer to Mom's rooms, my tennis shoes squeak on the linoleum floor. The closer I get, the more I lock away the scared little boy that knows his mom is going to die. Each time I enter this building, I don't know if it's going to be a good day or a bad day. My shields are in place by the time I knock on her door.

"Come in," Mom calls from inside, and I open the door.

Sunlight pours in from the windows, and the curtains are open to let in the light and view. Papago Park is right across the road, so the view of the mountains is killer.

"Hey, honey. How's your day going?"

Her eyes clear and bright, Mom waves me into the living room. Her eyes are always the first thing I look at. Some days they're hazy and unfocused. I hate the hazy days.

It started out small—with her forgetting an appointment or to pay a bill. There wasn't a pattern to it, no rhyme or reason, but when she forgot my birthday and called me by her dead brother's name a couple of times, we went to the doctor together.

Early onset Alzheimer's. Those three words scared the shit out of me, out of us. I knew nothing about the disease. Research helped me understand what was happening and what the future looked like. And it increased the fear exponentially.

I was twenty-three. She was fifty-two.

The doctor had explained it like it was a stroke of bad luck for her to get it so young, as if it was a cold she had caught. As if it wouldn't eventually kill her.

My mom is slowly losing her memories until one day she'll have none left. Memories of me, of her life. Everything. And there isn't a damn thing I can do other than make sure she's taken care of. So every day I wake up with the intention of working myself down to the bone. Because it's all I can do for her.

It sucks. But knowing it can't be cured, that it will keep getting worse, sucks harder.

Last year, it became clear she needed more support than I was able or qualified to give. Several people recommended this assisted living facility, so I got her on the waitlist, and we moved to Phoenix as soon as they called with an opening.

Since then, I've been scraping the monthly payment together. Some months there's a buffer, other months there isn't, but I do what I can.

I come as often as I can, but Thursdays are her favorite —bingo day. Each week we go to the activities center together, with me tucking away each nugget of her I can.

"Everything's fine, Mom. You ready for bingo?"

"You gonna steal my winning bingo card again?"

"If you get bingo before I do again. Absolutely." I grin.

The last couple of weeks I've come here to play, Mom's been the one to hit bingo first, if either of us gets it at all.

She narrows her eyes at me, but I'm not about to lie and tell her I won't cheat to win at bingo.

Not when it makes her laugh when I steal her card and shout before she can.

I want her to have all the laughter she can for as long as she can. If that means that I make a fool of myself, then that's what I'll do.

I stand and say, "Come on, let's get down there so we can get the good seats."

We walk the yellow, green, and then the purple hallways to reach the multipurpose room. There's a huge projector-style screen at the front of the room, and like Mom's apartment, more than three-quarters of the room is made up of windows that let in light.

Some of the other residents are already here and getting seated. I help Mom to her chair, though she doesn't struggle with mobility as much as some of the other residents here today.

Amy is standing at the front with the randomizer website pulled up. I tell Mom, "Be right back," and walk to the front.

"You need a hand?"

Amy hands me a stack of cards and the bucket of paint markers used to dot numbers as they're called. "Have at it, handsome."

Once I'm sure everyone has a card and marker, I make my way back to Mom. She's got her four cards in a square block and is double-fisting the markers. Her dark brown hair is pulled back in the same ponytail she wears every day. I know if I were to hug her, she'd smell like shampoo and home. I've never figured out exactly what the scent is, but it's the feel of comforting memories and safe spaces.

Someday, that's going to be gone. It's coming faster and faster with every day that passes.

Mom lifts her head and eyes me before putting her arms in front of her cards, as if to protect them from me.

She takes her bingo very seriously.

Not that I blame her—my competitive spirit is genetic.

I smile at her and settle into my seat, knowing the facade of cheer I wear like a cloak is starting to wane. Every visit is harder, and it's only going to get worse. How much longer can I do this without breaking?

As long as it takes.

THE ICONIC DIVING lady on the Starlite Hotel's retro sign comes into view as my quarry peels off Main Street and turns north on Lindsey before dipping between buildings. Pumping my arms for speed, I vault a chain-link fence right after him. Our feet pound on the asphalt, and I get close enough to hear the breath whoosh out of him. He's winded.

My heart thumps against my breastbone and my lungs work like bellows. The ringing in my ears signals I've reached my limit.

But he's so close I can almost touch the back of his stained white T-shirt.

I take a chance and leap, my shoulder clipping him mid-back and sending us both crashing to the pavement. Cement rips into my elbow as I land, and I hiss out a curse even as I scramble up to pin him down.

From my back pocket, I pull out zip-tie handcuffs and

secure his hands behind his back while digging my knee into his spine to hold him still.

My sweat is sweating by the time I drag and load the still uncooperative fugitive into the back of my car.

I slam the door shut and take a minute to bend over and catch my breath.

Goddamn, I feel old.

Once I catch my breath, I climb into the driver's seat and grab my water bottle to chug. Low muttered curses sound from the back seat, but I ignore them as I cap the bottle and start the car with a sigh. Sprinting after a bail jumper in today's heat has sapped the energy right out of me.

Blood from the elbow scrape has dried in a line down my arm. I'm gritty, thirsty, tired, and it's fucking hot. But I earned my pay today. Or at least I will have when I drop him off at the jail on Fourth Avenue.

A thirty-minute drive from Mesa to Phoenix will be more than enough time to cool off in the blessed AC of my car.

My phone chimes with a call, and I answer.

"Hey, top, what's the op?"

Bobby McIntire is one of several bail bondsmen I contract with. Bail enforcement agents can be freelance or work for a larger firm. Because of my need for flexibility, I freelance. Keeps things simple and makes my life a lot easier to juggle when other people don't depend on me.

"Griff, I've got a job for you." Bobby relates the basic details of the guy he wants me to track down as I navigate traffic, which is always a bitch.

"What's the pay?"

"A hundred K," he answers.

All of the air whistles out of my lungs as I do the math on what the guy's bail was.

"You posted a million-dollar bail? He must have had awesome collateral."

"His house in Paradise Valley. Appraised at two point two."

"Million?" And here I am willing to track the scum down for a paltry ten percent.

Oh, how the other half lives. Must be fucking nice.

"Why so much? What the hell did he do?" I ask.

"Domestic violence. He beat his girlfriend so badly the prosecutor tried to pin him with attempted murder. Didn't take, but the judge went hard on bail since the charge is aggravated assault. Guy was supposed to show to court this morning and didn't."

Bobby knows damn well I'll want this skip, regardless of the massive paycheck. After a particularly rough case last year, he found me at the bottom of a bottle of bourbon, questioning my life choices and ranting about the lack of justice for survivors of domestic assault to anyone who'd listen. I had just finished a case that still occasionally gave me nightmares.

"Send me the details. I've got a trace to drop off, but I'll swing by and get the POA when I'm done."

I exit the I-10 on Seventh Avenue and head south. Most of the cops working the desk here know me, so the drop-off should be quick.

I park at one of the meters set up along the road and pop in enough quarters to keep it from giving me yet another parking ticket.

I open the back door, and the smell hits me. Warm ammonia lights my olfactory senses on fire. I look at the crotch of the guy's pants—wet.

Dude is wearing a shit-eating grin, and I stifle the urge to sigh.

I've been doing this a long time—seven years to be exact—and if he thinks pissing his pants in the back seat of my car is going to deter me from turning him in, he's dead wrong. The only thing he's succeeded in doing is pissing me off because now I have to make another stop to get my car detailed before I get to Bobby's.

So much for getting to bed at a decent time tonight. If anything, my day just got a hell of a lot longer.

Gritting my teeth, I reach into the back seat and haul the asshole out while he laughs at me.

"Yeah, yeah, yuk it up."

Fucker.

3

MEADOW

Downtown Phoenix has always fascinated me. I love the commingled mom-and-pop places that have been here since the dawn of time and the newer shops and restaurants that have moved in more recently. There's perpetual light-rail construction, colorful graffiti, no parking, and the frenetic energy of traffic and businesspeople.

When I was young, I helped my mom volunteer at a race to stop domestic violence, and on the way home, she accidentally drove the wrong way on a one-way street downtown. When a cop stopped her and pointed it out, she burst out in panicked laughter, thinking the cop was going to arrest her and her own bail-bond-agent husband would have to post her bail.

Downtown to me is fun, frantic laughter in the car with my mom and sisters followed by ice cream.

I pull into the parking lot across from the nondescript building that houses Bobby's place. He has an official business name, but I never remember what it is. A bubbling fountain is quiet in the shaded courtyard of the building. The temperature drops ten degrees in the shade even though it's early evening and barely starting to cool off.

I'm gonna get in, get information, and get out.

I dropped Jenn at my place earlier with strict instructions to move into the spare room and keep the door locked and the alarm activated.

Normally I'd be hitting the pavement, accepting the trace and tracking this fucker down, but I need information first. Martin isn't the smartest guy I've ever met, but if he gets wind that I'm looking for him and bounces, Jenn will be living on pins and needles much longer than she needs to.

I pull open the office door, and a wave of air conditioning escapes to cool the light sheen of sweat on my forehead. The door doesn't shut fully before it's opened again and someone bumps into my back.

"Oh, excuse me," I say, moving out of the way.

"Flower Power?"

What karma god did I piss off to get saddled with so much shit on a Thursday?

"What the hell are you doing here?"

Gallagher and I speak at the same time, but before either of us has a chance to say anything else, Bobby pokes his head out of his office.

"Oh, good. You're both here. Come in, come in."

Bobby McIntire is a big teddy bear of a man with a perfectly groomed handlebar mustache who always wears a button-down shirt with a bolo tie. He and my dad have been friends since before I was born, and he's often at Sunday dinners.

I can count on one hand the number of times that I've gotten away with back talking to this man. So I do what I'm told and shut up and follow him.

Either it's professional courtesy or good manners, but

Gallagher follows me back into the cramped office decorated only with file folders that cover every square inch of horizontal space.

I take the only seat not covered, barely beating Gallagher to the chair.

Ha. Shithead has to stand.

I don't know why that makes me smile, but it does. It's a small cheap victory, but I'll take it.

My Spidey-senses are pinging. If he thinks he's getting this trace...

Sure, he can be here for any job, but I'd bet my bike that I'm about to get horrible news.

In the six months since he's moved in, I've lost a total of thirteen cases to him. Most of them skip traces, some of them process serves, all of them *mine*.

I've worked damn hard to get where I am in this career, and he just comes into town and starts to jump all over my jobs.

Oh hell no.

Sometimes bail bondsmen give jobs to one investigator, or firm, and other times it goes out on the wire to multiple private investigators, and whoever gets the perp first gets the pay. The first job he stole from me wasn't that bad. I've lost jobs to other agents—sparingly, but it happens. I was waiting to serve a corporate drone divorce papers when calm as you please, Gallagher saunters up, sweet-talks the receptionist that shot me full of chilly glares not five minutes before, and gets buzzed right up to the guy.

After that, it was the Nunez case. John Nunez got into a fight with his wife, went to a bar for a drink, and had several. Instead of calling a cab, he decided to drive home and got hit with a DUI. When he didn't show up for court, I accepted the trace on him only to have Gallagher once again swoop in and steal the bounty right out from under me.

Once I realized what was happening, I got sneakier in my case selection, and I've gotten him back a few times.

When one of us does manage to snatch a case out from the other, there's hostility and animosity to go around, but I don't think we've ever knowingly gone after the same guy.

Like I think is about to happen.

Bobby skirts around his desk after dumping a pile of papers on a filing cabinet. He needs a Jennifer in his life. His desk looks suspiciously like Dad's before we hired her and she worked to convert us to all digital files.

"You both know why you're here. Let's talk about Martin Hernandez."

My stomach sinks as Bobby rummages around his desk until he unearths a sage-green file folder. Opening it, he continues, "Martin was due in court this morning for the first hearing in his case, but didn't show. I got the notification and called Andrew immediately this morning, and then I reached Griffin this afternoon."

Umbrage burns my throat and I croak out, "Why would you give him this job? You know this case should go to me."

Gallagher makes a noise next to me, but before he can say anything, Bobby holds up his finger. Shooting me a look that says my question is as stupid as it sounds, Bobby says, "Mead, this job has a lot of money on the line. I want as many people on this as I can get, and I know hiring you means I get your sisters too. After talking with Andrew, we decided that it would be best if you and Griffin worked together using all of your combined resources to find him."

Shock closes my throat. He expects me to work with Griffin Asshat Gallagher? There's no way. Either he'll piss me off and I'll kill him, or I'll piss him off and he'll kill me, but either way neither one of us would survive the possibility of joining forces.

"Not just no, but hell no." I can't bite off the words fast enough. I know there are risks to me looking for Martin on my own. But it doesn't mean that I have to subject myself to working with Gallagher.

"Aw, Flower Power's afraid of a little competition."

"I'm not afraid..."

Wait. What if it *was* a competition? What if we each went about it our own way, using our own styles to track down Martin? I wouldn't be forced to work with him, but we'd still catch Martin. Win-win.

I turn to him. "Can I talk to you privately for a minute?"

His eyes go squinty, like he's waiting for the other shoe to drop. I stand, so he's forced to follow and step out of Bobby's office back into the reception area.

Gallagher trails behind me and shuts the door behind him.

"What?" he snaps.

"Look, I don't want to work with you any more than you want to work with me, right?" I whisper.

"Right."

I give him my best smile. "So, how about a friendly wager?"

"What do you have in mind?"

"We agree to work together to Bobby, but each of us uses our own ways to track Martin, with no one the wiser."

"And what about your family; won't they get suspicious?"

"No. My sisters will cover for me. They know"—I wrinkle my nose—"our distaste for each other." At least I hope my sisters will cover for me.

"How would the pay work?"

I roll my eyes. What's with all the questions?

"We'd split it, of course."

He's already shaking his head before I can even finish.

Contrary bastard.

"No can do, Flower Power."

"Why the hell not?" I whisper-squeak.

"Because as much as I'd love to find this asshole before you, which we both know would happen, I'm not about to piss off the guy who gives me a good fifty percent of my jobs, and definitely not on a job with this size of pay."

"One, you wouldn't catch him before me, and two, you scared of a little competition, Gallagher?" I toss his words back at him.

He scoffs. "Against you? Hell no. My answer's still no. We work together no matter how much that sticks in your craw."

Fucking hell. Maybe I did piss off the karma gods in a past life.

"Fine," I grit out.

He smirks at me. "Glad to do business with you, and just think—with all the time we'll be spending together, we're sure to be best friends."

Not likely. There's no way I can work with him—at least not without burning the city to the ground in the meantime.

But that doesn't mean it won't be fun to kick his ass at his own sneaky game.

By the time Martin's in handcuffs, Gallagher isn't going to know what hit him.

4

GRIFFIN

You've got to be shitting me. I did not see that coming. Meadow "Flower Power" Ridley suggesting a competition to see who can bring in Martin Hernandez first.

Since the day I moved into my apartment building, Meadow's poked at my nerves, and I've doubled down on antagonizing her back. Starting shit with her first thing in the morning is enough to make my dick twitch, and since I have no social life, I take my fun wherever I can get it these days.

It's perverse and makes me an asshole, but seeing the evil glint in Meadow's eyes right before she verbally eviscerates me is the most fun I have on a given day. I'm not going to stop anytime soon.

When we run into each other on jobs?

Even better.

Working together? This is going to be fun—well, for me at least.

So what if I snagged a couple of bounties out from under her; that's no reason to hate a guy, right? Open bounties are *open*. It means anyone can take them. Sure, there's been some friendly ribbing when I managed to snag a bad guy first in the past, but nothing like this.

She's been my neighbor for six months. We've traded insults and had pissing matches. I know a lot about Meadow, but why she hates me so much is still a mystery.

Looking at her now and that need to win firing her eyes up like gems? I couldn't pass up the opportunity to tweak her a little.

"Let's go back in."

She sails ahead of me. "Whatever."

I roll my eyes. She has to have the last word.

Bobby's eyebrow climbs up his forehead when we walk back in. "Did the two of you come to an understanding?"

I throw a thumb in her direction and fuck with Meadow some more. "Yeah. She'll give me the case; I'll find the guy and she can go and do—something else."

Hazel eyes shoot sparks at me as she says, "I'm not giving you anything, ass weasel—"

Bobby raps his knuckles on his desk.

"Enough. I don't know what the deal is between you two, and frankly I don't give a shit. Meadow, where are your manners? Griffin, you and I both know you can't be turning down jobs. Especially one as lucrative as this. Either you work together on this, or I'm giving the job to someone else and stonewalling you both. And that's my final say."

He holds out the folder and asks, "So, what'll it be?"

Meadow dusts her hands down her thighs and turns to me. "Don't fuck this up."

I stare at her dumbly as she starts to leave. "You don't want to see the file?"

She turns back and looks at me over her shoulder. "I

have my own copy. But you should brace yourself when you get to the pictures. They're...a lot."

I shut the file folder and look back at Bobby as the door closes behind her.

"Power of Attorney in here?" I ask. I can look for Martin all I want, but without a POA, I can't pick him up and return him to jail.

"Yeah."

That's all the confirmation I need. I can handle the initial research from my apartment, and I need to get started if I'm going to find this guy. The fact that Meadow has a file and has had ample time to look it over already puts me at a disadvantage.

I stand to leave when Bobby's voice stops me.

"A word of advice, son," Bobby calls before I can leave the room.

I turn back, but don't say anything.

"Meadow's like a daughter to me. Respect toward her isn't optional. Keep me up to date on the case."

And just like that, I'm dismissed.

What the fuck? What about respect for me?

Stomping out of the room would look childish, so I don't. I do, however, close the building door—firmly. High-tailing it out to the road, I don't see Meadow's car anywhere, and I'll be damned if I turn into a doormat to accommodate her.

Traffic on the way home is light, and soon I'm back at the apartment with a bag of Doritos sitting abandoned on the couch cushion next to me. My laptop is balanced on my left knee and a notepad on the right. I'm jotting down some notes from Martin's file. Meadow was right to warn me about the pictures. The victim's face was wrecked—the asshole did a number on her. My blood boils and I can't look at the pictures for long before I have to set them aside and start the search for him elsewhere.

My first order of business is to find Jennifer Sullivan and talk to her. I have her phone number and address in the file that Bobby gave me since she's a potential lead.

Might as well get it over with.

I call the number listed. At the same time, Meadow's phone next door starts to ring. It's a different ring tone than normal, though. Maybe she's dating a new guy?

The voice mail message on my call begins, and I drop the thoughts about Meadow's love life to leave a short message asking Ms. Sullivan to return my call.

Something Bobby said tugs at the back of my mind. *I called Andrew and then I called later and offered the job to Griffin.*

Who's Andrew, and why did Bobby call him before he called me?

Something isn't adding up here.

On a hunch, I pull up the website for Meadow's firm. Better to know your rival, right? I looked at the site briefly once or twice when I first moved to town and wanted to learn the professional landscape, but it's been a while since I was on it to look for anything specific.

The site lists client testimonials, services offered, and all of the accreditations and certificates the firm holds. I click the About Us link at the top of the page, and the first thing I see is a photo of an older man with *Andrew Ridley, Owner* beneath it. Meadow's unsmiling headshot screams professional capability. Next to her are the two other women who look damn near identical to her that I've seen coming and going from her apartment a few times.

Under the Additional Staff heading is a name that has

me muttering "Shit." And like dominos falling into place, I understand why Meadow would have a copy of the file.

Snatching the papers up, I scan them until I find what I'm looking for—the original emergency call about Martin and the subsequent arrest all started with Meadow calling 9-1-1.

Fuck.

A muffled knock comes through the walls, and I hear a door open and close to my left, in Meadow's apartment. I glance at the clock.

Her laughter carries into my living room. For as uptight as she is, her laughter is appealing as hell. It's throaty and more carefree than her sisters'. Like she doesn't care what anyone thinks of what she finds humorous. She lets it all out there without a care in the world.

I lean into my gut suspicions and redial Jennifer's number. Again, within seconds of the phone ringing in my ear, I hear ringing from next door.

Our prime lead is sitting right next door with the woman who's supposed to be working with me to solve the case, and she didn't think to mention it.

Oh, Flower Power. It's on.

My head of steam carries me out of my apartment and next door, but then I pause at her door.

"Come in, you idiot. We can see you standing there," Meadow calls through the door, and my blood sparks even as my cock reacts to the unrepressed irritation in her voice.

I shove the door open. "When were you going to tell me that Jennifer Sullivan worked for you?"

Meadow comes out of the kitchen, her hair tied up and face flushed. It'd be a good look if she wasn't a sharp thorn in my ass.

"Was I supposed to tell you? Oh, and when would I have had the time?"

"Maybe if you hadn't run out of Bobby's like your ass was on fire, you could have disclosed that little nugget of information. A little professional courtesy would be nice. That's probably asking too much from you, huh?"

Her gaze clashes with mine. "What's that supposed to mean?"

"Just because you're pissy I didn't go along with your asinine idea doesn't mean you get to withhold information, Flower Power." I add sarcastically, "It's not like this is your employee or anything. I figured you'd care more, but what do I know?"

Meadow's jaw drops. Before she can take aim and fire at me, her sister—Fawn, if I'm remembering the website photos correctly—steps between us.

"Hey now. Both of you. Chill for a second, okay."

Meadow's breathing hard, and my heart is hammering. I suck in a few lungfuls of air and work on bringing my blood pressure back down.

I took that way too far, way too fast.

I scrub a hand through my hair. "Look. I'm sorry. I didn't mean that. But I'm starting from zero here, when you obviously have history with the victim."

"I prefer the term survivor, if you don't mind."

I turn and meet impossibly blue eyes in a stunner of a face. She's no Meadow, but still a looker. I'm shocked for several seconds until it clicks.

"You're Jennifer Sullivan."

She smiles. "I am. You must be Griffin. Nice to meet you." She holds her hand out and I nod as we shake.

"You know what?" a fourth voice calls. "I can't do drama on an empty stomach. Can we eat yet?"

"Food's done. Gallagher, are you staying?" Meadow asks like the question tastes sour in her mouth.

The smell of garlic hangs heavy in the air, and my stomach gurgles. Those chips I had earlier aren't doing much to hold me over, and far be it from me to turn down a free meal.

I smile and say, "I'd be happy to stay if you'll have me."

One way or another I'm going to get more information out of this woman.

There isn't enough room for a dining table in our units, so we all crowd around the coffee table, sitting on the floor or the couch.

I don't know who made the chicken alfredo tonight, but it's fucking fantastic.

I don't realize that I'm wolfing down dinner until the absence of forks scraping bowls registers.

All eyes are on me, and heat creeps into my face. "This is delicious. So thanks to whoever cooked."

"That would be Meadow, but it's a family recipe," Willow says.

Meadow's hazel eyes flick to mine but don't hold. Even I can admit that it's weird that I'm sitting in her living room eating her excellent food when this morning I was ragging on her and asking her to grab me a bulk-sized lube when she did a grocery run.

My face grows hotter, and if I'd known this morning that I'd be eating dinner with them I'd...Nah. I still would have yanked her chain.

And yes. I do spend a weird amount of time on the warehouse's website to see what item I can ask her to grab for me that's most likely going to cause that murderous gleam to come into her eyes.

Not to mention me coming in guns blazing when I discovered she'd pulled a fast one on me.

To say that we're pushing each other's buttons today would be an understatement.

But one of these days she's going to snap that rigid control she has over herself, and I want to be there when it happens.

5
———

GRIFFIN

MEADOW TAKES THE LAST BITE OF HER DINNER, WIPES her mouth with a napkin, and says, "I'm going to start at the beginning, and you can ask questions when I'm done. A little over a year ago, Jennifer's mom called me to conduct an investigation on Martin. She was worried Jenn was being abused. During the six-month investigation, I found Martin was isolating Jennifer, was controlling and stopping her from seeing her friends, her family, and her coworkers. The night before I was going to approach Jennifer with an offer of help, I was tailing them downtown when he pulled her into an alley and assaulted her."

Fuck.

She reaches out and places a hand on Jennifer's knee. To comfort her or keep her silent, I don't know. "I called for him to get off her, and when he wouldn't, I pulled my taser out and he charged me. I fired, he went down, and I cuffed him and called 9-1-1." Her fingers twitch, like she wants to sink another fifty thousand volts into the man.

"Has he contacted her since he jumped?" I ask.

"We believe he has, but he didn't talk and the number

was unknown, so we can't confirm if it was actually him or not."

I look at Jennifer. "You were with this guy for a while, right? Any idea where he'd be, or where we can start to look for him?"

She shakes her head. "He has a couple of cousins left alive, but not any who'd harbor a fugitive. That side of his family doesn't really talk to him, and his parents died right before we met, so he's alone."

"No other family? Friends? No one who would know how to get hold of him?"

Jennifer shakes her head again. "He never introduced me to friends. But I wasn't very keen on meeting anyone he'd consider a friend, you know? I did my best to keep my head down and survive."

"Okay. I'm assuming Jennifer's protection detail is going to come from you three?"

For the first time, Fawn speaks up. "That's Willie's specialty. So she'll come up with a schedule for us, and we'll juggle our other cases around making sure Jenn has someone here with her at all times."

"What's your specialty?"

Meadow jumps in and says, "Fawn and Dad are in charge of background checks, and Fawn does most of our cyber investigations. I skip trace and work process serves—the more active cases we take—while Willow heads up the protection services arm of the business. We all float across each other's specialty as needed."

I nod. "What about Jenn's work?"

Willow says, "She's our office manager. She keeps us all in line like a drill sergeant on peppy steroids."

Meadow stands and starts to gather bowls. A voice in my head that sounds suspiciously like my mother demands I get my ass up and help with cleaning.

When she tries to take my bowl, I lever myself up from the floor, grab everyone's silverware, and follow her into the kitchen.

She stands at the sink, loading dishes into the dishwasher, and asks, "Did you see the pictures?"

"I did, but I didn't get much further than that."

"He shattered one of her cheekbones, broke her nose. When I got there, he was shoving her against the wall and trying to lift her skirt. She was trying to fight him off blind because both of her eyes had swollen shut by that point. She spent almost two weeks in the hospital for the concussion and surgeries..." Her voice breaks, and her swallow is audible as she tamps down her grief.

Some cases fuck with us. We all learn to cope with it as much as we can, but there are some that affect us. This is one of those for her.

I nudge her out of the way to rinse the pan she's washing. "How'd you two get to be friends?"

A ghost of a smile flits across Meadow's lips. "She sat down next to me at lunch our freshman year in high school and said we should be friends. It was history from there."

"You knew her before..."

She nods. "I did. I didn't catch the warning signs...totally missed them to be honest. I assumed she'd gotten busy. Life gets busy, you know? It wasn't until Cathy—her mom—called me asking if I'd heard from her when I started to get worried."

"This is personal for you."

"She's my best friend, Gallagher. So yeah, this is personal. I'm trusting you with her."

I nod. There's not much else to say. Jenn's covered, so we just have to find him.

Once we have the dishes done, we go out into the living room and I tell Jenn, "Can I have your cell phone for a bit? I'm going to draw him out, or get him to talk if he calls again, assuming that was him the first time. We'll get you a cell phone to use in the meantime."

Fawn asks, "Jealous boyfriend?"

I nod. "Maybe I can piss him off if he calls back—assuming it was Martin that called. Either way, I'm going to start digging."

Jenn says, "I can't let you do that. What if he..."

I place my hand over hers to stop her. "I won't ask you to trust me yet, but you can trust Meadow. Trust in her ability to keep you safe. I can handle myself; I promise."

Meadow answers the unasked question in Jenn's gaze. "He'll do his job. We're going to be as safe as we can."

The belief in her voice sets off an odd reaction chain in my chest that can only mean trouble.

BACK IN MY OWN APARTMENT, I dig into research.

Martin Hernandez is a trust fund baby. His parents were wealthy real estate investors in the valley, and they both passed away when Martin was twenty, leaving him a fortune of money. That money is the only reason he's walking free right now.

I pull up Facebook—it's a treasure trove of data in my line of work. There's a large amount of personal information housed in most profiles. When you share your entire life online, without regard for privacy settings, you open your-self up to someone like me digging through it. My social accounts contain no identifying information, and I post only enough so my profile doesn't get flagged by the bots and shut down.

Searching for Martin Hernandez, I get hundreds of results, but narrowing the results by state and then city doesn't give me anything matching the guy.

Of course not. That would have been too easy.

After double-checking the file, I look up his high school and college to check for groups created by the alumni. I request to join a few and turn my attention to his college. Martin is a true Phoenician. He was born and raised in the valley and decided to stay through his college years.

I pull up the website for his parents' company and start the painstaking process of digging through their social media accounts and cross-referencing any names listed in captions to see if those profiles have anything on Martin.

He was their son, so it stands to reason he could be in some of the business-related posts like charity events, auctions, and collaborations with other companies.

It takes about three hours before I hit pay dirt. Martin and his father stand beside Lucas Marks and his son, Kent, all holding their golf clubs in front of them while they say "cheese" for the camera.

Kent Marks's account is mostly locked down except a few profile pictures. Digging through them over the years, I'm able to make out "Acres" as part of the name of the country club.

Google tells me there are too many of those to visit every one, so I swap to Instagram and dig through the fully public profile he has there.

The corner of a neon sign catches my attention in one of the night shots and I grin.

I just got lucky as hell.

It's late, but I make a few calls. By the time I disconnect, it's nearly two in the morning. My eyes are strained, but I have some solid leads to start my morning.

My email dings with an alert announcing a payment for job completion. I breathe a sigh of relief at the balance showing in my bank account when I log in.

Finally.

Toggling over, I open up Mom's care facility portal, and after double-checking the amounts, I pay her bill.

The amount hasn't changed since we moved her in, but it's better to be safe than sorry when it comes to submitting a payment for such a large amount of money.

Ma's the only family I've ever had—she was an only child, and the guy who fathered me bailed as soon as she told him she was pregnant. She raised me entirely by herself, and I will work myself to the bone to ensure she has what she needs now.

I pay a couple more bills, then shut down my computer and head to the shower. I'll have brunch with Ma when I get up, then head to one of the country clubs in the photos I found online. I need to let Meadow know what I found out too, so we don't have a repeat of the argument in Bobby's office.

Dinner tonight was weird. I don't think Meadow and I have sat in the same place for longer than two minutes without it devolving into a fight. I certainly never thought we'd get through a whole meal together without verbally eviscerating each other.

I glance at the wall our bedrooms share as I crawl into bed. As a light sleeper, I'll probably hear her alarm go off tomorrow morning, but I'm not waking up early to ride.

I'm surprised she hasn't figured it out yet. My username on the stationary bike app is pretty obvious, but she hasn't kicked me in the balls for it yet, so I'm guessing she hasn't made the connection. And since my bike is in the second bedroom that doesn't share a wall with her bedroom, she's never heard me on it.

Being in proximity to Meadow multiple times today has messed with my head.

And nothing good can come of that.

Focusing on completing this job is my number one priority.

Too much depends on it for me to get distracted now.

6

MEADOW

My alarm goes off too damn early sometimes. The caffeine in my preworkout powder is the only thing that got my ass on the bike after the late night with my sisters. As an unexpected treat—thank you, universe—EagleEye was nowhere to be found when I logged in.

Thank God for small favors.

Riding high from my leaderboard victory before the sun came up, I beeline for the kitchen and coffee. Taking that first sip of strong hot coffee clears more of the cobwebs from my brain.

Dinner showed me a new side of Gallagher, one altogether different from the cocky, annoying neighbor I've been dealing with. And I don't know how to feel about it.

Where I expected crude jokes and innuendos, he was serious and focused on Jennifer's safety. He wolfed down his dinner, and the blush that tinted his cheeks afterward was adorable in a weird I don't want to talk about it way. Then he helped clean up as though it was our normal routine.

Thoughts about him keep getting in the way. I pop a couple of pieces of sourdough bread in the toaster. Does he know how to cook or does he rely mostly on takeout? Has he always lived in Phoenix, or is he a transplant like so many others? Has he experienced a desert summer yet?

And why in the hell do I have these questions about a guy I've abhorred for the last six months?

Griffin Gallagher in *off* mode, when he's not intentionally being a douche, is dangerously appealing. I still don't know if I should have told him about my friendship with Jenn, but the more information we both have, the better at this point.

"At least he's cute," Jenn says.

"What?" I squawk, my head snapping toward the living room.

Fawn, Willow, and Jenn are sprawled across my living room furniture with their laptops, the news playing quietly in the background.

She flicks her dark-blue eyes at me and points at the TV, indicating she was talking about the morning news anchor heartthrob she's got the hots for and not the guy floating around my brain like fruit in a punchbowl.

I'm twitchy. All the research and talking was yesterday. Now it's time to take action.

"Oh. Yeah. He's delicious," I reply dutifully.

"You know who else is cute?" Willow is practically vibrating in her seat.

My youngest sister is like a Pomeranian on cocaine at a Friday night rave. I know exactly where she's going with this, and if I don't nip this in the bud, she's never going to drop it.

"Gallagher?" I say and cut her off as she opens her mouth.

"Yep! You know what else I noticed? The hot looks he was shooting you between scarfing down dinner."

"I didn't notice anything of the sort." The only hot looks he aims my way are heat-seeking missiles of misery.

Fawn mumbles under her breath, "Yeah, because you were too busy not looking at him."

I should have expected it. They always team up on me. I look to Jenn for some sort of backup—hell, she's practically a fourth sister—but she gives me a shrug.

Calmly, I pick up a pillow next to me on the chair and chuck it at Willow and Fawn. Two of the corners manage to clip them, and I give myself four points for the double hit.

"Hey!" they shout in unison.

"He was not looking at me. I wasn't avoiding looking at him. He drives me bananas because it amuses him, and I expect some familial loyalty when I'm working with the bane of my existence to find and catch the bad guy."

"Can't you two get along? I mean, it's only one case," Fawn asks.

Out of the three of us, Fawn is the rule follower to the extreme. I don't know why I thought she'd cover my idea of competing with Gallagher. I have an odd sense of loyalty, and Willow is chaos personified, but if Fawn gives her word about something, she doesn't break it. Ever.

"Working with him and making his life easier are two completely different things, Fawn." If I can, I'm going to *work* with him as little as possible.

"Oh! This is going to be good. You can use your superpower against him. He'll never see it coming."

"My superpower?" I ask.

"You blend, Mead. You're like a freaking chameleon. Remember that one cheating spouse case we were on for the CEO a few months ago? God, what was her name?"

I know exactly what she's talking about. "Langham?"

"Yes! Her. You were parked in the hotel lobby for a solid hour before her husband realized you were there, and by that point you had already gotten the footage of him kissing his sidepiece goodbye. You weren't even trying to hid—there was no potted palm in sight—but you went unseen."

I'm shaking my head before she finishes. "That was just luck."

"Oh yeah? What about the Lopez case last year?"

"Can you call it a superpower when the guy was too busy admiring his gym gains to realize that I was taking pictures of him committing workers' comp fraud? I wouldn't exactly call that blending."

Fawn holds up a finger to stop Willow. "Didn't he only work out really late at night? How many people were in the gym?"

"Three," I grumble. They have a point, but I'm not going to say my ability to go unnoticed is a superpower.

It's more like a curse.

Being able to blend, as Willow calls it, can lead to some serious insecurity if I let it. Blending means nothing about me is intriguing or arresting at all.

In a crowd of a hundred people, I'm never the first to be noticed for anything. Hell, it's even worse when I'm next to Jenn. I fade away into obscurity when we go out, which makes me a wonderful wingwoman, but because of it I've had less than stellar experiences in my dating life.

So much so that over the last year or so, I've given up on dating.

I'm done with the time and effort men take.

"See! You should totally use it."

"How about I just do my job?" I face Jenn. "Can you

tell me anything you think might help? I know Gallagher asked you earlier, but can you think of anywhere to start the search for him?"

When they first started dating, she told me a little about him, then when it tapered off to her never bringing him up in conversation, I assumed that the puppy-love phase had worn off. I should have asked. It's another thing in the long list of my sins I kick myself over.

Jenn's gaze veers off somewhere behind me while she thinks. I want to throw him back in jail more than anything, but I have to find him first.

Under normal circumstances, we'd start with friends and family, but if what Jenn said is accurate—that he doesn't have any family left alive and she didn't meet any of his friends—then we're screwed.

"He has a few cousins around. Or you could look into his parents' business. I know he worked there as a sort of figurehead after they passed away, but he didn't have a real estate license, so he was 'in charge' in a very vague sense of the word. He might have had friends there, but I'm just not sure. He didn't exactly let me meet people close to him, and if we went anywhere, he made it clear I was meant to be seen but not heard."

"Did he have any favorite places to be?" Fawn asks gently. She's had her own past with assholes so she'd have better ideas on how to find them.

"He used to drag me to Talking Stick or the country club almost every weekend. At first, I couldn't go a lot because I'd have work or something, but then it got...worse... and he'd make me go with him. I always suspected it was because he didn't want me to run, because if I was going to, it would have been then."

"Why then?" I ask. Another question I've never asked.

"Because he'd go hours without contacting me while he was there, and I had to work at first. I think those were the times he was at the tables, or in the resort pool. When he went to the country club, his golf buddies had a strict no-phones rule as well, so if I was going to run, it would have been during one of those times."

"Do you remember any of the golf buddies' names?"

"I heard Martin refer to a Kent one time, and a John another, but beyond that no." She shakes her head before saying, "I can't think of anyone else. But the name of the country club was Green Acres, which made me laugh the first time he took me there. So you could start there."

"Why didn't you tell Gallagher any of this over dinner?"

Jenn smiles, the first full mischievous grin I've seen on her face since this whole ordeal started, and says, "Even if you have to work with him, it doesn't mean you can't ditch him now and then."

I return the smile. She could use this as a reason to fall apart, to whine that she needs to be protected, that she's limited in what she's allowed to do, but not my bestie. She's coolheaded, calm, and rational about this. Then again, if she were prone to hysterics, I wouldn't judge her, because this seriously sucks.

I snag my laptop and start to type up some notes. Like I told Gallagher, I have a copy of the file, and I've been studying it for anything I missed the first time around—some crumb or piece of information that could lead us right to the fucker's front door.

"If you think of anything else, lemme know and I'll look into it. For now, I'll swing by the country club this morning and see if anyone can tell me anything about Martin. Who knows? Maybe someone's seen him recently. I'll also stop at his old place and see what I can find there. He's gotta have a hole he's hiding in; we'll trace him back to it and trap his ass."

7

GRIFFIN

GREEN ACRES COUNTRY CLUB IS...INTERESTING. THE pueblo design of the main building climbs over boulders, rocks, and desert landscaping. From what I can see of the people outside, khaki is everywhere, the tans are as fake as the Rolexes, and a category five hurricane wind wouldn't move a single strand of any member's hair.

I bypassed the valet earlier and opted for street level parking. No way am I paying for some fresh-faced teenager to park my car for me when I'm more than capable of doing it myself.

I tug at the hem of one of my nicer button-downs. The dark-blue color has faded over the years, but it still looks okay—mostly.

My neck itches when I climb out of the car and someone turns my way. I shut the car door and shove the tail of my shirt into the waist of my black slacks.

Fucking country clubs. Fucking golf and tennis. What kind of sports are those?

Extracurriculars weren't part of my life growing up. Looking back on it now, I'm grateful Ma's job put food on the table and kept a roof over my head. But unless I was sponsored by another family or it was free, I didn't participate in a lot as a kid.

Golf is as foreign to me as grocery shopping probably is to these people.

Get on with it, Gallagher. Do the damn job.

My fingers dance along my thumb. I hate being out of place. The back of my neck gets hot as I approach the front desk, and the receptionist scrapes her gaze from my scalp to my toes before turning her nose up in a disinterested sneer.

I cross my arms and step up to the desk when I catch sight of an ass I'd recognize anywhere standing next to the bar that's visible from the front desk.

That juicy peach is one I want to bite and one that shouldn't be here.

Flower Power?

The guy sitting next to her is also very familiar, seeing as I spent the better part of the night digging into his connection with our skip. He's talking up a blonde on his right and isn't looking at Meadow.

Her hand traces the stem of a wine glass, and it distracts me enough that it takes a second to see she's taking notes on the conversation between Kent and his female friend.

How the hell did she find this place before me?

Of course.

Jennifer probably told her. Those two are best friends—if she had information on his whereabouts she's loyal to Meadow, not me.

This is the second underhanded technique the dirty little cheater has used.

My legs eat up the distance between us, and irritation drowns the discomfort of being here.

An earthy floral scent teases my nose when I get close

enough to take her arm in hand. I pull, spinning her around, and take an insane amount of pleasure from her startled, wide-eyed gasp.

"What are you doing here?" I hiss and glance around, hoping to avoid a scene. Kent and his lady friend are still too busy laughing a few seats down, and haven't noticed us.

Her stubborn chin kicks into the air, and I'd give my left nut to knock her down a peg, but I know this isn't the time or the place.

"Same as you. Looking for leads on Martin," she whispers.

The receptionist watches us, looking like she's about three seconds away from intervening.

"Outside, now." If I clench my jaw any harder, I'm going to crack a molar, but it's the only thing stopping me from yelling at her.

I should have expected this from her. We've only ever been at each other's throats. Why did I assume she'd play nice?

I won't make that assumption again.

A smirk covers her face, but she says, "Sure." She grabs her notepad as I tug her behind me.

I intertwine our fingers so she can't get away and ignore the thump in my chest at holding her hand.

Am I twelve?

Why she hasn't ripped her hand away yet is anyone's guess, but I'll use what leverage I have for her while I have it.

As soon as I get her outside and far enough from the door, I drop her hand. "What the fuck, Meadow? I thought after finding Jennifer in your apartment last night we agreed to share information."

"Jennifer told me *after* you left last night, and it's not like you'd have shared if you found out first."

"Yes, I would have." Maybe.

"Oh, really? Is that why you knocked on my door this morning with the lead?"

She's goading me, and it's fucking working.

I hate losing. Always have. Always will.

Wait a second.

"Why didn't *you* knock on my door with the lead this morning?"

"I left my apartment early and didn't want to wake you."

"Sure you did. Let's just assume that's correct. It didn't dawn on you to let me know *before* you came here?"

"I don't have to tell you everything the second I learn it, Gallagher."

"Us working together says you do, but maybe you're in it for the glory. I mean, you did catch him the first time, right?"

She winces before a strange look crosses her features, one that's part guilt and part secret.

"What was that?"

"What was what?" she asks.

"That look."

"I don't know what you're talking about."

It hits me like a bag of bricks.

"You're guilty. You feel guilty and that's why you're so hell-bent on finding Martin first. You'd do anything to make sure your best friend is safe again."

Her eyes cut away. "What I feel is irrelevant. It's none of your business if I slap a sign on my ass and shake it in Martin's general direction. How I catch him isn't anyone's business but mine."

"It's how *we* catch him," I bite out. She rolls her eyes at me and turns to leave.

Oh, hell no.

I reach for her arm, but as I do, she whips back around, her feet getting mixed up, and she trips. I catch her, but in the process, her cheek slides against mine and down until my face is buried in her hair.

"Jesus Christ, Flower Power, do you even know how to walk?" I can't look away from her lips. They were so fucking close two seconds ago. I nearly groan when her tongue slips out to gloss the plump lower one.

She shoves against my chest to right herself, but I don't let go of her arms. Her face is flushed, but she won't make eye contact with me so I can figure out what she's thinking. Regardless, I'm not done lecturing her, and she's going to stay put until I've had my say.

"Of course I know how to walk. And if you were trying to kiss me with that oh-so-subtle move, you missed."

That's it.

I've had it with her snarky ass. It's probably the summer heat melting what few brain cells I have left, or maybe I've gone temporarily insane. I'm beyond caring, or defining it, when I bury my hand in her hair and haul her to her toes to crash my mouth against hers. She wants a fucking kiss, she'll get one.

The soft strands of her hair rub against my fingers even as the perfection of her lips cushion mine.

The taste of cherries, tart and sweet, dances along my tastebuds.

Fuck. She's so fucking delicious.

She's not pulling back, and I haven't felt the crack of her hand against my cheek, so I take that as her permission and fully lose my mind.

Gallagher, you're an idiot. Meadow isn't the type to slap —if she wanted you to stop, she'd kick your balls into your throat.

Six fucking months I've wanted to do this. Months that I've been hungry for the feel of her mouth against mine. The sound of her hitched breath egging me on until I give in and steal the oxygen from her lungs. To claim something of her for myself.

Every taunt, every smirk and tease, every goading gauntlet has led us here. I wonder if she saw this coming, or if I'm the only one who's watched the locomotive barreling toward us at breakneck speeds. But fuck me, the wait was worth it. Every second of it.

I nip at her bottom lip, and she moans at the contact. Tunneling my fingers closer to her scalp, I tug at the roots of her hair, eliciting a purr from her that makes my dick jump to attention behind the fly of my jeans. There's a sharp sting in my pecs as she digs her hands into my shirt, twisting the fabric in her grasp, and the worn seams pop at the tension.

I leave the haven of her lips to trail my mouth across the sanctuary of her jaw, sipping at her earlobe, every inch of her skin the answer to my personal prayers.

A throat clearing penetrates the hazy fog of my brain, but I ignore it.

I'm gluttonous. I need more and more of this until I can't breathe, can't think, can't remember why I'm not allowed to have it.

Her hands loosen against my chest, press into me, then push me back.

A valet stares at us. He interrupted the best part of my year, of my life. An unforgivable action, for sure.

My gaze finds Meadow's again, but where I expected to find desire, or even softness, her expression is shock and awkwardness. A shutter of indifference falls between us, and fuck, that hurts.

I pull the tattered remains of my pride around me like a cloak, and in a voice steady enough to earn an award, I say, "Didn't miss that time, did I, Wildflower?"

Her jaw drops, but instead of being left with the usual satisfaction at getting a reaction out of her, something in my chest I won't examine too closely stings like hellfire.

I turn on my heel and stalk back inside. I have a job to complete, one that has nothing to do with Meadow Lark Ridley—though I'm not so sure it's a good thing anymore.

of Lucas Marks running for office when he retires. So his reputation needs to appear squeaky clean, which is what I'm banking on.

"You can't do that." Kent's voice scales two whole octaves, and I smirk.

"Oh, but I can." I pull my phone back and open a new email. I don't bluff.

"Wait. Wait. Just wait a second. I haven't talked to Martin in weeks." Kent's eyes shift back and forth like he's looking for someone to save him.

"Are you sure? You can tell us the truth," Meadow says and touches Kent's arm with concern. Her wide eyes and soft expression broadcast *trust me* vibes.

"Oh, come on, Wildflower. He knows something; that's why he's sweating buckets." I drop my arm and turn to Kent. "Tell us where he is or I'll make sure daddy dearest knows all about your weekend extracurriculars."

One little threat and he folds like an old card table. "Fine. I talked to him a couple of days ago. He called me to ask about selling his parents' place and how long it would take. When I asked where he'd been, he said his ex set him up and he was lying low."

"What'd you tell him about selling the house?" I ask.

He looks to Meadow and she nods for him to go on. "That we could get the team on it and touch base. I'm supposed to meet him next week for lunch at The Breakfast Club."

"Why next week?"

"He said he has some stuff to take care of with the house."

I add checking out the house to the top of my to-do list.

"You're going to keep that lunch appointment, and I'm gonna need the phone number he called you from."

After a few instructions for Kent, I have the beginnings of a plan in place. Unless we catch him before then, we'll meet up early next Thursday morning, and I'll stake out the restaurant where he's meeting Martin. Once Martin shows up, I'll apprehend him and turn him in. Easy peasy, lemon squeezy.

It only takes a few more threats to convince Kent if he calls or tips off Martin in any way he could be held as an accessory, which isn't technically true, but it *is* satisfying to watch the color drain from his face when I break it down for him.

Kent finally skedaddles, and I look around for Meadow. She stepped away a few minutes ago, and I assumed she was heading to the bathroom. But she never returned.

Why the hell would she leave before she got all the information on what I have planned? She's been cutthroat so far—she wants to know what's going on, right?

I grin. No. Meadow wouldn't leave if there was information to be had unless something else sent her running. Something more critical. And I'd bet it was the kiss to end all kisses.

A few more days and this case will be in the bag. The trap is set, ready to close on my quarry, but I have to make sure a stubborn, sexy private investigator doesn't get in my way.

You can run, Wildflower. But you can't hide.

9

MEADOW

How in the hell did things go so far off the rails so quickly?

One minute I was taunting Gallagher—finally getting one up on him—and the next thing I knew he was delivering a scorching kiss from which I still haven't recovered. My panties are damp and my core is strung tight, almost as if it's waiting for the other shoe to drop.

Damn Griffin Gallagher to the fiery pits of hell. He gave me a taste of something and then failed to follow through on the remainder, and my libido does not appreciate his lack of attention to detail.

When I taunted him, it was to cover up my own embarrassment at literally falling into his waiting arms. What am I? A damsel in distress? No, I think not. I'm a savage bitch with a heart of stone, and I'd appreciate it if my inner hormones would remember that.

I don't need a man to catch me when I stumble any more than I need a man to protect me from big, scary dragons.

But he's one hell of a kisser...even I can admit as much.

My original plan to sneak in and find useful information fell flat, and I was reduced to picking up the slack during Griffin's questioning of Kent, which galled the fuck out of me. But I'm nothing if not a flexible professional.

Maintaining a straight face while Griffin outlined Kent's plan to meet Martin should have earned me a medal or an award of some sort. I'm surprised he was willing to detail everything with me standing there.

Considering how bitchy he got about me "hiding information," I figured he'd shut me out of the first lead he got.

Maybe he's not trying to hide anything because I helped him get the information in the first place.

I refuse to think it might be because of the kiss.

No, of course not. It's because we have to work together. That's all.

Especially since I was trying to use my nonexistent flirting skills to get more information when Griffin came back inside and put a stop to it with one claiming move.

When he dropped his arm across my shoulder, the weight of his jealousy settled right along with it. He was seething.

And I'm a horrible person because I was thrilled.

For so long, I've only been the butt of his jokes. Now, after a single kiss, I was able to make him jealous.

But that's irrelevant. Because I cannot do it again. Especially when I'm actively trying to disappear without him noticing I'm gone.

Where the hell are you going to hide, idiot? You're neighbors, for crying out loud.

I shove the irritating thought away. If I can make it to my car, maybe I can get back to my place and then hide in my apartment while I dig into some of the information I gleaned today.

Heavy footsteps slap against the pavement behind me, and I pick up my pace. I'm almost at my car.

Please don't let it be him. Please don't let it—

A hand wraps around my bicep for the second time that day, and I jerk my arm, but his grip remains.

Gallagher pulls me against him, the heat of his body along my back overpowering even in the May sun.

"Where are you going in a hurry, Wildflower?"

Those stupid butterflies flutter around in my tummy again at this new nickname that I definitely dislike. My shoulders shiver at the husky tone, but I fight it back.

He's caused this itch that I can't scratch because I have no time for dating or any other shenanigans. And I'm certainly not scratching it with him—that would be madness.

We hate each other, right?

Then why did it feel so fucking good to give as good as I got in a simple lip-lock? Am I so sexually frustrated even Griffin Gallagher is starting to look good?

I sincerely hope not.

"What?" I do not have the mental fortitude to go to battle with him and come out the victor right now. I just don't.

I spin to face him, and he finally releases my arm.

"Earlier in the club. You were keen to stay in Kent's company after our *disagreement* outside." His eyes rake down me before a sneer curls his lips. "I mean, I guess I can't fault you for using what you have to get an inside track. I just thought you were better than that. Then all of a sudden you take off, so I wonder where you're off to in a hurry?"

Oh, no. He did not.

Because if he did, I am about to rip him a new asshole so

hard he won't be able to take a shit without thinking of me for the rest of his life.

A sweet, yet deadly, smile curls my lips. "I'm not sure I understand what you mean by 'using what I have'?"

He takes another step closer, and my breasts nearly brush his chest as he looms. I refuse to take a step back. Not only because I have limited space between my back and the car door, but because this motherfucker better learn real quick that he can't push me around.

Sure, I'll take the occasional ribbing or his juvenile requests when I do grocery runs, but I won't back down when he questions my integrity and skill as an investigator.

"You know what I mean," he continues, "using all of your *assets* to get what you want from someone to further your own aims."

I hold up a hand. "I'm going to stop you right there. If you try to tell me you've never flirted with a female to get information out of her, you're a damned liar." Considering I've seen it firsthand I know he has.

"That's different."

Yeah. Backpedal, asshole.

"Oh? How so?"

"It just is."

Lovely. Just lovely. I cannot possibly smack the stupid out of the man—my hands would fall off before I got the job done.

"Gallagher, it's not different, and your approval of my professional methods isn't up for discussion, because I. Do. Not. Answer. To. You."

I reach for the door handle.

"You realize you won't be able to catch this guy without my help, right?"

Every last ounce of patience I have for this man has dried up, and I'm done.

"You have that the wrong way around. Me? I don't need this job. My firm doesn't need this job. I want this job because it means protecting a friend and keeping her safe. But you?" He winces and cuts his gaze away.

That's what I thought. "The way you've been up my ass since this job started tells me you *need* it. And I'll only say this once; either you stay in your own lane and we bring Martin in or I'll tell Bobby to give the bounty to someone else. Do you understand me?"

My gut clenches, and I hate every word out of my mouth before I utter it, but he hit a nerve and that fucking hurt.

I've had to prove myself in this career for as long as I can remember. Never to my family, who know and appreciate my skill, but to every other bail bondsman, police officer, and *man* that thinks because I have a vagina, I'm somehow either using it to get ahead or I'm incapable of the same job they do. It's infuriating.

Gallagher's eyes narrow before going flat. "Is that so, Ridley?" The lack of a nickname pinches painfully in my chest.

I don't know why he needs the job, but watching him shut down tells me it's personal, and it's private. Two things that shouldn't mix with business, but for him they do and I stomped all over them.

Like you're one to talk about "personal," Ridley.

My temper got the best of me, and I shouldn't have lashed out like that. But still, I double down and kick my chin higher. "It is. Are we in agreement?"

"I guess I don't have much of a choice, huh?"

Instead of sticking around and giving him the chance to

back out, or worse, throw something horrible at me like I just did to him, I open the car door and climb in. Once the door is shut, I don't waste any time cranking the engine and getting the hell out of there. In my rearview mirror, Griffin's gaze follows me until I can't see him anymore.

Why does it feel like I broke something fragile between us?

10

MEADOW

After that disaster, I'm not in a hurry to get home and tell Jenn about the clusterfuck of the day, so I head to the office. I'll get some work done there in peace, so after shooting off a text to Jenn letting her know I'll be a little longer, I park my ass in my office.

It's a converted bedroom facing the street. When I need to think about a case, to turn it over in my head, I tend to stare out the window and let the details unravel in my mind.

Why would Martin jump bail? He has enough money that his lawyers will probably plead him down. Running exacerbates his situation—now he has a second arrest warrant and the prosecutors will strengthen their case against him.

I worry for a second he's going to come after Jenn, but dismiss it. Other than a breather call, which could have come from anywhere, there's not enough evidence to suggest she's under an acute threat right now. By staying at my place and having my sisters rotate through the apartment, she's doubly guarded. So he won't get to her.

There's a knock on the doorjamb, and my dad pokes his

head in. "Hey, sweetie, you got a minute? I can't get the program I want to open on this thing." He wiggles his iPad at me.

I haven't talked to him since Bobby dropped my new *partner* in my lap yesterday. This might be my chance to get some answers.

"Sure. Come on in." I take the iPad from him. "What are you trying to do?"

"I want to download a report, but it says it downloaded and I have no idea where it went."

I look at the address bar, and sure enough there's a little arrow with a circle. "It is downloaded. Remember, after the last update I walked you through the new way to view downloads?"

His hand comes up to his forehead and he winces. "I'm sorry, Sweet Pea, I forgot."

I hand the device back. "That's okay. While you're here, though, I wanted to ask you something. Why did you tell Bobby I should work with Griffin on this case?"

Dad takes a seat in the chair on the other side of my desk and blows out a breath. "I wondered if you'd be mad at me for that."

"Not mad, but confused. Do you think I can't find him?"

"No. Not at all. If anyone can find him, it's you."

"Then why?"

"I know how much you kicked yourself when we found out what happened to Jennifer in the first place. Working on a case this personal was bound to mess with your head. After talking it through with Bobby, we agreed you two working together on this case was more so you don't get overwhelmed trying to do it all yourself—because you have a habit of taking a lot on your plate."

If I was handed this case and I had no connection to the survivor, I'd probably just treat it like any other job, but because I know and love Jenn, it changes things.

Just like doctors aren't allowed to operate on family and friends, I probably shouldn't be working this skip, since it could be argued I'm not objective enough. Good thing that rule doesn't apply to us.

"Okay."

"How's that going?"

I laugh. "It's not."

"What's going on?"

"I can't stand Gallagher; he drives me fucking crazy. So we're butting heads, and I managed to go for broke and insulted and threatened his job."

Dad winces again. "I know you two don't get along, but he's got good instincts. He's a solid investigator and building a reputation in the city according to Bobby."

"Dad, those 'solid skills' are all charm. He sweet-talks people out of information he then uses to sweep jobs out from under me. The first time I could forgive, but the rest? Not so much. This is my career, and he's making his reputation out of making me a laughingstock."

"Now you're just being dramatic, Meadow. You're one of the most respected PIs in the city, and you know that."

Ugh. He doesn't get it at all. "I do know. But look at how hard I had to work to get where I am. It's taken me years to build my reputation. He's been here for six months and suddenly he's the first person you and Bobby think of when you worry I might be getting too close to a job. Never mind the fact I have two sisters who are also private investigators and plenty of business acquaintances who could fill in just as well."

Dad looks taken aback at my argument. Apparently,

today's the day I piss everyone off. Sure, I might be too close to this case since it involves my best friend, but instead of consulting me like an adult, a capable professional, or an employee, he made a decision that stuck me with someone who gets on my nerves more often than he doesn't. And damn me if his decision doesn't hurt like hell.

Maybe coming into the office was a bad idea. I gather my things and ignore the burning in my eyes. I will not cry like a child whose feelings were hurt. I won't do it. "I'm going to work from home until this case is done. I'll keep you updated." I don't bother trying to keep the hurt out of my voice; it would be impossible.

"Wait, Mead," he calls, but I don't want to continue to have a conversation where I won't be heard in the name of good intentions.

The drive home is uneventful and miserable. I have about ten more minutes I can possibly last in these clothes until they suffocate me. The slacks aren't too bad, but the flouncy dress shirt is uncomfortable.

When I slam into the apartment, Willow, Jenn, and Fawn spring off the couch. I hold a hand up to forestall the questions I know they have. My most pressing issue takes priority right now.

I head for the kitchen, grab a spoon because I have guests, and dig into my jar of almond butter.

If three women weren't watching me, I would have just stuck my finger in the jar like normal.

One heaping spoonful later, the creamy texture and nutty flavor soothe me.

My sisters and Jenn follow me into the kitchen. Fawn asks, "That bad, huh?"

I shake my head and shrug my shoulders while I work

the almond butter in my mouth, hoping I'll be able to swallow it at some point.

The day wasn't that bad, but I can't kick the feeling I hurt Gallagher—just like Dad hurt me—and that wasn't my intention. I have a horrible temper—I get it from my mom. I have a fairly long fuse, but once it's burned down? Take cover.

I shouldn't have lashed out like I did, and now the damage is done. The only thing we can do is move forward from it and catch Martin. Surely once he's back in jail, Gallagher and I will return to the status quo. He'll annoy the snot out of me, and I'll ignore him.

But then you won't get any more kisses.

Hell, no. I do not want more kisses from him. That just invites more drama and feelings into the equation. My job gives me an unobstructed view of how horrible people can be every single day, and I'm not lucky enough to find that one-in-a-million guy who is trustworthy and makes me laugh. I'm better off staying single.

My life is very comfortable, and kisses lead to complications.

I've got family and friends who love me, a job that I enjoy, and all the independence a girl could want.

Nah, dating is for later. Like *way* later in life.

With that thought comes another. I'm going to have to apologize to him. I hate apologizing. Not because I don't like to be wrong—show me one person who does—but because saying sorry means feelings are going to come into play.

Feelings are messy, and dealing with other people's is a pain in the ass.

I force down the last bit of almond butter as Jenn and

my sisters stare at me. Everyone's waiting for an update on Martin and what I found out at the club.

"Gallagher kissed me and I think I hurt his feelings."

That's...not what I meant to say. What the hell is wrong with me? The kitchen breaks out in a cacophony of screeching voices, and I can't pick out a single coherent question.

I shove my fingers between my lips and let out an ear-piercing whistle. The harpies crowding me go silent.

"Jesus God, you guys are loud. I'm changing my clothes before I get into this with you. Grab a bottle of wine, someone order something for lunch, and then I'll tell you about the country club and the kiss."

I'm exhausted. That's definitely the only reason I blabbed about the kiss.

I head back to my room and change into leggings and a T-shirt. If I'm going to dissect my stupidity in front of the class, I'm going to be comfortable while doing it.

A glass of merlot is sitting on the coffee table when I return to the living room, and Willow says, "Pizza will be here in about forty-five minutes."

"Did you get extra ranch?" She and I always fight over it, and I'm not in the mood for that today.

She nods. The three of them are looking at me with the identical expressions of *spill it!*, so after taking a hearty sip of wine for courage, I say, "I went to the country club and was eavesdropping when Gallagher came in and got really mad."

I run through the rest of the story for them, finishing it at the car conversation with my promise to undercut him and hand over the bounty to someone else.

"Oh, Meadow, you didn't," Jenn says.

I drain the remaining wine in my glass in one giant, guilt-ridden gulp. "I did."

"You know," Fawn says, "when I asked if you could get along, I didn't mean for you to burn that bridge down at the same time, but talk about multitasking."

"Wait. Can we go back to the kiss? Was it at least good?" Willow asks.

I grab the bottle of wine, knowing that I need more liquid courage to get through this next part. After a deep drink and an even deeper breath, I say, "It was the hottest kiss I've ever had in my life."

Willow crows, Fawn's mouth drops open, and Jenn smiles at me. Normally I'm the one giving my sisters shit, especially Willow. She gets more action than all of us because she hasn't been fully disheartened by men yet. Fawn goes out occasionally, but considering she's raising Landon by herself, she's resigned herself to waiting until he's older before diving back into the dating pool. And obviously Jenn's not super excited about meeting new men since she got away from Martin.

Dating is a minefield of insecurities, narcissism, and doubt mired in a shit-ton of small talk, and those are all things I'd rather not be involved in.

"What do you think it means? You said he kissed you, right?" Willow asks.

"He did. I tripped and his face kinda smooshed into the side of my hair, so I snarked that if he was trying to kiss me, he could have done a better job or something and then *pow!* He laid one right on me." As for what it means, I have no idea. Especially now that we're assigned to the same case.

"So he kissed your brains out, you kinda worked together to set up a sting for Kent, and then you insulted him and threatened to take his paycheck away?" Fawn clarifies.

The second glass of wine bites the dust, and I sigh contentedly. "That about sums it up."

"That's an eventful day for you. Especially considering —" Jenn stops with a faraway look on her face.

"Considering what?"

"I can't remember the last time you texted me about a date or a hookup. How long has it been, nine months or so?"

I blush. Leave it to her to call me out on being off the dating scene.

"About that long, yeah. But don't read anything into it. I tossed a gauntlet at his feet, and he picked it up, nothing more or less than that."

Jenn says "Hmm" and takes a sip of wine.

"You know he could technically make this job very hard for you too, right, Mead?" Fawn asks.

"I do."

"She's right. You need to make nice with him," Jenn says.

I'd already come to the same conclusion. "I'll apologize."

It'll make me look like a fool, but it's worth it if it gets that asshole behind bars faster. I can't afford to alienate him any more than I already have, and I stepped in it big time today.

Willow's hand slashes through the air. "That's not the only thing you can offer, Mead. We're Ridleys."

"And?" I ask.

My sisters roll their eyes, and I shoot a glance at Jenn. A small shoulder shrug tells me she's as clueless as I am.

Fawn and Willow speak at the same time. "Cook for him."

"What? Cook?"

Jenn nods enthusiastically. "Oh, yeah, he was scarfing down dinner last night. I bet if you make him something and apologize, it would smooth things over between you two."

The idea has merit. My mother's been perfecting her red sauce recipe since before we were born. Some of my earliest memories are of her in the kitchen, and she had the three of us cooking and baking by the time we were teens.

"When?" I ask.

"Tomorrow morning. There's nothing like a big breakfast to start the day off right. Plus, with the three of us rotating through here, you need to go to the grocery store."

That's true. I didn't anticipate feeding anyone other than me, and my kitchen is already near empty. I need to make my own grocery list.

I could make him something, take it over, apologize for overstepping, and restore the balance between us.

If you could even call whatever we had going on before balance.

Let's hope I can earn his forgiveness through food.

Between him and Dad, I'm batting a thousand in the relationship department today.

But remembering the way Gallagher's face shut down earlier, I'm not optimistic.

11

GRIFFIN

I'm TOWELING OFF AFTER A SHOWER WHEN THERE'S A knock at my door. I haven't had time to install a peep camera—though I really want to—so I glance through it the old-fashioned way.

Meadow is standing at my door, holding a covered...something.

What the hell is she doing here?

I'd intended to touch base with her later today and let her in on the plan I devised to catch Martin, but I've been putting it off. Her threat to tell Bobby to give this bounty away rankled. I know I pick on her a lot and we're at odds much of the time, but I'd never thought she'd have the potential to impact my career like that, never mind that she'd actually threaten it.

I open the door and lean against the frame. "Meadow."

Her eyes drop to the towel around my hips, and a lovely blush starts to cover her cheeks as she shifts her feet back and forth. Looks like Ms. Meadow Ridley is flustered by me in a towel. Considering the quick way she brushed off my kiss yesterday, that's surprising.

"Oh, um. You're not dressed. I can come back."

I must not have learned from my mistake yesterday—and yes, it was a mistake to grab her and kiss her and lose my ever-loving shit when it came to her—because I snag her hand.

"Wait up. Did you need something?" Against my better judgment and grudge, I rub my thumb across the back of her hand, letting it coast over her knuckles.

"Just wanted to talk about yesterday, and you know...all that."

Yesterday, huh? I figured she'd said everything she needed to say.

"Okay, come on in and have a seat. I'll throw some pants on. Gimme a second."

I leave the front door open and turn toward my bedroom. It takes seconds for me to pull a pair of jeans off the top of the laundry pile and, to be on the safe side, quickly sniff them to confirm they're clean before putting them on.

Forgoing a shirt—I want to see if I can get any more color into her cheeks—I walk back out to the living room.

Meadow is still standing by the door, holding the covered plate.

"What's that?" I ask.

She lifts it a little higher. "Oh, this. Well, I was kinda hoping it could be a peace offering and I could say sorry for yesterday."

"A peace offering, huh?"

"Yeah. I'm sorry for what I said out by my car—it was out of line. So that was on me."

I want to grab her apology and hold it tight while I kiss her again, but I know her regret for the work threat doesn't give me leave to lay my lips on hers again. I still need to feel that part out, and if the way she's got the plate in a death grip is any indication, I've got a lot of feeling to do.

"What's my peace offering?"

"I made sourdough French toast, scrambled eggs with chorizo, and home fries."

My mouth waters, and my stomach gurgles. I haven't had a chance to eat breakfast yet and that sounds amazing. The only thing in my pantry is some lonely toast. My fridge is even sadder.

I take two steps forward and snatch the plate from her, peeling back the foil and taking a deep whiff of the hefty breakfast. My eyes nearly roll back in my head.

A few more steps and I'm grabbing a fork, then pulling up a barstool at the breakfast nook. I nod for Meadow to sit down, too busy shoving chorizo eggs into my mouth to form words. The spicy heat spreads across my tastebuds, and for the second time this week, I'm thrilled my neighbor knows how to cook damn well.

I groan. Fuck, this is so good. I've barely swallowed that bite before I fork up a bite of her French toast, and it's just as good.

"Marry me."

Meadow's eyes bug out of her head. "What?"

"You may not realize it yet, Wildflower, but I'm a catch. You could do a lot worse than me." I toss a wink her way. A lot of my sore feelings are being nursed back to health with this meal.

I'd totally marry her for this cooking every day.

Just for her cooking, huh?

I hush that internal voice and go back to systematically plowing through breakfast.

"Do you want me to make some coffee?" Meadow asks.

I shake my head. "I don't drink it. But if you want something, I've got some water and juice in the fridge."

Her eyes widen. "You don't drink coffee?"

"I don't."

"Bu-but how do you function?" she sputters.

I chuckle around a bite of food. This isn't the first time I've gotten asked that question, or the first time someone is surprised I don't drink coffee.

"I don't like the taste. And caffeine makes me jittery so I stick with the soft stuff—caffeine-free drinks, water, juice. It's healthier and I like it better that way."

"Huh. Well, okay then. I guess I wouldn't have pegged you for a health nut."

"What would you have pegged me as?"

She shrugs. "I don't know. But definitely not a health nut."

She shoves her hands in her pockets. I'm not sure if it's a nervous tell or just comfortable for her, and it hits me that while I know a lot about Meadow, I don't really know her at all. We've lived next door to each other for months, but other than me silently lusting after her and some ribbing, what I do know about her is surface level.

"I wouldn't say I'm a health nut. I take care of myself. Caffeine makes me jittery, so I don't drink it as a rule. Simple as that."

"I guess that makes sense."

"Tell me something about you."

Two slow blinks later, she asks, "What?"

I grin at her. "You heard me. Consider it part of the peace offering."

She finally sits down next to me, and a strand of her silky hair falls over my bare arm. Goose bumps sweep to my elbow.

Her shampoo smells spicy with a kick of citrus, and I just barely bite back the request she tell me what it is so I can buy it if only to smell it.

"I, um...."

"Come on, Wildflower, it can't be that hard to share a little something about yourself."

"It's not. I mean, it is. But only because I don't know what to say."

I wait, letting her gather her thoughts. It started off as something I blurted out to fill the dead air between us, but now? Now I'm invested and curious about what she'll share. I'd like to get to know her better if she'll let me.

This peace offering is one I'm taking. Sure, we could go on the same way we have been—me teasing her, her avoiding me—but I don't want to anymore. And I'm pretty sure she doesn't want to either; otherwise why would she go through the effort of even offering peace?

"I eat the same thing every single day for breakfast." She stares at me with those hazel eyes that are more green than blue as though she's waiting for a specific reaction. But I don't know what she expects. "And some days I eat it more than once, depending on how shitty my day has gone."

"What's the thing?"

"Almond butter toast. Sometimes I'll switch it up and have almond butter on waffles or a cinnamon raisin bagel, but most of the time it's toast."

"And that's your favorite? This toast?"

"I can take or leave the carb it comes on. I'm in it for the almond butter."

I file that piece of information away.

"Can't say I've ever had almond butter toast. I'm a regular peanut butter guy."

"Have you ever tried almond butter?"

"Nope." I pop the *p*.

"Maybe I can bring you some the next time I go to the store."

"Didn't you just go?"

She smirks. "Yeah, but that was for my own stash. I'm not sharing."

That gets a chuckle out of me. "I'd like that." I stand and take my now empty plate to the sink and wash it. Maybe I was wrong about the cutthroat threats she made yesterday. Maybe, like me, she was caught off guard by the kiss and finding out that catching Martin might be easier than we originally thought.

"So, um, anyway, I should probably be going. Fawn had to run my nephew to an appointment so it's just Willow and Jenn next door."

"Okay. Can I swing by later to go over some stuff?"

She eyes me suspiciously. I get it. My tune has changed, but maybe we're going about this the wrong way. Maybe we can find a balance working together. Maybe we don't have to be at odds.

I don't know her well enough to determine where her strengths lie, but I know what mine are, and if I can figure hers out, maybe we could complement each other if we met halfway.

"Actually, my parents are throwing a block party, so we're going to that. Get Jenn out of the apartment, ya know?"

"A block party?"

She tucks that strand of hair behind her ear again. "Yeah, about one Saturday a month my dad fires up the grill and he and their neighbors get together. It's a lot of fun. You should come."

Her eyes widen, but before she can take the invitation back, I say, "Sure. What time?"

"Um. It runs most of the day, so you could show up whenever." Her voice is higher than normal, and I tuck away the little tell for later.

I make Meadow nervous. How about that?

"Okay, where's it at?" I pull out my phone, and she rattles off the address.

"Okay. I guess I'll see you there. Also, sorry, again for... you know...yesterday," she stammers.

"Water under the bridge now. Thank you for breakfast." I drop my phone back into my pocket and dry her plate before handing it back to her.

"Um. Wait. Sorry, but I was just curious. Since we're kinda not yelling at each other right now, or trying to snark each other to death..."

"Yeah?" This is the most time we've been within five feet of each other and been civil without it pertaining to work.

"It's just that yesterday when I said you missed...I didn't expect you to..."

"Kiss you?"

"Yeah. Why did you?"

I take two steps forward and snag the strand of hair brushing her cheek. The air between us goes heavy, and her chest rises and falls faster as I let the dark blonde silk glide between my fingers for a few seconds before tucking it behind her ear.

"Wildflower?"

"Griffin." I've never heard her call me by my first name, and damn me if I don't like my name on her lips. We lock eyes, neither of us blinking. I don't want there to be any misunderstanding between us.

"I kissed you because I've wanted to kiss you for a long time, and you finally threw down a challenge I couldn't walk away from."

Color rushes into her cheeks, and she breaks eye contact first. This new shy side of her is different, but good different. I'm used to the ballsy, take-no-prisoners Meadow that meets me joke for joke. I don't know what to do with her when she isn't tearing into me, but I kinda like the calm of this. It's nice.

"Um. Okay then. Well, I'm gonna go." Her voice shakes on the last two words, and I fight off a smile.

As she backs slowly toward the door, I lock my leg muscles to stop myself from following her. I wonder what she tastes like after I've made her blush. My guess—fire and sin.

Her eyes stray to my bare chest before shooting back up to my face, and again she snares her lower lip between her teeth. With her hand out behind her, she finds the door and disappears.

Well, shit. That changes the playing field.

I'M TYPING up an outline for Thursday's "nab Martin" plan when a new email notification catches my attention. It's a reminder message from my doctor's office in Flagstaff that I'm overdue for a physical.

Going to the doctor is tricky. I recognize the need for routine medical care, but after Mom's diagnosis, medical offices have become suffocating for me.

If I think too much about it, I start to fixate on my own behavior, looking for the same signs I saw in her and discounted until I couldn't overlook them anymore.

There are tests to determine whether I carry the genes for Alzheimer's. I've been advised getting them is relatively easy, but fear holds me back.

The test only provides a scale of likelihood, not certainty. Which somehow feels even more reckless to me.

What if I test negative, start a family, and then develop Alzheimer's? The point of the test is to avoid becoming a burden to anyone, and yet the negative result won't have prevented anything.

Knowing how isolating it is for Mom, and how alone I feel at times, makes me never want to be responsible for making someone else feel this way.

And if the genetic test is positive...Jesus. Then I *know*. And I'll drive myself crazy for the rest of my life looking for signs of the disease, whether they exist or not.

It's better for me if I go about my life the same way I have been. Take care of Mom. Stick to casual dating.

Enough melancholy, Gallagher. Pull up your big boy boxers and get to work.

I scroll through the email and click the unsubscribe button. I need to find a doctor down here anyway.

After dicking around my apartment for a few hours, it's time to head to the block party, so I gather what I need and head to the front door. I don't know what makes me do it, but I look back and consider that Meadow was in my space.

Somehow, the space is fundamentally altered. On a cosmic level, it's never going to be untouched by her again. I can't help but wonder what she thought of the place. What she thought when she saw my threadbare old couch, the sparse amount of furniture, and the lack of art hanging on the wall.

Hell, the most important and expensive things in my

house are my bike and my surveillance equipment, and they're hidden in the second bedroom.

And that's just another sad thought to go along with the rest of them.

I need to shake off this funk, and I bet a block party will do it.

12

MEADOW

I kissed you because I've wanted to kiss you for a long time, and you finally threw down a challenge that I couldn't walk away from.

What the hell was I supposed to do with that? I made the joke about him missing my mouth due to acute embarrassment from tripping over my own two feet.

When he reached out to tuck a strand of hair behind my ear, I sincerely thought I was about to be struck by lightning. I was hyperaware of how close we were. Goose bumps still prickle my arms even now when I'm safely out of his apartment.

Tuck it away, Meadow. It doesn't mean anything.

The little pep talk isn't doing anything to help me forget the way his lips took mine, or the way my toes still curl thinking about the taste of his desire as he ate at my mouth.

Let's not forget the fact the man has a chest that should be outlawed nationwide. Watching water droplets drop from his shoulders and slide down his pecs when I first entered his apartment was pure torture. The fact I wanted to trace them with my tongue didn't help either.

I push open the door to my place and find my sisters and Jenn pressing their ears against the wall separating Griffin's living room from mine.

"What the hell are you three doing? And when did you get back, Fawn?" She left while I was making breakfast, and I hadn't expected her to return this quickly.

The three of them turn toward me, and the only person who isn't trying to look serious is Willow. A grin creases her cheeks as she says, "What do you think we were doing, dummy? Listening in. How'd it go?"

"Oh my God. Are you three in elementary school? What do you mean you were listening in?"

"You can't honestly expect me to stay in this apartment with nothing to do while you go next door to talk to your hunky neighbor who kissed your brains out yesterday," Jenn whines.

She's got a point. If it was one of them, I'd be all up in their business too, so I guess I can't get upset they're doing it to me.

I tell Willow, "It was fine. I apologized. He accepted and ate my breakfast." I set the plate down on the breakfast bar and head back toward my room. "I invited him to the block party today."

"What?" three voices screech in unison, and their stampeding feet follow me down the hallway to crowd into my room after me.

"He wants to go over some stuff for next week. I told him we wouldn't be home today and invited him along. It's no big deal." I throw open my closet door. Block parties aren't anything fancy—they're more about hanging out and having a good time. Kids watch the movie my dad puts on the projector in the garage. There's plenty of food, alcohol, and lawn games, and the best part is it's the safest way to get my stir-crazy bestie out of the house without compromising her safety.

Normally I'd wear the shorts, tank, and sandals I put on this morning, but maybe I should dress up a little. Not for Griffin, *obviously*. But for myself. There's nothing that says I can't feel pretty while hanging out with my sisters and our friends.

"If it's no big deal, then why are you in your closet? You've already showered and gotten dressed for the day, so there's no reason for you to change."

Fawn's logic has no place here, and I ignore her until they start singing off-key, "Meadow and Griffin sitting in a tree..."

"There will be no sitting in a tree for either of us, so you can just knock it off."

"Better than you two sitting in a car," Willow says.

"What's that supposed to mean?" I ask.

"Oh, come on, you guys totally have heard that, right?"

"Heard what?" Fawn asks.

A devilish grin covers Willow's face for the second time in two minutes, and I brace myself.

"Meadow and Griffin, sitting in a car," she sings. "Are they fucking? Yes, they are."

My mouth drops open, and the squawk of a dying bird emerges while Fawn and Jenn dissolve into laughter.

"Willow!"

"What? Are you guys seriously telling me you didn't learn it in middle school?"

I shake my head, but both Jenn and Fawn raise their hands, admitting they've heard it.

"Jesus, Meadow," Fawn says. "I knew you were a goody-goody in school, but I didn't think it was that bad."

Jenn says, "Well, she is the oldest of y'all. It makes sense she's the good girl."

"I'm older by three minutes. That doesn't count."

Willow points at me. "Sure, it does. You're the rigid rule follower, Fawn's the middle child mediator, and I'm the youngest one, which makes me the wild child and instigator. Think about it..."

"Stop. I don't have time for this. I need to change and then we need to get going because Dad asked me to stop and grab a case of water on the way. I don't have time to play your weird little mind games right now, Willie. Everyone out." I throw a hand at the door for emphasis.

Willow waves her hand in the air. "We'll leave in a minute, but I have one question. Did you ask him why he kissed you yesterday?"

I don't mask the confirmation quick enough and Willow jumps on it. "You did. What did he say?" When I don't answer, she wheedles, "Come on, you gotta tell us. This is better than my daytime soaps."

I know full well she doesn't watch daytime soaps.

"Only if you promise to shut up about it and get out." Heat climbs my cheeks, and I wish I could get a handle on these blushes.

Willow holds up three fingers in the Girl Scout salute. She was never a Girl Scout.

"Fine," I concede. "I asked him why he kissed me, and he said he's wanted to kiss me for a long time and because I threw down a challenge he couldn't walk away from."

Three pairs of stunned eyes stare at me for a beat of time before they all erupt into squealing giggles. Their dog-whistle-pitched excitement sends ice pick shards of glass through my newly formed headache.

I grab a navy spaghetti-strapped sundress from my

closet and pull it on. Letting my hair down from the clip I threw it in after drying, I tousle it around my shoulders. The same sandals I wore today complete the look, and a simple swipe of lip gloss and coat of mascara have me as ready as I'll ever get.

It's just a block party. Nothing more.

Even I'm starting to hear the lie in that.

MY PARENTS HAVE LIVED in the same neighborhood since before my sisters and I were born. Over the years, some of the neighbors have changed, but mostly it's the same people who bought these houses a generation ago and never left. I pull into the cul-de-sac, and Jenn and I climb out of my car as Willow and Fawn park behind me. Opening the hatchback, I pull out the last minute items Dad asked me to pick up. Why he asked me instead of my sisters isn't lost on me—he's trying to get me to talk to him. Sure, I'm still irked at him, but I feel better than I did in the office yesterday.

The scent of grilling meat spices the air as I walk toward the curve on the street where everyone is set up. Dad has his smoker out, and the Nelsons have their grill going too. Kids zoom back and forth on bikes and scooters, and the adults congregate around the food tables. There's music blasting from Dad's giant subwoofers, and the newest kids' monster hotel movie is playing.

"Girls!" Mom meets us on the sidewalk and pulls all of us into a hug. Then she draws back and holds me at arm's length. "Wow, Meadow, you look nice. What's the occasion?"

Shit. I'm obviously overdressed, and I'm an idiot for

thinking it would be overlooked. Mom's wearing a baggy denim shirt and some cut-off khaki shorts that used to be pants, and her light brown hair is braided.

Dummy me showed up in a dress and wearing makeup.

Goddammit. I should have stayed in my shorts.

"Uh, no occasion. Just wanted to do something different this time."

I duck out of that conversation fast and cart the case of water over to the coolers. It's cooler than expected for a May afternoon, hovering in the high eighties. The trees in everyone's yards go a long way toward cutting the heat, and there's a slight breeze that helps.

The Musas have their sprinklers running, and a number of kids are running full-bore at a Slip 'N Slide so it's easy enough to stay cool.

After nestling water into the coolers, I make my way over to Dad and Bobby, who are manning the smoking grills.

"Hey, Dad, anything I can help with?" It's another peace offering. I might still be annoyed, but I won't let it ruin our day. And based on the look of relief on his face, it's the right step.

"Hey, Sweet Pea, you look nice. No, we should be fine. How's the case going?"

"It's going. Griffin uncovered a lead that's supposed to be meeting Martin for lunch. We're going to stake out the restaurant and hopefully nab him this week."

Bobby raises his eyebrows. "That was fast. Any issues with Gallagher?"

I shake my head. I'm not about to announce to my dad and his best friend who stuck me with Griffin that we're at each other's throats more often than not, or that he knocked my socks off with a single kiss I can't stop thinking about.

"All good here."

"Hmm," Bobby hums, while watching me suspiciously.

Little does he know Dad's interrogating stare is much more terrifying—and Mom's? Forget about it.

The sound of a car pulling up draws their attention away, and for a brief moment I think it's going to be the reprieve I need.

Sadly, it's not. Mom whistles lightly under her breath—where the hell did she come from—as Griffin exits his car and starts toward us with a bouquet of flowers and a six-pack of beer in his hands.

"Who's that?" Dad asks.

"Meadow's boyfriend," Willow practically shouts.

I swipe a hand at her. Any hope Griffin didn't hear that dies as I watch a grin spread across his face. I rush to meet him halfway, but Mom and Willow beat me to him. Elbowing my annoying sister aside, I say, "Ignore Willow. Mom, this is Griffin Gallagher. We're working together to find Martin. Griffin, this is my mother, Susan Ridley."

"It's a pleasure to meet you, Mrs. Ridley. Here, these are for you." He hands over the flowers. "Where would you like me to put these?" he asks as he lifts the beer a little higher.

A sneaky smile curls Mom's lips before her eyes slide to me, the gleam of a seasoned schemer shining in that gaze.

What the hell is wrong with me? I know better than this. I shouldn't have dressed up, I shouldn't have invited Griffin, and I absolutely shouldn't have told my sisters any of this because they will throw me under the bus at the first opportunity.

Susan Ridley's mission in life is to smother grandbabies in affection and love. To her dismay, she only has Landon, and all three of us have been adamant that he's all she's gonna get for the time being.

Bringing Griffin here and having Willow call him my

boyfriend is exactly what I didn't need. My mother is about to break out the crochet hook and yarn and start making baby blankets.

I sidestep my sister and snatch the beer from Griffin's grip before saying, "Come on, let's put these away and then we'll grab a drink." Under my breath, I mumble, "A really stiff one."

Griffin's head swivels between Willow, sporting a very evil grin, and my mother, who has stars in her eyes. When he looks at me, I'm pretty sure the panicky terror is plain on my face because he says, "A drink would be good."

I don't bother trying to smother the snorting laugh that pops out.

How is this my life right now?

13

GRIFFIN

I almost didn't come to the block party. I could have gotten together with Meadow later tonight or sometime this week to hash out the details of what was going to happen. But for every excuse that I came up with not to show, my curiosity got the better of me, and before I could debate it anymore, I was stopping by the store to pick up a pack of beer and a bundle of flowers.

It's hotter than Hades out, and I have no idea why anyone would believe that May is an appropriate time to BBQ in Phoenix. But here I am, sweating my ass off following Meadow toward a bunch of tables and coolers.

Once there, she drops down and then pops open the cardboard box of beers and starts to layer them in with the other beverages.

The dark blue little sundress that she's wearing rides up the back of her toned thighs, and I clench my hands at my sides. It's either that or I'm going to go over there and slide my hands along her skin to see if she's as soft as she looks. Considering Bobby is giving me the equivalent of the evil eye, that'd be the exact wrong thing to do.

When she swung by my place earlier, she was in shorts and a tank top. Nobody else here is dressed up—most everyone is casual in deference to the heat.

Maybe she has a date after this? My heart hammers at the thought and even more sweat beads on my brow.

The reality of it is that I don't know her well enough to know if she's dating. And that makes my stomach churn. I kissed her at the country club without even knowing if she belongs to someone else, and the thought that she might— that someone else could have a claim on her—punches through my sternum like a pair of brass knuckles.

"Are you seeing someone?" The question blurts out of me, harsh and angry.

Meadow turns toward me. "What?"

I wave a hand at her outfit. "You heard me. You're awfully dressed up for someone who's hanging out at their parents' block party."

Willow called me her boyfriend when I arrived, but maybe she was fucking around and Meadow is waiting for an actual boyfriend.

"Um. No. I'm not seeing someone. I wouldn't have let you kiss me if I was seeing someone."

My pulse spikes at her response, and I know I should stop, that I should be relieved. But before I can make myself chill out, I say, "So what's all this? You weren't that dressed up this morning when you came to my place with your *peace offering.*"

Peace offering sounds dirtier than I meant it to, like I'm criticizing her efforts to bridge the animosity between us. Why can't I control my reactions when I'm around her? Her jaw kicks forward as her lips purse, the muscle in the side of her cheek working double time and telling me that she's grinding her teeth.

"The dress is for *me*. You're a douchebag. There's snacks and stuff you can help yourself to and fuck you very much. The only reason I'm not walking away right now is because my mom would skin me alive for leaving a guest alone, but if I could, you'd be on your own, buster."

The effortless way she delivers the barbs along with her hostess duties is hilarious and a little scary.

"You're right. I'm an asshole. I'm sorry. I just—"

Her gaze narrows on me, but she doesn't say anything.

Good going, Gallagher. Alienated your host in less than two minutes. Fantastic.

"I kissed you yesterday, ya know. I kissed you without considering that you might be seeing someone, and that messed me up for a minute. But I shouldn't have taken that out on you. I'm sorry."

"Thank you for apologizing." Prim and proper Meadow is back, and I hate that. I hate that her shoulders are tight, that she's closed off again. I want the Meadow that hummed and sighed as I sank into tasting her. I want the Meadow that fisted my shirt as she tasted me right back.

I fucking hate talking about it, but here goes. "I'm the result of what happens when you don't ask questions or you get involved with someone who's already taken. My ma was the other woman, though she didn't know it at the time. She never talks about it, but from what I've gleaned over the years, my dad was her boss. As soon as she got pregnant with me, she found out that not only was this prick married, but that he'd been stringing her along the whole time. So it's a sore spot for me."

Meadow's shoulders drop a little bit. "I'm sorry to hear that. It'd be a sore spot for me too."

"We okay?"

"Water under the bridge. Just don't do it again."

"I won't," I promise her.

Smoke is billowing from a couple of grills, and through the haze I see Bobby and who I'm assuming is Meadow's dad watching our exchange. Bobby nods his head in a "come here" gesture, so I reach down to grab a bottle of water and say, "We're being summoned."

"Of course we are."

We weave through adults and kids milling about, Meadow introducing me to people as we go. She has a word with just about everyone, and it takes us three times longer than necessary to make it over to Bobby and her dad.

"Dad, this is Griffin. Griffin, this is my dad, Andrew Ridley."

I nod to Bobby and shake Andrew's hand. "Nice to meet you."

Meadow looks like her dad. They have the same hazel eyes and high cheekbones, but his hair is a lighter blond than hers.

"Meadow says you should have Martin in hand by the end of next week?"

"Yes, sir, that's the plan. Meadow and I have a few more details to work out, but I have high hopes that we'll be able to wrap this up quickly."

"Hmm. You know what they say about good intentions."

"I do. But we're going to do our best to bring him in safely."

Andrew nods. "I'd like the emphasis to be on the safely part."

"Dad," Meadow says, the warning clear in her tone.

"What? I'm not allowed to look out for my baby girl?"

"You're allowed to look out for me, but only while you respect that I'm capable of taking care of myself."

"Hmph. It's my job to worry about you."

Meadow rolls her eyes. "My black belt in Krav Maga says you should worry more about the person who crosses me."

I try and fail to stifle my snort at that. She's got a point, though.

Bobby asks, "Something funny, son?"

"No, sir. We'll stay safe. It's not my first rodeo or hers, and I have complete faith in her abilities."

Andrew pulls a giant spatula from the side of the grill and raps it across the top of the lid. "That's what I like to hear. Now go grab some plates—these burgers are about done."

There's a flurry of activity as everyone gets their food, kids are corralled, and plates are made before people find their seats. Half a dozen folding tables sit in the shaded parts of yards, and I manage to snag a seat at the crowded Ridley table.

This is the third time in as many days a Ridley is feeding me. Meadow wasn't joking when she said that her family likes to cook. I'm thankful that I get to enjoy the fruits of that labor.

Willow leans over and whispers something to Fawn, but she's too far for me to hear. Meadow squints at them before picking up her dinner roll and firing it at her sister.

It smacks Willow in the temple, and Meadow whispers, "Shhh!"

Willow sticks her tongue out and lifts her own roll. Just as her arm cocks back, Susan, who's circling the table with a tray of corn on the cob, smoothly snatches the roll from Willow's hand.

"Aww, c'mon, Mom! She threw it first."

"Just because your sister is challenging her spiritual

karma for the day doesn't mean you have to. What's the rule?"

Dutifully, all three girls recite, "Everyone deserves respect and kindness."

Meadow turns toward me. "Mom's a total hippie. Ignore her."

"How does that work with what you do?"

This family fascinates me. Susan takes a seat next to Andrew, both of them listening to Jenn and Fawn talk over each other about a case. Willow's making faces at a kid from a neighboring table.

"She expects us to conduct business with 'the rule' in mind, but understands that there are circumstances that don't allow for it. Mostly she stays out of business and sticks to her volunteer work."

"What kind of volunteer work?"

Meadow finishes chewing a bite of food before answering. "Oh, just about everything. She and Willow like to help out at the women's shelters and with domestic abuse survivor programs around the valley, she and Fawn will volunteer at Landon's school, and she and I like to do community outreach events for food drives. Community service is a very large part of what we do."

Conversation is fast and seems extra passionate as it buzzes around the table. Finally, I realize why and lean over to Meadow to whisper, "Why is everyone using sign language?"

"The little guy next to you? That's my nephew, Landon. He's deaf."

The kid is shoving potato salad in his mouth like his life depends on it as his eyes ping around the table to follow the conversations.

After a quick jog down memory lane, I turn in my seat

and introduce myself using the little bit of ASL that I remember from my days at summer camp. Here's to hoping that nothing has changed in that time.

The kid stares at me wide-eyed for a minute before he signs back and I have to ask Meadow, "What'd he say?"

"He said nice to meet you. And then asked why you're sitting with the family."

When I was growing up, it was just me and my mom. To see a whole block of households come together and act like family is surprising. And kind of nice. We never lived in a neighborhood that had this kind of cohesion. Community often feels like a foreign concept to me, and it's a little scary to know that one day I'm going to lose Ma. She's my only person.

Meadow sneaks a bite of burger to a dog that comes sniffing.

"You know, kid, I've been asking myself the same thing," I mutter to myself.

I'VE GOT a beer in my hand and I'm talking about the morality of law with Miguel from three houses down when the first balloon pelts me. It bursts against my chest, water rushing up my nose and into my eyes. The cool liquid is welcome after the heat of the day, but I want to know who fired on a noncombatant. I look around to find Meadow standing across from where I'm sitting, a teasing smile on her lips. A mischievous glint makes her eyes look more green than blue.

I wipe my hand down my wet face and say, "Run."

She squeaks and takes off, and I scramble out of the

chair after her. To my right are two kiddie pools, one filled with water but the other full of balloons.

Veering off, I grab three pieces of ammunition. One goes in my throwing hand and the other two are balanced in the opposite hand.

Meadow is hiding behind a paloverde tree, and I fire off the first balloon at her shoulder. It narrowly misses her and smashes into the tree, splattering everywhere. She scoots off to the left as I throw the second balloon, but I manage to clip her.

"Come out with your hands up and you won't get hurt," I call.

"Never surrender," she yells back.

I take two quick steps to the right and get a clear view of her juicy ass. Before she can alter course and find coverage, I whip the third balloon at her and watch in satisfaction as it splatters all over her dress, drenching her.

"Steeeeerike! And the crowd goes wild."

Meadow's head tips back and she laughs. "Yep, you got me all right." She bends down, and I realize that she chose this tree, this tree away from all of the other balloons, for a reason.

A green garden hose sits at the base of the tree, and she wastes no time in snatching it up and aiming it at me.

"Hey, there. Hold up now, Wildflower. That's not fighting fair." A balloon hits my back, but I ignore it because I know the second that I look away from her, she's gonna soak me.

"It's not?" she asks with a laugh. Her infectious smile is brighter than the sun. Goddamn, she's so fucking beautiful. I grin right back at her and mentally calculate how quickly I can reload or get out of hose range, but the odds aren't looking good for me either way.

"You know it's not, Wildflower. But I can see why you'd need more ammuni—"

She blasts the hose at me, and I get a face full of water. The lukewarm liquid soaks me down to my boxers.

I rush her.

In a few quick strides, I have one hand wrapped around the hose and the other arm scooping her into me. And because turnabout is fair play, I turn the hose on her, lifting it over her head and letting the water run over the both of us. She screeches and squirms, but I've got a good hold on her, so she's not getting away.

I toss the hose down and wrap my other arm around her waist. For a second, everything falls away. The case, her family, though they're likely watching this, the conversation that we still have to have about this week—one that I know she isn't going to like—it all disappears as I stare down into her face.

Something in my chest shifts before clicking into place. I'm too scared to think about it, so instead I lean down and capture Meadow's laughing lips with my own.

14

MEADOW

I DIDN'T INTEND FOR HIM TO KISS ME AGAIN. HELL, I barely know what to do with the first kiss. But once the kids broke out the water balloons and set up their battle stations, I couldn't help myself. The wine coolers I had at lunch helped me release the stress of the last few days.

His lips coast along mine, light and teasing. I want to grip him by the hair and demand that he kiss me the same way he did yesterday, but I have to remember where we are.

I pull back, breaking the kiss, and watch his eyes open. We're both out of breath, which is weird considering how light this kiss was. My heart is thumping away, and heat rises in my cheeks before I can mentally will it away. His eyes flick to mine. There are gold flecks in the dark brown irises that I've never noticed before.

Of course you've never noticed before, dummy. Up until recently, you hated each other's guts. What is wrong with you?

I don't *do* things like this. I don't go around kissing random guys, and I don't insert myself into other people's issues, but that's just what I did at lunch. I don't know what the deal was with Griffin's family, but he looked a little lost when Landon asked him why he was at our table, and that tugged at me. There was so much longing and sadness when he looked out at my family, and damn it, I felt that in my soul. If I could erase the sad even for a few minutes, then I wanted to do that.

Soaking him with the hose wasn't part of the plan either. When he said "run," I did just that. After seeing him scoop up water balloons, I changed course for the Laffertys' lawn since their hose is always at the base of that tree for easier watering. Dad's told them multiple times over the years to install a dripper, but they continue watering their plants each morning and paying their astronomical water bill each month.

Getting soaked with the hose was expected once I fired on him, but it was poor planning on my part since I don't have anything to change into.

His full grin and dripping hair mean I did my job in pulling him out of whatever sad he was stuck in while we ate. "Um."

Really, Ridley, that's the best that you can come up with?

"And that's how you win something, Wildflower."

A quip is on the tip of my tongue to question if he really did win, a snarky way to take us back to our safe place of arguing and bickering, but before I can say anything my mom yells, "Meadow, come grab a towel and dessert."

And just like that, the moment is broken.

I step back and run my hands down my wet dress, now plastered against me. If I stand in the sun for five minutes it's going to dry, but my nipples are hard under the material, and I'd really like it if the breeze would stop blowing over me.

Yeah, Meadow, the "breeze" made your nipples hard.

That's my story and I'm sticking to it.

"What's for dessert?" Griffin asks. His tongue darts out to swipe along his bottom lip, and I'm swamped with heat and tension.

"Sex in a pan," I blurt out.

"What?" His eyebrow kicks up.

"Oh, shit, um, not like actual sex. *Obviously*. It's a layer cake thingy. Super delicious and sugar rush guaranteed."

He stares at me for a beat, then roars with laughter.

"What's so funny?" I snap. My face is on fire right now, for no good reason, and *this right here is why I don't get involved with other people's issues.*

Griffin shakes his head and says, "Nothing, Wildflower. Absolutely nothing."

"Then why are you laughing?"

"You looked like you swallowed a pickled lemon."

"Shut up." I drag him behind me to where Mom is passing out towels and paper plates of cake to everyone. Once we have our slices and are sitting near one of the tables I ask, "So how are we going to work Thursday?"

I'm dragging us back to the land of professionalism if I have to do it kicking and screaming.

"I'll be inside waiting," Griffin says. "There are only two exits at the restaurant patrons can use, the one in the front and the one along the side of the building. That's if we're not counting the kitchen exit. I'm going to stand by the side and Kent agreed, after some persuasion—"

"You mean after you threatened and blackmailed him?"

"—to sit near the front of the restaurant and wait for him. Once he shows up, I'll cuff him and we'll escort him back to jail."

"And what will I be doing?"

"You're going to sit in the car and wait to see if he tries

to make a break for it. If he slips by me, then you follow him in the car until I can catch up."

I'm shaking my head before he even finishes his statement. "No. That's stupid. It's more effective for me to be in the restaurant as well, not sitting outside waiting to take off without you if he gets by you."

"Meadow. Be realistic. You're too fucking recognizable, or did you forget that you're the one who originally stopped him and tased his ass so hard that he's probably still tingling?"

Recognizable? Ha, not likely. "A disguise—"

"Is too risky and you know it. Even if this guy isn't a huge threat, you're the one who stopped him the first time. If he catches sight of you, he's gonna be off in the wind and then where will we be? Standing around with our thumbs up our asses again. This is the best chance that we have to catch him without drawing out this investigation, so you're not coming in and that's final."

He did not just throw down a command at me.

"That's final, huh?"

With that expression carved from granite, I know—I *know*—I'm not going to get him to budge on this. That's all right. I can pick my battles.

"Fine. I won't come in, but I'm not waiting in the car either. There's a coffee shop across the street with a clear view of the restaurant. I'll sit there and wait."

He opens his mouth to argue, but I interrupt. "You don't think it would be a little suspicious for me to be sitting in a parked car...in May...in front of a trendy bistro...in the middle of a Thursday morning? That's more suspicious than me sitting in the café with a ball cap on. You know I'm right."

"Fine. You can sit across the street. But if he gets by me, you have to promise that you'll wait for me to go after him."

"What? No."

"Meadow. Listen to me. This guy is gonna be mad. Who do you think he's going to take that out on if he gets the chance? Your dad said to keep you safe, so that's what I'm trying to do."

This fucking asshole. It's a fact that this career is predominantly male driven, but every single time the patriarchy tries to shove me back into the corner I want to start throwing throat punches.

"I'm fully aware of my capabilities as a skip tracer and investigator. Your mistake is assuming that I don't know how to prepare for or succeed in my own career. I've apprehended bail jumpers before. I am also fully aware that if given the chance, Martin would try to beat the snot out of me. The difference? He's not going to get the chance. I'm smart, capable, and armed. So how about you pull your head out of your ass and join the cool kids' club where it's understood that I'm damn good at my job. Until then, you can take your myopic opinions about my experience and fuck right off with that nonsense."

I stand and walk away rather than continuing an argument that would ultimately burn a bridge that no amount of peace offering food could repair.

Everyone deserves respect and kindness.

That inner voice? It sounds suspiciously like my mother, and I'm choosing to ignore it for the first time in my life.

He may kiss like a fiend, but he's a misogynistic asshat.

AFTER SOME STUMBLING, awkward goodbyes, Griffin took off. Mom eyeballed me for all of ten seconds before shaking her head and busying herself with cleanup. I don't really blame her. I'm a mess and don't know what to do with myself today, so why should I expect her to know what to do with me?

Leftovers are boxed and divvied up, but before I can slink off to grab Jenn and head out, Mom hollers for me.

Might as well get this over with.

I head into the house and notice that she's repainted the living room again. What was a pale blue a couple of months ago is now a sage green that works really well with the deep chocolate leather of their sofas.

Each room in this house has been repurposed multiple times over the years. I never knew if there was going to be a new change when I got home from school each day. Mom's always been a homemaker, a crafter, and an artist, and our house is her canvas.

I walk toward the kitchen and find my mom pouring herself a glass of Zinfandel.

She looks over at me and raises her eyebrows. "What's the deal with you and Griffin?"

"We're working together. That's it."

"I didn't know that working together meant flirty kisses after water fights. Good thinking, heading to the Laffertys' yard, by the way."

Hell. There goes any hope we went unnoticed this afternoon.

"Yeah. Great thinking."

"What's going on, my little lark? Why do you look so sad? Was it because of the disagreement you had with him before he left?"

"I'm not little, Mom. And I don't know. I guess...I guess

it just sucks when you find out how little someone actually thinks of you."

"What does that mean? Break it down for me."

I snag Mom's glass and take a swallow. The crisp wine tastes way too good. Maybe I'll have another glass when I get home to make up for the roller coaster of the day.

I take a deep breath and tell her about the last couple of days. The country club, the peace offering, and then this afternoon, ending with, "Griffin doesn't trust me as an investigator. He doesn't trust in my ability to protect myself and expects me to sit on the sidelines."

"Which you'll never do."

"Nope. So it doesn't matter how good his kisses are, or how well we seem to get along once he stops being an obnoxious asshat. None of that matters."

"But it sounds like you want it to matter."

I did want it to matter. I thought that maybe this was the sign I was waiting for. The sign that it was okay to consider dating again. To maybe take something for myself. But it's not.

"No, not really. Once Martin's dealt with and Jenn's safe again, everything will go back to the way it was."

Mom cocks her head to the side and her eyes narrow on me. I'm a shit liar, always have been, but she doesn't call me on it.

The truth of it is I'm sad. I thought that Griffin coming to the party, the flirting, the back-and-forth teasing, meant more than it did.

I've never been someone who can easily flit in and out of a relationship. In a world of swiping left and right to find a hookup, I'm the odd man out because I need time and a connection with someone before hopping into bed with them all while keeping it as surface level as possible. I thought maybe, just maybe, that time and connection were pointing me toward Griffin Gallagher, but I guess I was wrong.

"Meadow, answer me this. Would you say Griffin considers you incapable, that he doesn't respect you as an investigator, or is it more likely that he does and he's just trying to protect you, much like you're trying to protect Jennifer right now?"

Griffin Gallagher has "overprotective" written all over him, and maybe Mom's right. I would say that I don't need protecting, but as someone who continually looks out for my completely capable family members, I know it's a weak excuse at best.

"I, uh, I don't know, honestly."

Mom grabs her glass of wine and tips it in my direction. "Something to think about."

Yeah. I have a whole lot to think about.

15

GRIFFIN

My irritation at my stubborn next-door neighbor burns through the night and still glows like banked embers when my phone alarm goes off the next morning.

Why can't she just listen to reason? She got involved in this whole mess because she wants to protect her friend. I get it. It's asinine but also admirable. What does she think of me if she believes I'd blithely let her place herself in harm's way without being as smart as possible about it? It already rankles that she's not locked in the apartment with Jennifer and her sisters for safety.

Haven't I compromised enough? Why can't she meet me halfway?

Ugh. Women.

I snag a water bottle from the kitchen and head to the second bedroom for my morning ride. Crowded gyms aren't really my thing, but this does the trick for me.

I strap on my heart rate monitor and clip in while pulling up the class menu. In the lower right-hand corner of the screen, there's an indicator that a follower is online. I only have one follower, and Meadow's morning schedule is as structured as always.

She's up and on her bike first thing. Her workouts have a distinct pattern that I've picked up through our shared bedroom wall. And though it sometimes makes me feel like a seven-year-old boy teasing the girl he has a crush on rather than a grown-ass man, I take a ridiculous amount of pleasure out of crashing her workouts.

It's Sunday so that means it's cardio followed by leg day. I click into the same class that Meadow's in, crank my resistance up, and start to pedal.

Everything goes wrong about ten minutes into the heavy metal ride.

I adjust my weight to stand up, something rips, and the pedal clips don't brace me like normal.

I tip over the handlebars, my left leg flying in a wide arc now that it isn't locked into the pedal. My head bounces off the tablet display and my ribs crash against the handgrip.

Fuck!

I shove away from the handlebars and plant my left foot for balance just as the pedal slams into my calf like a wrecking ball.

The weight and momentum of my right foot, still clipped in, drives the pain into my left leg. With a grunt, I kick my left foot forward.

And then the bike falls on its side. With me still attached.

I crash to the floor, the bike landing heavy on my left thigh and the seat racking me hard in the nuts.

The pain doesn't register for an adrenaline-spiked second or two, but when it does, I'm engulfed in agony and nausea. I moan weakly, trying hard not to throw up.

I'm gonna lie here for a second. Try to breathe. Remain conscious.

My front door crashes open, and Meadow calls, "Griffin? Are you here?"

She pushes through the bedroom door, a pistol lowered in front of her in a two-handed grip. Willow follows her in.

"Oh my God. Are you okay?" Meadow asks.

My balls are still resting somewhere just barely south of my Adam's apple, so I can't answer her right now, but I manage a grunt. Maybe they'll leave me to die in peace.

"Okay, let's get you up."

She unbuckles my right shoe and slowly works my foot out of it. Once it's free, she and Willow pull the bike off me. The screen is dark. I either broke it or snagged the power cord in my blazing crash of glory.

I pull myself to a seated position with my back against the wall and breathe through the last of the pain. I'm gonna be tender for a while, but I don't think anything is ruptured.

Jesus. Just the word makes me queasy.

"Thanks," I croak.

"Are you okay?"

"How'd you get in?"

We speak at the same time. I wave her on to answer my question first. She's kneeling next to me, her hand braced on my knee, and something about her smells fruity through the light sheen of sweat she managed to work up in the first part of our ride.

"We heard the crash, and I yelled to see if you were okay. When you didn't answer, I had Willow pick the lock." She looks up at her sister and they silently communicate until Willow nods and leaves.

Fuck.

As much as I'd love another Meadow lecture, I'm not in fighting form right now.

"Can I get you some ice?"

I tip my head back against the wall and try to slow my ragged breathing. "Ice would be good, but I don't have any."

"I'll grab some from my place—be right back." Her hand rubs along my thigh before she stands and turns. My dick considers twitching, but the pain in my balls shuts that shit all the way down. Now is not the time to get turned on by the woman who drives me batty, no matter how good she smells or how appealing it would be to bury my hands in her hair and kiss the shit out of her to distract me from the pain in my groin.

Nope. Now is definitely not the time considering the dumpster fire of last night.

I manage to stand and hobble to the bathroom. Everything looks and feels like it should, but I'm going to be sore for a few days.

Good thing I don't have any carnal plans on the horizon.

I'm gingerly lowering myself onto the couch when the front door opens and Meadow carries in a drug store ice pack and a towel.

She passes them to me. I wrap the towel around the ice pack, then tuck it into my crotch. The cold is shocking for a second before it cuts away to relief.

Ah. Thank fucking God.

Meadow is a busybody—she's always moving or doing something, never settles for long. Before I can invite her to sit down, she heads back to the bedroom. A minute and a few grunts later, I hear the mechanical hum and beep of the bike starting up.

The screen must work because Meadow sucks in a sharp breath.

She sticks her head out the door. "You're EagleEye-BeastPI?"

I nod. She doesn't sound as pissed as I thought she would be. She doesn't look angry either. Her eyes are narrowed on me though. I don't know if I prefer her suspicious curiosity over her anger, and I don't have the energy to decide right now.

She shakes her head and plops down on the couch next to me. After a second, her head tips to rest on my shoulder. "I've hit more PRs in the last six months of trying to keep up with you than I have in the last two years of having the bike, damn you."

"Same, but I haven't had the bike as long as you."

We both chuckle, and then we lose it, laughing our asses off.

"How did you even find me on there?" she asks.

"I got your work email from your business website and took a chance. Sure enough, you popped up."

She laughs harder, and I can't help but join in.

Once I catch my breath, I say, "You really had no idea?"

"No, Willow made an offhand comment the other day, but I didn't think anything of it. I mean, how many PIs have Pelotons, ya know? Why am I the only person you follow? Don't your friends have bikes too?" She leans back into the couch, and her temple finds my shoulder again.

I shut my eyes and drop my head back against the cushion. "I don't have other friends, Meadow. I had a couple that I went to school with, but we lost touch when I moved down here."

"What about your family?"

"It's just my mom and that's..."

"That's what?"

"Complicated."

"I'm sorry." She says the words softly, but there's no pity in them. I don't think I could handle it if she pitied me. I used to have friends. I had a good group of guys, but once Mom was diagnosed and I became the sole provider for us both, it became tough to keep in touch, and we slowly drifted.

"It's okay." I lay my hand over hers where it rests between us. "About last night. I know that you're a solid investigator and that you can handle yourself."

"But you said—"

"I know what I said, but I could have said it better—or explained. I want you to stay out of the line of fire because it's not safe to dangle yourself in front of him like a red flag in front of a bull, Wildflower. You can't expect me to stand back and watch you put yourself in jeopardy. I can't do it no matter how many salient points you make about your experience or skillset. I can't."

"Griff, are you trying to protect me?"

I scoff. "You bet your ass I am. If you think for a single hot minute that I'm going to let you be in a dangerous situation with no protection—"

She kisses me.

I expected her to get angry, to rail and rant at me for wanting to protect her. I didn't expect her to place a hand on my jaw, turn my head toward her, and fasten her mouth to mine.

Her lips are so damn soft. I nip at them, encouraging her to open for me, and on a hitched breath she does. I trace my tongue along her bottom lip before dipping inside.

Suddenly, she breaks the kiss. My stomach swoops when her hand reaches between my legs, grabbing the ice pack and tossing it aside. Before I can blink, she throws a leg over and straddles me.

I bury my hands in her hair, fingers close to her scalp, and tug. Her breath is shaky, and she lets out a tiny sound when I go back in for a deeper taste.

I need more. The desire to taste her all over rises like a tidal wave, and I dip my mouth down her neck, scraping my teeth along her skin. Her hips crash against mine, creating a delicious, aching friction.

Grabbing the dip of her waist, I yank her down along my dick.

"Griff." Her eyes snap open and lock on mine. The green flecks in them are sharper than normal, her cheeks flushed with arousal.

I don't know what's happening, but I don't want it to stop.

"Wildflower. Give me your mouth again."

With a cry she does, and I ravish her mouth. The spicy sweet taste of her is everything I want and not nearly enough.

Breaking the kiss again, I move her hips against mine. "There you go. Just like that. Keep rubbing that pussy all over me."

Her heat carries through her pants and my shorts. She's going to burn us both up.

Take her to bed. Make her yours.

A harsh knock comes from the front door, and Willow calls, "Meadow, Dad just called. I have to head into the office for a bit. I'll be back before lunch."

Meadow scrambles off my lap and falls to the cushion next to me so fast she almost ends up on the floor. She clears her throat and replies, "Okay, I'll be right over."

She stands and straightens her clothes, though nothing was out of place.

From making out to awkward interruption all in the space of a heartbeat.

Roll with it, Gallagher.

I stand with her and ask, "Are you staying close to home today?"

"Yeah. We're all working from my place today."

"Okay. I've got an appointment and then I'm going to run by Martin's house and take a look." I grab my phone. "Do you want to go with?"

She shakes her head. "No, I'll let you do that while I do some online digging. Keep me updated?"

"Sure. Give me your number so I can text you."

She takes the device and punches in her number. She doesn't look at me before turning to leave again.

Fuck this.

I grab her elbow to pull her around to face me.

"Where are you running off to, Wildflower?" I ask the question softly, because she's frozen like a deer in the woods. One sharp sound and she's going to bolt.

But I have questions first.

"Um. We're keeping two people with Jenn at all times right now."

"That's not what I'm talking about, and you know it."

Questions run rampant through my head. Why is she so awkward now? And how do we get back to the wanton woman who just rode my clothed dick like it was her mission in life? Why'd she kiss me? Does she want to see me again? Is this even considered seeing? I'm out of my depth here.

"I don't know, Griffin. I don't know, okay? One second you're driving me insane being obnoxious, the next you're kissing the brains out of my head and asking me about my plans for the day. I just don't know."

I drop her arm. "When you figure it out, let me know. But, Meadow?"

Her gaze meets mine, and the heat we found together on my couch is absent now, her expression almost scared. I don't blame her; this shit is terrifying.

"Yeah?"

"Don't keep me in the dark too long."

"Okay."

She takes the brightness of the day with her when she pulls the door shut behind her.

16

GRIFFIN

AFTER MEADOW LEAVES, I GET DRESSED AND HEAD OUT. I want to visit Mom and do a drive-by of Martin's place before it gets too late in the day.

Moving forward on the investigation without Meadow almost makes me feel guilty until I remember she's doing work of her own at her place.

I don't want to wait till Thursday to grab this guy. If I can get him now, then there's no reason for Meadow to be in the line of fire.

Overall, this guy is an unknown. We think he called Jenn the day he skipped bail, but that could have just been any creep. Or even a creep misdialing and Jenn wasn't the intended target in the first place. There've been no new calls, no new developments that suggest that he's an active danger to Jenn or Meadow.

Not that either of us plan to let him get close. I get why Meadow's worried, especially if she didn't notice signs of Jenn being abused the first time.

Hindsight's a bitch like that.

The drive to Mom's is pretty smooth, but the second I

open her door, I know today's a bad day.

She's sitting in her pajamas by the window, her hair down around her shoulders instead of up in her usual pony-tail, and she's absently doodling on a pad of paper.

Her head turns toward me, and the tiny flame of hope that I might be wrong evaporates. Her normally bright brown eyes are cloudy and confused.

She slightly smiles at me and says, "Richard, it's so good to see you." Gingerly, she stands and comes to wrap her arms around me.

Mom's always had a small frame, but she feels so much smaller now.

I brace myself and say, "Hi Celia, how's it going?" My uncle passed away before I was born, but this isn't the first time she's confused us. I've seen pictures of him, so I know that I kind of look like him.

Mom's lips pinch together, and she looks around the room as though seeking the answers to how her day is.

I hate that she's confused. That she doesn't remember me. She didn't choose to forget about me or anything else in her life. Helpless rage at being unable to fix this choked the life out of me for the first year after her diagnosis.

"Let's get some tea and then we can sit by the window."

I move toward the kitchenette and ignore the pinch in my chest while I make us drinks.

She's getting worse, and I'm not prepared for it.

I sit next to her by the window and ask inane questions about what she's drawing, her plans for the day, most of which I already know the answers to, but it makes her happy to have the conversation.

Mom stops talking midstory to stare out at the moun-tains. I know that she's not going to come out of the confusion today, and I curse the lost day. Lost because there are only so many days left I get with her.

I'm in a vicious cycle. I want to spend all the time that I can with Mom, but I need the work hours and income to pay for this facility. And now I've added in a new element with whatever the hell is going on with Meadow.

My phone pings with a notification from a process serving company that has a few open projects. I accept them and then stand to clean up our drinks. I can knock them out this afternoon and pad my bank account a little.

"I need to head out," I tell Mom.

She doesn't respond, just stares out the window.

My nose stings and my eyes burn as I bend to kiss her cheek. Another day with her gone.

Amy's at the front desk, and her face pinches when she sees me. "Bad day?"

I nod, the clog in my throat preventing me from speaking.

"Griffin..."

I hold up a hand. I can't do this right now. Clearing my throat the best I can, I croak, "I'll swing by later this week. Call me if she needs me, okay?"

The bright sunlight mocks me when I plug Martin's house address into the GPS and pull out of the parking lot.

Mom's doctors urged me to go see a grief counselor when she was first diagnosed, and I did for a little bit. I kept going until I got a handle on feeling helpless in a shitty situation. I kept going until we moved down here. It might be time for me to go again.

Seeing her like this, watching her slowly drift away one memory at a time, frightens me. It scares me that she's disappearing right in front of my eyes, and it scares me that I might disappear one day too.

It's a sobering thought. One that makes me question exactly what I'm doing with Meadow, why I'm pushing for more from her. What is it about her that makes me *want*? Dragging someone else into this mess will just end up hurting more people in the end.

I pull off the freeway and down a private drive. Martin's last address is in a wealthy neighborhood where each house sits on sprawling property. Bobby's paperwork includes the code for the gated community, so I punch that in and follow the GPS's monotone directions.

The structure is almost entirely glass. How can anyone live in a house with so much visibility? It makes me itchy just to consider it. But then I notice the tint on the windows.

The two-way film lets light in but keeps prying eyes out. *Wonder how much that cost for this much glass?*

The driveway is empty as I pull in. I can't see anything through the front windows of the house, but I figure it's better to be safe than sorry as I make my way around the front yard in search of the gate that will let me in the back.

The wood and metal fence is surprisingly unlocked. I unlatch it and pull it closed behind me. In this neighborhood there're probably cameras everywhere, so I'd better be fast and stealthy.

I round the back of the house, skirting the sparkly blue pool. The rest of the landscaping looks maintained as well. I need to ask Bobby about that. If there's staff maintaining the property, maybe someone's seen Martin.

Through the back of the house I can't see anything, but when I press my face to the back door, it slides open an inch.

Maintained yard and pool. Unlocked back fence. Unsecured back door without an alarm.

Warning bells chime in my head. Someone's been here recently.

Usually I try not to break the law, which is both an "I don't want to be arrested" choice and an honor thing, but I'm going to make an exception.

Lightly I step through the back door and into the spacious kitchen littered with trash.

Dirty dishes are piled in the sink. Old takeout boxes are scattered across the counter. The trash smells like it should have gone out a couple of weeks ago.

I cross into the living room. The rest of the house isn't much better.

My taser in hand, I work through the house, kicking along trash and clothes as I clear the rooms.

It looks like a hoarders' convention in here. Each room is more of a pigsty than the last. Clothes are tossed everywhere, dishes that double as science experiments cover every flat surface, and the smell of a dead *something* is coming from under a pile of trash in the bathroom that I'm unwilling to investigate.

I don't find anyone here, but I do hit pay dirt in the study. In a small notebook, the name of the restaurant that Kent said he and Martin were meeting at is circled.

Martin was clearly staying here while he was out on bail but isn't here now.

If I was a bail jumper trying to evade the authorities, I wouldn't stay at my last known address either.

What the hell is this guy thinking? And where is he now?

I finish up at the house and leave through the back door again, making sure to pull it shut.

Back in my car, I call Bobby to give him an update.

"He's been staying at his house?" he asks.

"Looks like it, but not anymore."

"Why do you say that?"

"The place is trashed, but it's old trash. A week or so since he's been here, I'd say."

"Hmm. And you think that appointment is going to be the best bet to catch him?"

"Maybe. I'm hoping for it, but something isn't adding up."

"What do you mean?"

"I don't know. Just something not sitting right. He stays here and leaves the place a dump, but then reaches out to a friend to try to sell the place after skipping bail? If I were him, I'd have tried to sell it before I skipped so that I could be in the wind by the time anyone noticed."

"Maybe he's not the sharpest pencil in the box. Does he have any family?"

"A couple of cousins, all of them claiming not to have seen him since before his parents died. None of them seem like the type to harbor a fugitive they barely talk to."

"So we shoot for Thursday and if we can't nab him then, we keep digging. We'll find him. Meadow with you?"

"No. She had to stay behind with Jenn." While it's not technically a lie, it's not the whole truth either.

"Hmm."

"Hmm what?"

"Nothing. Update her and keep me in the loop. We'll touch base closer to Thursday."

"Sounds good."

The phone clicks in my ear, and I toss it to the passenger seat. This situation doesn't make sense.

I start the car and pull out of the neighborhood, the glare from the glass in my rearview mirror enough to blind me.

The notebook in the study is too convenient. Martin may not be the smartest, but even the least intelligent criminal knows better than to leave behind traceable information just lying around for anyone to find.

"What the hell are you up to, Martin, and where is your hole?"

17

MEADOW

I RAN LIKE A SCARED LITTLE RABBIT.

Yeah, we're trying to keep two people with Jenn at all times, and I'm glad that Willow let me know she was leaving. And I have work I can do from here, but I totally used it as a reason to bail without talking to Griffin about the kiss.

I went from worried about him to taking care of him, and then I'm kissing him and grinding against him on his couch.

What is wrong with me lately? Is my libido finally rebelling for neglecting it for so long? I don't know for sure, but what I do know is that I lost my ever-loving mind for a few minutes there.

I return to my apartment, mumbling to Jenn and Fawn that I'm taking a shower.

The hot water beats along my neck and shoulders, the tension easing with each pulse of the shower head.

Even if I do want to break my dry spell, do I really want to break it with Griffin? Just last week, I wanted to pluck his eyeballs out with tweezers, but this morning when he demanded my mouth again, I turned into putty in his hands. How crazy is that?

I learned three things this morning. Griffin Gallagher's kisses are addictingly dangerous. He's a lot more complicated than I gave him credit for. And for some reason, he's chosen to be very alone in the world.

Griffin, what in the world am I going to do about you?

I don't have the answer to that, and I'm not sure that I want to figure it out right now. I didn't get a chance to finish my own workout, I haven't eaten yet, and I still have some research to do on the sting we're executing in less than four days, plus I need to follow up on all of the other cases waiting in the wings.

I need some thinking time.

Thinking about my combustibly hot neighbor and grinding all over him is not on this morning's agenda. Making a decision about what to do with the combustibly hot neighbor is also not on the books for the foreseeable future.

I dry off and dress before making a beeline for the coffeepot. After dropping two pieces of bread into the toaster, I pour myself a cup of coffee and take a deep drink, narrowly avoiding scalding my mouth.

Jenn and Fawn are sitting at the breakfast nook, watching me. Guilty, I look away but still see them share a look out of the corner of my eye.

I preempt whatever they are about to say. "I'm going to get some digital work done this morning. Jenn, were you able to pull up the floor plan of the restaurant for me?"

She cocks an eyebrow at me before nodding. "It's in your email. I'm going to work on pulling some of the background reports Andrew requested. Once this is over, y'all are going to have your hands full."

"We know, but you come first."

Fawn jumps in. "I have to run Landon his swim trunks around lunch, so if Willie isn't back by then, can Griffin come and back you up?"

The first rule of providing protection services is making sure you know where the client is at all times. The second rule? Have adequate backup in case shit hits the fan.

"I can ask him."

I snag my laptop and head for the couch, eager to bury myself in enough work that my brain shuts up for the time being.

A TENSION HEADACHE thrums in my temples and my eyes are dry when I surface from my case files.

Willow returned just as Fawn needed to leave, and she and Jenn settled in with some work. Fawn came back after about an hour, and we've all been working since.

We could have gone into the office, but none of us felt like loading everything up for a couple hours of work and then lugging it all back here later this afternoon.

I roll my neck, the muscles tight from sitting for so long.

I nudge Jenn with my toes. "Wanna get out of here for a bit?"

She smiles and stretches her arms above her head. "Absolutely."

We pile into the car and head to one of my favorite places.

Great Skate has been around probably longer than I've been alive. My sisters and I were here constantly as kids, for birthday parties and school skate nights and summer afternoons when it was too hot to play outside.

We pull into the parking lot and grab our skates from the trunk, then go inside. I texted ahead, and open skating doesn't start for another hour, so we'll have the place to ourselves.

"Well, if it isn't my favorite ladies," a familiar voice calls out.

Cameron's manning the front desk, and his eyes skip over us before settling on Jenn. A shy smile curls his lips.

His crush on her is adorable.

"Hey, Cam, how's it going?" I ask.

Willow gives him a playlist as we all strap on our skates, and soon music is pumping through the speakers as we circle the rink.

I love to skate. It's a hell of a workout, fun, and there's music—all wins. One of the first times that Jenn and I hung out our freshman year, I brought her here and she was a hot mess on skates. But after a little practice, she'd gotten the hang of it, and now she's a pro. It's still one of our favorite places to get away and just have a good time even though it's meant for kids.

I let my hips move to the beat of the music and my thoughts go as I circle the rink.

When I have a particularly hard case, or something isn't adding up and I need the thinking time, I come to the skating rink. Willow's not a fan, but that's only because her attention span is too short to go in the same circle over and over again for the fun of it. She gets bored with the monotony and usually ditches us for the arcade.

Fawn likes to race around the track—it's all about the speed for her, and she's in a roller derby league. She and Landon come pretty regularly too, but he wanted to stay with my parents today and hang out in their pool.

Something about the ease of picking Martin up on

Thursday doesn't sit right. He's not stupid. He was smart enough to cover up his abuse of Jenn well enough that none of us realized what was going on until it was too late.

I haven't heard anything more from Griffin about his conversation with Kent, but if he had more information, he'd pass that along, right?

Maybe Griffin knows more than he's letting on.

We've never worked together, so I don't know what his methods are or what he's thinking about the case, but the same can be said for him considering that we've been at odds for a lot of the time.

I add it to my list of things to talk to him about. We need to be on the same page by Thursday.

I skate off the floor and toward the water fountains to grab a drink. As I cross onto the carpet, Cameron rolls up beside me.

"Is Jenn okay? When you called earlier..."

Cameron's had stars in his eyes for Jenn since the first time he saw her, but he's always been too shy to make a move.

I bump my shoulder to his and gesture toward a bench. "Come on, let's sit down for a minute. She's as good as can be expected." Cam's gaze is glued to Jenn on the rink where she's skating backward and swaying to the music.

"You're going after that asshole?"

"We are. We have a plan and hope to grab him later this week."

"Is there anything I can do to help?"

"We've got her, Cam."

"How's the case going? Your mom was in here earlier this week and said something about you working with another investigator?"

Mom loves to skate as much as I do and comes once or twice a week.

"Yeah. His name's Griffin. Bobby hired him to work with me on the case."

"And is this the same guy that you were looking cozy with at the block party this weekend?"

"You were there?"

He shakes his head. "Nah, I had to work, but I got it from the grapevine." He nods toward Willow, who's bumping her hip against a videogame and cursing.

I laugh. It just figures that she'd gossip with Cam about my love life. Those two are thick as thieves.

I roll my eyes. "In this *one single instance* your grapevine is correct. He kissed me at the block party."

"*Just* at the block party?"

With a huff, I give in to the interrogation and tell him about the weirdness of me and Griffin.

He squints at me like he's trying to figure something out. "So he's doing what you're doing and that makes you mad? He's trying to protect you like you're trying to protect Jenn."

Mom pointed out the same thing, and now Cam? Is there something in the water?

"No. It's not the same at all. I'm an investigator just like him, and I'm more than capable—"

"You don't think Jenn is capable of taking care of herself?" he interrupts.

"I didn't say that. I'm just saying—"

"You're saying that you're more capable of taking care of yourself than Jenn is. Is that what you think?"

"No, not at all."

Cam stands and shoves his hands into his pockets. "If I were you, Mead, I'd take a long hard look at the similarities between your actions and Griffin's. Because to me, it sounds like you're both just trying to look out for the people you care about."

He shuffles across the carpet to get back on the rink just as the disco ball drops and "Dancing Queen" starts.

Mom insinuated the same thing—that Griffin was trying to protect me, and I shoved it to the side and chalked it up to him being an asshat. Then he confirmed it this morning. Can I really fault him for it since I'm doing the same thing for my best friend?

Being thrown together with Griffin both personally and professionally has me off-kilter when I can't afford to be.

18

GRIFFIN

Process serving is one of the easier aspects of being a private investigator and the bulk of my work today.

I park a few houses down from the most recently known address of one Allen Kapowski. Based on the thickness of the envelope holding his court papers, he's either getting a divorce or he hasn't been paying his child support.

The details of what I'm actually serving aren't provided, but I've done enough of these to guess.

I yank my ball cap a little lower and start down the sidewalk. A dog barks in the distance. Double-checking the numbers on the side of the house, I approach the front door. This neighborhood is full of cookie-cutter houses that are all similar enough I don't want to get them mixed up.

A quick knock at the door sets off a dog inside, but based on the yapping, it sounds small.

The door cracks open, revealing a skinny guy in his boxers who looks like he hasn't shaved or slept in days.

"Allen Kapowski?"

"Who's asking?"

"Are you Allen Kapowski?" According to the DMV

photo I pulled up, I know that it's him, but I need his verbal confirmation.

His shoulder slumps, and he says, "Yeah, that's me. What do you want?"

I hand him the envelope, and once he sees the court seal on it, he swears. "I don't have any more money for her. She's running me ragged with all these child support claims, and I never even see the fucking rats anymore. I shouldn't have to pay for them if I don't see 'em."

Child support. Called it.

I nod and turn away. "You have a good day, sir."

Contrary to what Hollywood would have you believe, I don't have to stick around after serving someone papers or tell them they've been served. Most of the time, they know and aren't evasive or aggressive, even when you catch them off guard. But I want to be anywhere but here right now.

My mother never petitioned my father, whoever he was, for child support or custody. His name isn't even on my birth certificate. I never met the man and don't want to. But that meant there were times I had to watch my mom decide if she was going to pay our light bill or feed us that week. Those aren't things kids should see.

I finish up two more process serves, but I can't seem to kick my irritation. As a result, I'm testy as fuck when I pull into the apartment parking lot to find the Ridley women and Jenn all climbing out of Meadow's car and laughing.

Anger snaps through me. She told me they were staying home today.

I slam my car door and stride across the lot. "Where the hell were you, Meadow? You said you weren't going anywhere today."

Meadow looks at the others. "You guys go ahead. I'll be right up." She stares at me for a second, then says calmly,

"We went skating. It wasn't planned or I would have said something about it this morning."

"And you didn't call or text me because?"

Her eyes flare, and she rolls in her lips. "Because I don't answer to you. I don't know where this attitude is coming from right now, or why you're so mad about me leaving my house, but you need to get over yourself. If I want to cart-wheel naked through the Deck Park Tunnel during rush hour, then I'll do it. Now, if you want to have a rational discussion about today, you know where to find me."

She whips around and stomps down the sidewalk. Most of my temper bleeds away at the logic in her argument.

She's right.

I don't have any say in what she does or where she goes.

I follow her and slap a hand on the elevator door before it can close. The temperature in here is thirty degrees below zero, and the frosty glares Meadow sends my way hit the mark.

I bide my time, waiting until Meadow's nearly to her apartment before I snag her fingers in mine and tug her after me. "I'm sorry. You're right. Can we go to my place to talk?" I feel like since this whole case started I've spent most of my time putting my foot in my mouth and apologizing to Meadow.

"Why does it always have to be your place? There's nothing wrong with my apartment."

"Your apartment is like Grand Central Station right now, so this is the only place I can get you to myself."

Her eyes find mine and hold steady. "Is that something we're doing now?"

I unlock my door and pull her inside behind me. "I'd like it to be."

Her fingers squeeze mine when she says, "Me too."

But the second that I close the door behind her, I take her mouth and back her against the door. Her arms wrap around my neck and she meets me halfway.

The crisp taste of her rights the tilt of my day, and I take my first full breath in hours.

"How was skating?"

"Why were you mad?"

We speak at the same time.

She waves at me. "You go first."

"It was a shitty day and then seeing you coming home when you said you weren't going anywhere irked me. But I overreacted. I'm sorry."

"It's okay. I understand. We're both under a lot of stress right now."

"And skating?"

"It was good. Have you ever been?"

I shake my head. "No. The last time I strapped death shoes to my feet I was a little younger than your nephew."

She laughs. "I'll have to take you sometime—it's one of my favorite places to think."

I rub my face along her arm and breathe her in. "I'm game."

"Why was your day bad?"

"I went to see my mom. Swung by Martin's place and did some process serving that put me in a shit mood."

Meadow nods. "Did you find anything?"

"About six months' worth of trash and a notebook with Kent's meeting time and place circled, but that's it."

"What do you mean 'trash'?"

"The house was trashed, like he never cleans up after himself and when the mess gets to be too bad he just moves to a different room."

"And the notebook with the meeting was just sitting out?"

"Yeah."

Meadow's brow furrows.

"What is it?" I ask.

"Something's not right. Martin's not that dumb. He wouldn't just leave something like that out after skipping bail. And the trash thing is weird. I remember Jenn telling me about one of their fights because she left her makeup out on the counter. He didn't *do* clutter or mess."

I gently hug her a little closer. "We should go talk to Jenn. But I'd like it on record that I'm good with staying right here holding you for a second."

"I'm good with being held, but I think that it's best if we go talk to Jenn. Plus, I'm hungry and it's close to dinnertime."

"What are we having?" I place a nibbling kiss along her collar bone.

"I'm thinking some chicken stir-fry. It's easy and makes a lot." Her response is breathy.

As much as I'd like to spend all day with her here, alone, to explore all the ways I can make her breathless, we can't. At least not yet.

I drop a kiss on her mouth, brief and nowhere near what I need. "Delicious."

And the stir-fry sounds good too.

JENN AND FAWN are both sitting on the couch with laptops open when we walk into Meadow's apartment.

"Jenn, Griff went to Martin's place today." Meadow nods at me.

"The house was trashed. Like he hadn't cleaned it up since he got out on bail."

Jenn's brow crinkles. "Are you sure Martin was staying there?"

"It was the address listed in the file, but other than a notebook with the details of his meeting with Kent on them, I didn't see a definitive sign that he was the one staying there, no."

She's shaking her head before I finish. "What kind of mess? Can you be more specific?"

"Trash, dishes, and clothes were everywhere. Like two hoarders were setting up residence." I pull up some of the pictures that I took today and hand her my phone.

Jenn takes it and shakes her head again.

"Martin wouldn't do that. He had a cleaning lady come three times a week and would freak if dishes weren't done right after dinner." She points to the screen. "That broken vase in the kitchen? It's Meissen and cost Martin just over six figures. I don't think he did this."

I look over at Meadow and she asks, "Do you know who would?"

"No. Unless he went crazy in the past few months, I can't see him letting the house get like this."

That's what I'm scared of. But before I can voice my concerns there's a knock at the door.

On the screen Meadow has set up next to the door, Susan, Landon, and Andrew Ridley are displayed standing in the hallway with a covered dish.

Meadow lets them in and offers me a wincing smile. "I forgot it's family dinner night and my turn to host."

I nod and offer, "Should I go?" I don't want to intrude.

"Of course not," Susan says. "I made enough for everyone."

Laptops are put away, Susan and Meadow head into the kitchen to warm up dinner, and the already crowded apartment gets a little bit smaller with her parents there.

Andrew hands me a beer. "So, how's the case going?"

Meadow's eyes find mine and she smiles slightly. I hold that smile close because I'm about to watch it die. I pop the top on the beer and take a sip.

"Something's off about the case. Things aren't adding up." I break down the situation for him and finish with, "I'd prefer that she not be included in the trap to catch him at lunch later this week. It's too dangerous."

"What?" Meadow's head whips toward us.

"If he's the one that was staying at his house and trashed it, then he's more dangerous than we originally thought since it's so out of character for him. If he's not the one who trashed his place, then we have another party involved that's an unknown. Considering you were the one who caught him after he assaulted Jenn, you're most likely on his shit list. It's not safe for you to be there."

The muscle in her jaw pulses, and I know that she wants to argue with me. But she stays silent because she knows I'm right.

"Which is why I'll be across the street at the café."

"Even that might be too close, Wildflower."

She opens her mouth, but before she can say anything Andrew asks, "And you believe we have reason to worry about Meadow?"

I nod. "I'd rather be safe than sorry. Jenn's under protection right now, and I think Meadow being cautious would be a good thing."

"I gave her this case because I believe she's capable of it. What makes you think she isn't?"

"Dad. What the fuck?" Willow cuts in.

I hold up my hand. "I believe she's more than capable of handling herself against the common threats of this job. But when the case doesn't add up against a known threat—one that she was responsible for putting in jail, and now has an unknown element, I believe it's better to be safe than sorry. I wouldn't suggest this unless I needed to."

Andrew nods. Willow, Fawn, and Jenn glare at me, but none of them sting as much as Meadow's spurned gaze. She's erasing what little progress we've made and wiping our scorecard clean.

Keeping this thing growing between us separate from the case is already harder than I thought it would be.

It's a good thing I'm a patient man.

19

MEADOW

I can't sleep. I feel like shit, my brain won't quiet down, and I'm pissed at Griffin.

I thought that we had come to an understanding—I'm more than capable of taking care of myself—but he just cut me out without hesitation at the first tiny sign of perceived danger.

All because *something* doesn't add up.

What a crock of bullshit.

I've been a private investigator for eight years. In that time, I've had a handful of close scrapes, but no one has ever questioned my abilities as an investigator like Griffin has.

Being betrayed by my own family fucking sucks—and that's exactly what it was, betrayal. Once Griffin got done with his analysis of the case, everyone unilaterally decided he was right, and no amount of arguing from me changed their minds. I did something that I've never done in my entire life. I gave up and hid in my bedroom. Let my sisters handle the guard duty tonight, because I'm done with the day.

Mom knocked on the door and told me dinner was

done, but I faked being asleep until she left me alone. I don't know if Griffin stayed for dinner or not, but if he did, I hope he choked on a chicken bone.

When cornered, I usually come out swinging with logic and facts until I've pulverized the opposing arguments. But how do you fight against feeling and emotions? Especially when you're outgunned and up against your family?

You don't.

My stomach gurgles hard. I'm starving, but the low sounds of the TV in the living room keep me in my room. I'm not sure if anyone is still awake, but I'd rather not deal with any of them right now.

A faint knock sounds through the wall behind my headboard. Probably just Griffin getting ready for bed. My phone buzzes on the table next to me.

I snag the device and unlock it.

Griffin Asshat Gallagher: How're you feeling?

I start to rage text but then waffle on what I want to say, typing then deleting over and over.

"Meadow, I can see the floating dots. Just fucking send it already," Griffin calls through the wall. He's a little muffled but understandable.

Fuck. I should have turned off read receipts.

Me: *middle finger emoji*

There's a snorting laugh from the other side of the wall before a new message comes through.

Griffin Asshat Gallagher: I guess I deserve that, huh?

Me: You do.

Griffin Asshat Gallagher: Wildflower...

Me: Nope. You do NOT get to use a cutesy nickname when you stabbed me in the back.

Griffin Asshat Gallagher: Okay. Let's get something straight.

Me: This oughta be good.

Griffin Asshat Gallagher: I did not stab you in the back. I agreed that you're capable didn't I?

Me: That doesn't count when you turn around and tell my father that I can't be involved in the more physical aspects of the case. Do you know how stupid you made me sound? How awful that felt?

And the fact that my dad *sided* with him? That sucked too.

The bubbles bounce and disappear for a few seconds before they just don't come back.

Good riddance.

That doesn't hurt at all. Not one bit. The ache in my chest is acid reflux.

I throw my phone on the side table and am punching my pillow into shape when my bedroom door opens and Griffin barges in.

He's shirtless, the wide expanse of his chest on full gorgeous display.

I can't help it; my eyes drift down to the basketball shorts that ride low on his hips. The belt of muscles there plays peekaboo.

Oh. He's fighting dirty now.

"We're not having this conversation through text messages." Without waiting for me to respond or, I don't know, offer a fucking invitation, he pulls back the covers and crawls into bed next to me.

"What the hell are you doing?"

"I want snuggles. And we're going to talk."

He fluffs my spare pillow a few times before settling down on it. My arms are crossed over my chest, and everything about my body language says back off, but apparently he doesn't get the memo.

"Now. Come here." Gently, he pulls my arms apart and tugs me close until my head rests on his chest. He smells like soap and radiates enough heat to power the city, which should be annoying. It should be so annoying, but it isn't.

"Griffin..."

"Shh. Lemme hold you for a second. Now I'm going to talk, and for once, you need to shush and listen."

I try to push up from him, but his hold tightens, locking me in place.

"You're the most capable person that I know. But you're also the most stubborn. Do I think that you could be there in the restaurant with us and we'd get the job done? Sure, but not at the expense of your safety. That's nonnegotiable to me. Even being across the street is too close. Whether you're here with Jenn or in that restaurant with me doesn't negate your abilities as an investigator. I'm sorry if me kicking you to the sidelines made you think that, but we already cleared up just how capable I think you are, right?"

He doesn't wait for me to confirm. "But your capabilities have limits, and you being in the restaurant wouldn't be smart, which I know you are. It makes no sense to have you anywhere near there, which could complicate the whole thing. Having you in any potential line of fire scares me because I fucking care about you and I don't want to see you hurt. I *can't* see you hurt. Not because I doubt your usefulness on the case. I'm sorry I made you feel small or stupid. That wasn't my intention. You're a fucking Amazon warrior to me, okay?"

His hand finds my hair and his fingers burrow in, tugging lightly at the scalp. I want to fire back with something witty. Something to keep my distance, but the exhaustion from the day has caught up with me, and my eyes drift shut.

I WAKE up to the sound of a camera shutter clicking, then realize a steel bar of an erection is nestled between my ass cheeks.

Griffin's breaths tickle the back of my neck, steady in their intensity. I look up to find Willow holding her phone over us, snapping pictures.

"Willow, what are you doing?" I whisper yell.

"I needed photographic proof of hell freezing over."

Getting up to kick her ass is out of the question since I'm pinned under the bulk of man meat that has taken over my bed. Griffin said he wanted snuggles, and I guess he's not above chasing me across the bed and wrapping himself around me like a vine to get them.

Weak sunlight filters through the window. I have no idea what time it is, other than morning with the way it's slanting into my bedroom.

Fawn pokes her head around the corner of the door. "Willow! Let them sleep."

I lift my head as much as I can. "I'm awake. But Griffin isn't so you both need to get the fuck out. I'll be out in a minute to kill you."

Fawn skirts around the door to grab Willow by the elbow and drag her away.

My head hits my pillow again as I burrow back under the covers and blink the sleep from my eyes. I've been waking up cold lately since Jenn and my sisters like the air conditioning set at "winter wonderland." But the heat pumping off Griffin is wonderful, and I snuggle as close as I can without waking him up.

The arm around my waist tightens, and a warm,

scratchy kiss dances along my neck, causing goose bumps to break out down my arms.

That feels really good, but I don't know if I'm still mad at him or not, so I stay silent.

"Good morning, Wildflower." His voice is rough and slurred with sleep, and his hips flex against my ass.

Don't squirm. Don't squirm.

The hand around my waist sneaks under my sleep shirt and then his whole hand is closing over my breast. My nipple perks right up and hardens, waiting eagerly for him to move his hand and give it the attention it craves, but he never does.

I want to scoot my hips back and rub along the length of his dick so bad, to thrust my breast into his palm, but I can't. First off, I didn't get to say my piece last night, and second, my sisters are less than twenty feet away from us, so nothing is happening.

"Breakfast is ready!" Someone—I think Fawn—yells from the living room.

Griffin flexes against me one more time and squeezes my breast before he rolls to his back and stretches. I listen to his joints and back popping, then turn over to watch him.

His eyes meet mine, and he throws a cocky smile at me as he gets out of bed. "I'm gonna shower at my place. I'll be right back."

There are a few muffled giggles from the living room and then the front door shuts.

Five seconds later, my bedroom door is thrown open again, and three women bounce into bed with me.

The fact that they say nothing and just smile at me has heat rushing to my cheeks. Jenn dances her eyebrows at me, making them do the wave. "Sooooo, Griffin spent the night?"

I roll my eyes. "Obviously. But nothing happened. He talked and then I fell asleep."

"That wasn't nothing happening in his shorts this morning, honey." Willow smirks.

I toss a pillow at her head. "You shouldn't have looked, you hussy!"

She tosses it right back. "How could I not look at all of that?" she cries.

I wind up to throw again when Fawn stops my arm. "She's right—he walked right past us, and it was really hard to miss how...ahem...excited he was."

Jenn grumbles, "You both are lucky asses."

"I would thank you for not invading my privacy this morning, Jenn. You've officially been promoted to favorite sister status."

Fawn and Willow gasp in outrage, but Jenn smiles mischievously. "Don't thank me yet—I got an eyeful while he was walking out."

"What did he say?" Fawn asks.

"He just explained about why he sided with all of you about the restaurant."

Fawn cocks an eyebrow. "You know that he's right. Otherwise you wouldn't have hid in your room—you'd have doubled down and fought dirty to be included. Though he could have gone about it a better way." Out of all of us, she's the most serious but also the peacekeeper. If you need someone to understand both sides of the story without taking sides, she's your girl. Her objectivity is something I usually love, but having it turned against me sucked.

She's not wrong. I do recognize that there's an increased risk in being included in the physical boots on the ground investigation, but that doesn't make it any easier to swallow.

I missed the signs that Jenn needed help the first time,

and now I'm being relegated to the sidelines. But holding on to my anger about being banished to the back end of the investigation is childish and petty. Two things I have no business being.

Plus, waking up to Griffin's superior snuggles pretty much vacuumed the vengeance-seeking wind out of my sails.

Now I'm wondering when we can do it again—and this time without an audience waking us up.

Maybe it's time I do something about that.

20

GRIFFIN

I FEEL LIKE A NEW MAN AS THE HOT WATER BEATS against my shoulders and head. I can't remember the last time that I slept so hard.

Energy courses through me. If only I hadn't trashed my cycling shoes because I need some sort of outlet for all this. Normally I walk around in a haze of exhaustion, but this morning I'm bound to bounce off the walls if I don't find a way to burn off some of this.

I could always burn some energy the old-fashioned way.

I brush that thought aside because I don't think Meadow's ready for it. As much as I loved spending the night with her, it's hard to be intimate when your sisters and best friend are in the next room.

Part of the reason I made such a hasty escape this morning after a brief bout of cuddling was that I didn't trust myself not to take advantage of having Meadow in a bed with me.

I had her tit in my hand and her ass cradling my cock in a lover's embrace. It was either give in or suffer through the most severe case of blue balls the world has ever seen. I elected to get the hell out of Dodge.

The urge to rub one out while I'm in the shower sounds appealing, but empty—I'd rather wait for the real thing with Meadow.

It may not happen any time soon, but no one's died of unfulfilled lust so thick you practically drown in it, right?

I climb out of the shower and wrap a towel around my hips. Jenn said something about pancakes, and I'm absolutely going to weasel my way into a stack of those. Plus, I want to talk to Meadow more about last night. She fell asleep before she could say anything, and I want to give her a chance to communicate with me.

The only thing that I've got going on today is some light work and organizing some case files.

Maybe I can take Meadow out to dinner. Or at least order in and have a quiet dinner in my apartment.

Romancing a woman is new to me. I dated some in high school, but after Mom's diagnosis, I didn't have the time or energy for a relationship. Casual one-night stands have been the norm until now because Mom has always been my first priority.

I've never really made an effort with women before, but I want to for Meadow.

And it can't hurt to ask her out. I've asked her weirder things before and survived to tell the tale.

I walk into the bedroom and stop short when I see someone there already.

"Jesus. Wildflower, you scared the shit out of me."

Still in pajamas, Meadow is cross-legged on my made bed. She's not wearing a fucking bra, and my hands clench reflexively, wanting the weight of her tits in my palms again.

"Sorry. I didn't mean to startle you."

"I told you I was coming back. What're ya doing here?"

Instead of answering me, she stands and drags her sleep shirt over her head and off.

Every trace of oxygen backs up in my lungs, and I nearly choke at the sight of her full breasts. Her nipples, a few shades darker than the cream of her skin, pucker in the cool air. A rosy flush that I want to trace with my tongue is already spreading across her chest.

Her flared waist tapers into thighs so thick I'd happily die with them as my earmuffs.

Meadow shuffles her feet, antsy under my gaze. I have to grit my teeth and close my eyes, dropping my chin to my chest to hold it together long enough to say, "Wildflower, I need you to be real sure. Because I'm hanging on by the skin of my teeth."

"I'm sure."

I take two steps forward, which brings my chest flush to hers. The scrape of her nipples across my pecs confirms that she really is here—in my apartment, feet from my bed, ready and willing.

I keep one hand on my towel and sink the other into her hair to guide her mouth to mine.

From bickering in the hallways to unlikely allies and finally now lovers, the rightness of her in my bedroom is inescapable.

She tastes faintly of mint and mine and I want to kiss her for days. To get lost in the silky texture of her mouth. To slowly discover every spot that makes her gasp and tremble, to unravel her just for me.

Her hands find my shoulders, her fingertips pressing in, and I urge her down onto the bed until she's lying under me.

I abandon the towel and slowly drag her shorts down her legs, tossing both away.

Her legs are smooth under my fingers, and I take a second to just look at her. Never in my wildest dreams did I imagine having Meadow Ridley in my bed, hair spread out across my pillow, waiting for me to fuck her.

She stretches her arms, and the motion lifts her breasts higher. If that's not an offering, I don't know what is. Propping myself up on one arm, I let my lips fall to one breast, slowly swirling my tongue around the underside before sucking the peak into my mouth. Her hips flex, seeking, and I move my mouth to her other breast and pinch the tip of the first.

I could do this all day, but her breathing is coming faster. Her legs are sawing against my blankets in impatience. As much as I'd like to see if I could get her off by only sucking on her, I don't think either of us is going to make it this time.

I dip a hand down to her core, and my fingers glide through her folds easily.

"As much as I'd love to eat your cunt, I don't think I'd survive it, Wildflower."

Her eyes lock with mine, and she nods even as she chases my fingers with her hips.

"Ah-ah, I'll touch this pretty clit when I'm ready to."

"Fine. Then I'll just have to find something to play with until then," she taunts, and then the smooth skin of her hand is closing around my cock. My dick jumps in her hand, and I groan at the pressure.

"Fuck, yes. Squeeze me harder, Wildflower."

Her fingers tighten on me and I grunt, before burying my face in her neck and sinking my teeth into her shoulder.

My fingers circle up and around the swollen nub of her

clit. Her hand falters at my first passing glance. I don't want her to stop, but we're both going to blow before we get to the main attraction if I don't stop her.

I push her hand away and stroke myself. Her wetness provides enough lubrication that my hand shuttles along the length easily.

"In the side table. Grab a condom." I lever up to give her room to move.

She leans over, her legs outside of mine. The curls covering her sex are shiny, and my mouth waters for a taste.

"Fuck it," I growl and scoot down the bed until I can lie on my stomach. With her thighs gripped in my palms, I squeeze lightly before spreading them and burying my face in heaven.

The first taste of her coats my tongue, tart and sweet, addicting.

"Oh, Jesus. Wait. Griff, wait."

I pull back. "Is this not good for you?"

Her cheeks go pink. "No, it's really good. I—just, uh—haven't showered."

I roll my eyes and pull back far enough to bring my hand down on her pussy in a pawing slap.

Her eyes snap open. "Did you just smack me?"

I let my hand fall in another slap, this one right against her clit.

She could stop me with one word. One word and I'd pull back and just fuck her, but I don't think she's going to stop me. Her hips shift back and forth, alternately thrusting against my fingers and squirming away.

"I did, and I'm gonna keep spanking this clit and eating this cunt until you come all over my tongue."

Her breath puffs out in a stunned exhalation. "Fuck, why is that hot?" she mumbles.

"I don't give a single shit if you haven't showered; you taste like heaven. Now get out of your head."

"I'm not in my head."

I snarl. My girl would argue with a brick wall if I let her.

I let my hand fall in another slap, this one a little harder. Her whimpered sigh is my permission.

Yeah, she's not gonna stop me.

"If you're worried about showering, you're in your head."

I go back to her clit and circle with my fingers, but I don't break eye contact with her. "Wildflower, stop thinking and let me make you feel good." I accompany my statement with a swipe of my tongue across her clit.

"Oh, fuck."

Her jaw pops open, and I take her stunned silence as my green light to continue.

I get lost in her. In the sounds she makes, her taste, in the way her breathing changes when I alternate between sucking on her clit and fucking her with my tongue. Every discovery is a revelation and new addiction all at once.

Time means nothing, and it's not until her thighs clench around my ears and she lets out a low keening cry that I realize she's coming.

Right on my tongue.

A rush of arousal greets my lips as I work her through the orgasm before eventually slowing my movements.

I'm desperate to sink into the heat of her.

I scoot forward on my knees, and she sits up, foil packet in hand.

"I thought you used all of these?"

It takes me a second to understand what she's saying, and when it registers, I bark out a laugh.

"Yeah. I don't know who could go through a hundred

condoms in less than a month, but the look on your face when you thought I did was priceless."

Her eyes go heavy-lidded and she asks, "Wanna give it a shot?"

"Don't fucking tempt me, Wildflower. I have half a mind to keep you in this bed for the rest of the week, work and the case be damned."

She tears the foil with her teeth and slides the condom down my shaft. Just the light touch of her hand is nearly enough to set me off.

My declarations aside, spending a whole week in bed isn't going to happen. I'm not twenty anymore, and I don't have the stamina or the electrolytes on hand needed for shenanigans at that level.

I run my shaking hands up her thighs, enjoying the feel of her under my palms. Once my hands are securely in the dip of her hips, I yank her closer, the slide of her skin on mine more seductive than anything I've ever felt.

Am I finally going to get all of Meadow Ridley to myself? Dream come fucking true.

Every teasing taunt, every challenge brought us here. To me notching my dick at her entrance, one swift thrust away from what I'm sure is perfection.

I don't know if I'm ready for it. Meadow's hazel eyes hold me steady as I slowly push inside of her.

The snug clasp of her around me is more than I could have ever hoped for, and too much all at once. With every inch I press inside her, more and more of me is fundamentally altered. Before Meadow, I was Griffin Gallagher, private investigator and Celia's son.

Now? Now I'm Meadow's as well. For good or ill, I'm hers.

And I sure as fuck hope she's mine too.

21

MEADOW

I'VE NEVER HAD GOOD SEX. IT'S ALWAYS BEEN OVER TOO fast, or too hyped-up with not enough follow-through, or plain ol' boring.

In previous experiences, by the time it was all said and done, I'd wished that I'd spent the time differently, like catching up on my favorite TV shows or reading a book. That would have been time better spent.

Griffin pushing into me slowly along with the devastating kiss he gives me has already ruined me for sex for the rest of my life.

The way his gaze locks with mine for the initial thrust? It's everything I can do not to immediately come all over his dick.

An inarticulate sound falls from my lips, and I couldn't tell you what I meant to say if my life depended on it.

He bottoms out inside of me, and I focus on my breathing. If he moves, I'm going to lose it, and I'd really like this to last longer.

A hard nip at my lips sends lightning through me.

"Your cunt's quivering and shaking already, Wildflower. You gonna come hard for me?"

"Oh, Jesus." His words nearly send me crashing over the edge, but I hold on just barely. I've never been more turned on in my life.

Achieving an orgasm other than by myself is a struggle nine times out of ten. But by some act of fate, Griffin Gallagher has the key to my passion, to my body, and I'm helpless against him.

With his head thrown back, the veins in his throat stand out as he grinds the base of his cock into my clit.

And it's all over.

"There you go. There you go, Wildflower." He grunts.

Wave after wave of pleasure rushes through me. My toes curl and the muscles in my calves contract hard as his hips press against mine, the slightest friction causing more ripples.

By the time my body relaxes, I'm panting and my hands are locked on his planted forearms. Who the hell comes on the first thrust? Apparently me. My cheeks heat in embarrassment.

What the hell devil cock magic was that?

"Sorry." The apology comes out sheepish, and I cross my arms over my face. Whatever the hell this feeling is, it can fuck right off.

Griff stills, then his hands come up to grab mine and pull them off my face.

"Don't hide from me. I want to see all of you."

His cock throbs and jumps inside of me. Like the sight of my vulnerability is arousing, and for all I know it is.

"That was..." I stutter.

"Red hot. Like witnessing something divine and catastrophic all at once."

I don't have the words needed to respond to that, but the ache in my core has yet to subside. Something about the earnest way he's looking at me along with his understanding makes me want to try something I've only read about.

I clench my inner muscles and have the satisfaction of watching his eyes roll back, a gruff groan accompanying his sloppy retreat and thrust back into me.

Apparently, I have the power to wreck him as much as he does me.

"Fucking Christ, Meadow. Do that again."

I clench harder around him, engaging my core muscles and shifting my hips at the same time for good measure.

Griff bares his teeth at me and grips my hips hard before he pulls back and thrusts into me.

"Now that you've come for me, your cunt is relaxed enough for me to fuck you how we both need."

"And how's that?" I pant, timing the rhythm of my hips to meet him until we're moving together. Each jarring press feels more permanent than the last. I may live the rest of my life with an imprint of his dick inside me.

"Hard. Deep. Fast." Each word is punctuated by a devastating thrust, and the tightening in my core shifts to a kaleidoscope of sensation unfurling inside of me.

I cry out at the suddenness of the orgasm. I always thought that multiples were a myth, but the shaking in my thighs and pulsing release crawling through me right now are proving that wrong. I'm pissed that I've wasted twenty-nine years of my life on shitty sex and subpar orgasms.

"There it is. Good girl," Griffin growls in my ear before pulling out and rolling me to my stomach. I start to lift to my hands and knees but stop when his hand lands on my ass in a hard, slapping grab. His grip transfers to my hip and he lifts just enough to shove a pillow under my stomach before lining his legs up outside of mine and shoving back inside of me.

"Holy shit, Griff." With my legs closed, the pressure escalates until I can feel every inch of him.

"I like the sound of my name on your lips. Let's see if we can get you to scream it, hmm?"

Things get chaotic after that. The only thing that stays constant is the unrelenting barrage of his rhythm, and before long the familiar tension builds in my gut again. My abs tighten and pull taut. This orgasm is going to wreck me. That doesn't stop me from pushing my hips back and riding his cock like my life depends on it.

His headboard slaps against the wall with the movement of the bed. The few scattered pillows left on the bed not helping my hips stay in the air fall to the ground, something tips off his nightstand and crashes to the floor, but I don't give a rat's ass about any of that. Not one single fuck to give when every muscle in my body locks up as a mind-numbing orgasm rushes through me.

Over the blood pounding in my ears, I hear Griffin's harsh grunt and his guttural "Wildflower" before his cock kicks hard deep inside of me.

I either black out or transport to another plane of existence, because when I come back from la-la land, Griffin's arms are banded around me and we're lying on our sides. He's still inside of me, still hard, and my body is as limp as an overboiled noodle.

He brushes a soft kiss on my nape, and I hum. I don't want to leave whatever this is.

"Did I hurt you?" he asks.

"Hmm? No, you didn't hurt me."

Slowly, he pulls out of me. My skin is covered in a light sheen of sweat, and I probably look like a train wreck, but that was worth it, and I'd do it again in a heartbeat. As soon as the feeling comes back into my legs.

My stomach growls angrily, and I shift to my back and stretch.

Griffin stares at me.

"What?" I ask.

"You're so beautiful." His expression is serious.

Compliments usually make me uncomfortable, so I don't know why I want to preen at his words.

I smile back at him. "You're not too bad yourself, stud."

His blinding smile moves us back to the safe space, away from the heaviness that I don't think either of us is ready for yet.

ONCE WE'RE DRESSED, we go back to my apartment only to discover that it's empty. A sticky note on the microwave reads, "Holy wall banging, Batman! Went to the office for the day. Take a load off. Breakfast inside. - W."

I snatch the note down in hopes that Griff didn't notice it, but the chuckles that shake his shoulders tell me otherwise, and I try my best to rein in my blush.

"Sorry. My sisters don't really understand boundaries. Wait. That's wrong. Fawn understands them—it's Willow that's a problem."

He kisses my temple. "And Jenn?"

I lean against him for a second before answering. "Jenn's no different. She's a sister from another mister at this point."

"That's good. I like how you have your own mini gang. I thought Willow was going to shank me last night. That saying, 'glared daggers,'—she could be the poster child for it."

"Yeah. Willie's the fiercest of us. She's always the first to jump in when something isn't right, the first to throw hands if needed, and the first person you want at your back in a war. She's calmed down over the years, but back in high school? Most of my parents' gray hair is from the antics that she pulled."

"And she runs the protection service side of the business?"

I step out of his arms and hit the reheat button on the microwave. "Yes and no." I make my way to the fridge and pull out juice. "She takes over the bulk of those jobs, like Fawn and Dad do for the private investigations, and I do the skip tracing, but we're all trained to work any part as needed." Once I have two glasses poured and the plates warmed up, we take a seat at the breakfast counter.

Before I finish a single pancake, Griffin's already worked through a quarter of his breakfast. "Do you always eat like that?"

"Like what?"

"Like every meal is going to be your last?"

Color comes into his cheeks, and I wish I could pull back the question.

"Sorry, that came out wrong..."

"No, it's okay. Uh. Yeah. I guess so. It helps that you guys can fucking cook. Seriously, I haven't had food this good ever." He accompanies the compliment with a smile, but it's off. Almost fake.

Something tells me that isn't the full story, but I let it go to ask, "What about you? Does your mom approve of your work?"

Griff polishes off the last of his pancakes—much slower

now—and takes a deep drink of his juice. "Mom's never said otherwise, so I'd assume that she's fine with it."

The dismissive tone tells me to drop it, but my curiosity can't. "You haven't asked her?"

He grabs his plate and moves around the counter to the sink.

Message received.

He's not looking at me now. His gaze is locked on the water flowing from the faucet. The plate is rinsed clean, but he doesn't turn off the water. Maybe I shouldn't be grilling him, but I don't know of a better way to get to know him than to ask questions.

I just had him inside of me and I barely know the basics.

Abandoning my breakfast, I move close to him and lightly touch his arm. "Griff?"

My hand on him breaks whatever spell he was under, and he says, "I've never really talked to her about it honestly."

I nod. But the flat delivery of that statement tells me there is way more to the story that he's not ready to share with me yet.

When will he be ready?

This thing with him is getting more dangerous for my heart by the second.

22

MEADOW

I finish eating while Griffin cleans up and puts everything in the dishwasher. He disappears into the pantry for a second and returns with a loaf of bread.

"Did you not get enough to eat?" I ask.

"No, I'm good."

I nod toward the bread as I rinse my plate. "Then what's that for?"

The laugh lines around his eyes stand out when he smiles at me. "Almond butter toast. You said you eat it every day, and since we have work to do today, I don't want you to be thrown off your routine. I need Meadow the ace investigator, not Meadow the tight ass who likes to give me a hard time."

I swat at him with the towel I'm drying my hands on. "Ass. I'm full though, thank you."

Honestly, I never expected him to remember such a mundane thing I told him, but I'm learning that the charming playboy exterior he puts up is a facade.

Oh, he's still charming under it all, but not the fake smarmy charming that annoyed the shit out of me before.

He's the grinning, teasing charming that guarantees I'm going to spend most of my day laughing at his antics.

With everything going on I haven't really taken the time to figure out what we're doing, or what it means, but I do know that after this morning and then breakfast with him, I ought to give it a chance and see where it goes.

"What is this to you?"

"What's what?" he asks, eyes on mine.

"Us. What are we to you?"

He doesn't answer immediately, and I hold my breath. We've moved so fast. Just last week, we were at each other's throats, but now, we're snuggling, having sex, and eating breakfast together like a couple. These constant flips to a new version of our relationship are making my head spin.

"This is more than casual to me," he says. "Work aside, the case aside, I want to see more of you. I want to see where this goes."

My tummy goes *swoosh* at his words, and I breathe out a relieved sigh.

I've had my fair share of casual relationships with guy friends, and if that's what Griffin wanted I'd have been okay with it. Mostly. After an adjustment period where I got my emotions under control.

But him calling this "more" is a huge relief because somewhere along the way this evolved beyond casual for me too.

I can't stop a smile. "So we'll see where this takes us?"

Griffin hooks his arm around my waist and tugs me closer to him before dropping his lips to mine in a smacking kiss. "I'm good with that. What do you think?"

"Works for me. There's just one thing..."

"What's that?"

"Can you talk to me about any decisions you come to about the case before broadcasting them to my family?"

He winces. "Yeah, I'm sorry about that. I should have come to you first with my concerns."

"You should have." I step up to him and lay my lips against his, nonverbally giving him my forgiveness.

He nips at my lower lip. "It won't happen again, Wild-flower. Partners?"

Partners.

I like the sound of that more than I should, but I'm too far gone on him to care about should or shouldn'ts.

"Partners," I promise.

He snags the towel from my fingers and snaps it at me.

I jump back with a shriek and run for the bathroom. "Last one in the shower is a rotten egg."

Griffin's steps behind me are loud as we fly through the apartment, and I barely make it to the bathroom before him. We both start to strip, but I have the advantage since I just threw my pajamas back on after his place this morning. Since I don't wear underwear to bed, he's got extra articles of clothing to take off, and I jump in the shower right before him.

"Ha! I win. You lose."

He drops his boxers, and every breath in my body whooshes out. Carved muscle on display makes my fingers tingle. I reach out, unable to stop myself from touching him, and let my fingers dance along his broad chest, the crisp hair tickling my palms.

He steps into the shower, wrapping his arms around me and dropping his mouth to mine. Kissing Griffin is like riding the tallest roller coaster—every time his lips capture mine, my insides go *wheeeeeee*.

His hands massage my hips, and after a lingering kiss,

he drops to his knees, pressing me back against the wall of the shower while urging my legs apart.

Again?

His tongue makes contact with my clit, and my entire body shudders with pleasure.

My head thumps back against the wall, and I get lost in the sensation of his fingers and tongue playing across my flesh like a master.

When my gut tightens and my legs start to shake, I look down. Griffin's eyes are locked on mine. One hand grips my thigh while the other is wrapped around his cock, stroking himself in the most primal definition of jacking off that I've ever seen.

The sight of his mouth buried in my pussy and his dick sliding through his fingers sends me over the edge. The orgasm punches through me in the best way.

Griffin grunts against my folds, and rippling aftershocks flow through my system. I pant my way through them while his release paints the shower floor.

I chuckle weakly.

When did I become this woman? The one who let her lover chase her through the house before eating her out in the shower.

Whoever she is, I want to keep being her.

Griffin stands and pulls me into another kiss, wrapping his arms around me. I can taste myself on his lips, and it's easily the hottest, kinkiest kiss I've ever had. My fingers trace his sides and drop down to his cock. I lightly run my fingers over his balls and shaft until he shudders and pulls my hands away.

I'm so lost in his arms that I don't realize when his hand leaves my back until freezing cold water pelts my back and I screech.

"Griffin!"

He flips us around, taking the brunt of the icy water on his back while laughing, kissing me again and murmuring against my lips, "No, that's what winning looks like, Wildflower."

Being around Griffin lets me release the weight of the world for a moment and laugh while I shiver.

For as long as I've been dating, I've never found someone who can take the seriousness of my life and inject fun and playfulness into it. But now that I know this exists?

I'm greedy for more of it.

———

IT'S late morning by the time we settle on the couch to get some work done.

Griffin asks, "Can you send me the floor plans for the restaurant? I want to double-check my plans against what Jenn was able to get."

"Sure. What are you thinking?"

Griffin eyes me suspiciously.

"Don't worry, I'm not going to crash your party. I'm just curious."

He opens the file and points at his screen. "I'll be here. Kent will be sitting here waiting for Martin. Once Martin shows up, I'll wait for him to get comfortable with Kent before moving in. It'll be an easy in and out."

The restaurant has three exits, including the kitchen door. I point to one of the corner sections of the floor plan. "Your best bet is to sit here with your back to the corner so you have a full view of the place."

"But with the walls and the tables, if he decides to run, I won't be able to maneuver fast enough to grab him before he makes it to a door. It's better if we're in an open area even if it leaves my back exposed."

I know he doesn't want to hear it but... "It wouldn't be exposed if you had someone there with you. Like maybe a *partner*."

"Mead," he says warningly.

"Griff. You know I'm right."

"And if he recognizes you?"

"Then we both chase him down until we catch his ass."

I bite my lip and wait for him to think it over.

"Fine. You can be there..." I fist pump, but he holds his finger up to stop me. "But you're going to do everything that I say and if you deviate at all, I'm going to haul your ass out of there, the bounty be damned. Are we clear?"

"We're clear."

"Okay, let's dig into this." Cognac-colored eyes lock on to me, and I fight the urge to fidget. "I'm going to be really pissed if you get hurt, do you hear me?"

"I do. We'll be careful, I promise."

We discuss that we'll both get there early but at separate times in case anyone is watching. I'll disguise myself, but considering how pathologically self-centered Martin is, I doubt he'd recognize me even if he did see me.

Once Martin makes contact with Kent, we'll wait a few minutes, then Griffin will stand to approach him with me bringing up the rear. When I suggested that I go first because Martin wouldn't consider me a threat, the look Griffin gave me was way intense and a little scary, so I backed off and let him take the lead.

Fawn and Willow will stay with Jenn at the office while we're at the restaurant, so she's taken care of.

I can recite the plan in my sleep by the time we break for a late lunch. And I was a good girl and didn't roll my eyes during the discussion no matter how much I wanted to a few times.

The only thing left for us is to do the job and wrap this case up.

I just wonder how finishing this project will affect this new and fragile relationship we're building.

23

GRIFFIN

Bright and early Thursday morning I park at The Breakfast Club. Meadow pulls into the parking lot right behind me and kills her ignition. My skin is buzzing with the need to catch this fucker and close down the case, especially after this week.

Meadow and I spent most days together, working quietly from our respective corners of the couch. By the end of every day, her feet were propped on my lap, and I could get used to that shit. Naturally, that is terrifying.

Like plummeting off a cliff, I'm falling fast. And I can't. I'm not supposed to. All morning I've been second-guessing my agreement to let her be involved today, but trying to shut her out because I'm nervous doesn't make sense. I thought being with Meadow would be light and fun, something to help me pass the time and release a little steam every once in a while.

But I'm getting stuck on the stubborn woman, and that wasn't in the cards at all.

Especially considering the anvil I have hanging over my head.

An anvil I haven't even told her about.

I won't be a burden on someone later in life. I won't have her working herself to the bone like I'm doing for my mother. It's not fair to her.

Which is why I didn't stay with her last night.

Jenn and her sisters showed up shortly after dinner when Meadow and I were polishing off the last of a pizza, and when she smiled at me over the rim of her glass, her sisters laughing at one of her jokes, the pinch in my throat scared me.

I wanted nothing more than to take her back to bed, to cuddle up next to her, and crash out for another night of the best sleep of my life.

But sleepovers? Spending nearly every second of every day together?

I have to get my head screwed on right. I'm too close to the situation—to her—so I left after making a lame excuse.

She didn't ask me to stay either, which made the decision simple for both of us.

After parking, I climb out of the car and wait for Meadow to join me. She has her hair pulled back through the loop of a ball cap and sunglasses that obscure almost all of her face.

If you look closely enough, you can make out the bulge of her taser on her hip, which is covered by a light sweater that's buttoned to just below her breasts.

My Glock is tucked safely in the holster at the back of my pants with my T-shirt loose and hanging over it.

"You ready?" I ask. My throat is dry, and my gut has jumping jellybeans in it.

"Yep. You okay?"

No. I'm not okay. I nod anyway. "You go ahead. I'll be right behind you."

I watch silently as the woman I'm starting to have feelings for walks through the front of the restaurant and takes a seat to the left of the door, right in the open part of the floor plan like we talked about.

I shoulder my laptop bag and follow. Once I'm settled in one of the corner tables, I order a cup of coffee and open my laptop, so it looks like I'm working. Meadow has headphones in and looks engrossed in her own computer.

Now we wait.

There aren't many patrons for the breakfast crowd, but I keep a keen eye out for anyone who might look even a little bit like Martin.

When I'm on an investigation that requires a public confrontation, my senses are dialed up to a twelve out of ten. With Meadow here? I'm at twenty. I track people as they move in and out of my visual field, cataloging what they're wearing, who they're with. The table to my left is whispering about a first date gone wrong while the barista at the front is dealing with a frustrated customer.

About eleven thirty, Kent shows up—right on time. He takes a seat at a nearby table and doesn't so much as look at me, which is perfect.

I prepped him on what to expect—what to do and what not to do. Simply mentioning that I still have the proof needed to morally bury his father's political dream in the cleavage of strippers and land of lap dances was enough to scare the shit out of him.

Fear is a fantastic motivator for getting others to do what you want, though it leaves a smarmy feeling behind.

I have nothing against Kent or his father. But I have a problem with scum assholes who beat their girlfriends, so the gloves came off for this case.

The clock on my laptop shows that it's after twelve.

Martin is late. I glance around the room. Meadow's eyes meet mine before she raises her eyebrows in question. I shake my head, telling her to stay put.

Maybe he's running behind.

Kent gives me a questioning look, and again I bob my shoulders and slightly shake my head, telling him to stay put before I go back to my "work."

Minutes turn into a half hour and then an hour, and it's clear that Martin isn't going to show. Patience is necessary for stakeouts and public takedowns. But every gut instinct that I have is telling me he won't be making an appearance. I glance up just in time to see Kent type something on his phone, then shove the device back in his pocket before his gaze darts to the front of the dining room.

Oh, hell no.

I shove my laptop into my bag and head toward Kent's table. Meadow stands as well.

Sweat slicks the guy's forehead, and he looks nervous as fuck. Come to think of it, if Martin looked in through the windows and saw the fear clear on Kent's face, he probably bailed.

I know I would have.

Unless...

"Gimme your phone, unlocked if you please."

Kent flings a chair at me and sprints toward the exit. I kick the chair away as Meadow runs after him. She hits the door first, and I'm just a step behind her when she collides with someone and falls to the sidewalk.

I vault over them to avoid stepping on anyone. Kent is half a block up, pulling open the door of a moving car, then diving in. The car roars away, tires squealing as it rounds the next corner.

I turn back to find Meadow sitting on the ground with blood streaming from her forehead.

"Meadow, Jesus!" There's a kid holding his skateboard next to her, and I grip him by the collar. "What the hell happened?"

The kid's eyes go wide. "I'm sorry! I wasn't looking. The dude just came rushing out and then she did too, and I couldn't stop before I hit her."

I let him go and squat next to Meadow. She's got her sweater off and balled up against her forehead.

She grimaces and says something, but I can't hear through the blood rushing in my ears. Everything sounds tinny and I'm breathing too fast.

I take a deep breath and try again. "Are you okay?"

How could I let her get hurt? I knew that I shouldn't have let her come with me. I *knew* that she would have been better off at home, but I was too busy thinking with my dick.

"I'm okay. I just clipped the corner of the planter over there with my head."

Kent got lucky with the kid on his skateboard. Chances are he wouldn't have gotten away if Meadow hadn't gotten knocked on her ass.

I should have guessed. Kent doesn't seem like the most up-front and honest guy to begin with, so assuming that he wouldn't tip off Martin was a miscalculation on our part. Even fear only goes so far.

I think back, trying to remember if Meadow gave her name to the dick weasel when we were talking to him at the country club and come up blank.

If Martin was the getaway driver is anyone's guess, but I don't have time to think about that right now. I need to take care of Meadow and then get back to figuring out a new way to catch this guy.

And now we're back to the drawing board.

MEADOW TRIED to talk me into letting her go home and dealing with the head wound there, but that wasn't happening, so I dragged her to an emergency room.

Which is why, hours later, I've barely dropped Meadow on her couch when the door at my back snaps open and the whole Ridley gang barrels inside.

"Meadow, what the hell happened?" Willow's question sets off the waterfall, and soon the living room is filled with voices.

"Wait!" Meadow shouts. "Wait. What the hell are you all doing here? I thought you guys were at the office?" She looks around the room, and I clear my throat.

"I called them."

I called her parents when they started her paperwork to leave. I didn't expect them to get here this fast, but I shouldn't be surprised.

"Are you okay, honey?" Andrew asks, sounding pissed. If I had to guess, I'd say he's not angry at Meadow, but at the helplessness he feels.

"I'm fine. Just a bump on the head. You know head wounds bleed a lot."

"What the hell happened?" Fawn says.

I explain the restaurant and resulting ER trip. Before I can finish the story, Andrew interrupts.

"You're off this job. Both you and Jenn are going to come stay with your mother and me. Fawn and Willow can work with Gallagher to find Martin."

Meadow bristles. "No. Absolutely not, Dad."

He slices a hand through the air. "Not up for discussion, Meadow Lark. Go pack a bag. You too, Jennifer."

"Now let's just take a second to calm down," Fawn says. Like me, she's watching Meadow and probably knows my Wildflower is about to lose her shit.

"I'm not going to calm down when a case sent my daughter to the hospital."

The talking escalates to four people shouting again until a shrill whistle cuts through the air, silencing everyone. Susan pulls her fingers out of her mouth. "All of you need to mellow down. Andrew, I told you that Meadow wouldn't take you removing her from the case well."

"Maybe he's right," I say before I think better of it, and now all eyes are on me.

Meadow's jaw drops. "What?"

Fuck. I shouldn't have said anything. I shouldn't be putting myself in the middle of this argument, especially after we cleared the air on Monday. But *fuck,* she scared me today.

"You got hurt, Mead. Maybe you should hang back for a bit."

Meadow stands, her face devoid of expression when she says, "Unbelievable. Me getting hurt today had nothing to do with the case, though neither of you give a damn about that. You want the case all to yourself, so go ahead and take it, Gallagher."

My last name on her lips is jarring, and I fucking hate it. After hearing her call me by my first name and then shorten it recently, the way she moaned it, husky and strained, when she fell apart in my arms is miles away from this clipped version she spits out like it tastes bad.

I know that it's her way of slapping me back. Like I retreated to my own place last night, she's drawing her own line in the sand, restrengthening the walls around herself. And though I'm doing the same thing, it doesn't stop the pinch in my chest that screams we're doing this the wrong way. That we took a wrong turn and need to backtrack.

Backtracking is scary. It's being open and vulnerable. It's admitting your flaws and faults and hoping—just fucking hoping—the person on the other side will still want you.

I'm not ready for that. And I don't know why I thought I was.

The stony expression hides her hurt, but I know it's simmering under the surface.

Hurt that I caused and don't know how to fix.

Exhaustion weighs on my shoulders, and I want to crawl into bed and claim a do-over for the day.

"Douchebag," Willow says. She wraps a hand around Meadow's arm, and they walk to the bedroom, slamming the door behind them.

Even with the lights on, the room is darker when she's gone.

24

MEADOW

MEN ARE COMPLICATED CREATURES, NO MATTER THEIR claims otherwise. If you'd told me that I'd spend a whole morning in bed with Griffin, followed by several days of working together side by side, only to have him go ice king on me the next day, I wouldn't have believed it. Not considering how things changed so fast between us.

I won't lie and say that I don't have my own misgivings, but apparently not large enough to make me take a step back like he did last night.

Insecure isn't something I've ever really felt outside of the raging hormones of my teenage years. But I feel insecure now. And I want to smack myself for it.

Willow made us dinner last night, and this morning I decided I'm taking the case back into my own hands.

Fuck Griffin. If he thinks that I can't do the job because I'm not good enough, then I'll show him just what I'm capable of.

This is what I get for leading with my emotions in the first place.

We've been looking for Martin for a week, and all I have

to show for it is some fancy time at a country club, a shit-ton of research, a head wound, and a sore heart.

It's time to go back to the basics. Jenn and I got into the office early to comb through the information we have on Martin, digging for new leads. We're not even there for an hour before Dad pokes his head around the door frame.

"You got a minute, Sweet Pea?"

I clench my jaw and glance at Jenn. She gives me a small but encouraging nod.

I stand and grab my now cold coffee. "Sure. I'm due for a refill. Walk with me?"

I was too much of a coward to come out of my room last night after Griffin said his piece, but Fawn gave me the breakdown this morning, and it was pretty much the same drivel I heard last night. They want me off the case, I can take a few days off with Jenn, Griffin will wrap it up—blah blah blah.

"How long have you been here?" Dad asks.

Longer than is wise, but I'm not going to tell him that. That would just open the door to all the sticky things I'm not ready to talk about.

I shrug. "Did you need something?"

Dad scrubs a hand through his hair and blows out a breath. I haven't talked to him since he unilaterally decided that I'm incapable of my job, but I'm absolutely not ready or willing to have that conversation now. If that's his plan, then I'm going to sneak back to my desk until I'm ready to embrace the confrontation that's going to bring.

I know that he's been on the fence since this whole mess started, but *some* faith in me wouldn't be remiss.

I splash coffee into my cup and scoop some sugar into the mug before angrily stirring it. If Dad thinks I'm going to crack and say something first, he's dead wrong.

"Look, Mead. Last night..."

I hold up my hand. My temper isn't up to this challenge today.

"Am I off the case?"

"It's not that simple."

"You made it that simple last night when you valued Griffin's opinion over mine. So I'm asking you now, not as your daughter, but as an employee and investigator, am I off this job?"

"And if I say yes?"

My heart hammers in my chest. "Then I'll go write up a resignation letter and have it on your desk within the hour."

"Sweet Pea..."

"Dad, no. You don't get to call me Sweet Pea when I've worked with you for eight years and you decide at the smallest *incident*—because that's what yesterday was—an incident, to yank me from a case that involves my best friend. Either you trust my ability to do the job or you don't. If you don't, then I'll find an employer that does."

"No."

"No, I'm not kicked off the case, or no, I'm not allowed to resign? Because you only get to make the decision regarding one of those options."

"No, you're not kicked off the case." He bites out the words.

"Fine."

"What about what you told Gallagher last night?"

"I'll talk with him."

"Okay. Be careful, Sweet Pea." My heart rate spikes in relief, and I want to slump against the counter.

I'm so tired of being treated like glass. My father has *never* stepped in on a case like this, and I've had it with the *protect Meadow* mindset everyone has lately. If anyone needs protecting, it's Jenn, for crying out loud.

But then, we've never had a case that's so personal to all of us.

If I had made mistakes before now, them being worried would make sense, but I haven't. Yeah, I'm guilty that I didn't get to Jenn fast enough the first time, but I've been objective. I've kept my head as clear as I can.

This drama isn't like my family and I don't know what to do about it.

Dad's keen gaze is on me, and the dark circles around his eyes speak to a sleepless night. "Look, Dad. I'm going to go and do my job. The one you trained me to do. I'm going to be smart and careful. I'm asking you to trust me."

A short nod later and he leaves me in the breakroom.

When did things get so complicated, and why does it suck so much?

I HEAD BACK to my desk, ready to dig into finding this fucker *without* Griffin's help.

The second that I cross the threshold into my office, Jenn jumps up and shuts the door behind me.

"What's going on?"

"Martin's using his credit cards."

"What? How?"

"I took a chance. This is insanely illegal, and I wasn't even sure that I'd be able to pull it off, but I tried his normal username and password on the off chance that he hadn't changed them since being released from jail and he didn't."

She turns her computer toward me, and right there on the screen is his transaction history.

"Will he find out?"

"I don't think so. I didn't change anything that would trigger an alert or notification to go out to him, so as long as we're careful, we shouldn't run into any issues."

"Holy fucking shit, Jenn. Good job!" Normally I wouldn't use this information. I obey the laws that uphold our society even being in my position where I have information at the tips of my fingers, but fuck that.

This is Jenn. And she's more important than my licenses or reputation.

I sit in the other visitor's chair and tug the computer closer to review the list of transactions. There's a lot. Most of it local motels and food.

"He's changing locations every couple of days, by the look of this," I say.

"Yeah, there's a lot of transactions to look through."

"We need to get this out of the office." I don't want to take the chance that my dad walks in when we have an illegally obtained credit card statement sitting on a company computer.

"Take it back to your place?"

"Take what back to your place?"

I jump, my phone flying out of my hand, and whip around.

Leaning a hip against my door is none other than Griffin Gallagher. My back was to the door, and I was so caught up in Martin's credit card statement that I didn't hear it open.

Just my luck.

"Nothing," I say coolly.

"You sure?"

"Yep," I confirm. "We're heading out. Did you need something?"

I throw the strap of my laptop bag over my shoulder and start toward him, Jenn following me.

He takes a step back and says, "Nope. Just here to talk to Andrew." He's miles away from the smiling, smug Griffin I spent the last week with. Which is a good thing because the carefree, laughing Meadow that he somehow pulled out of me is long gone.

And that doesn't hurt at all.

Pfft. Partners my ass.

Feeling used and irritated about it, I snark, "Good luck with that."

Jenn and I manage to get out of the office without running into anyone else. Willow's meeting with a potential client and Fawn had an appointment for Landon, which was why we were at the office. So my apartment should be empty.

Once we're safely behind my locked door and security camera, she brings up the page again.

I scan the list for patterns. "There's at least one charge from Sunset GC each night, what's that?"

Her fingers fly over her keyboard. "Strip club. Off the 202 and Baseline."

"He's been there every night this week. What are the chances that you think he'd make an appearance tonight?"

Jenn grins. "I'd take those odds."

I'M DRESSED to the nines and have more makeup on my face than I've worn in the past five years combined. In my eagerness to see if this lead would pan out, I convinced Willow to come with me, and we showed up way too early, so we're waiting for the doors to open.

I'm shooting birds at evil piggies while Willow scrolls through her Instagram feed. We've got a few minutes still before we can get inside.

A knock at my window startles me, my phone flying out of my hand for the second time today.

Son of a bitch. Griffin is standing outside my car.

It's not truly surprising. He might be an asshole about personal matters, but he's a pretty good investigator.

Today someone clearly shit in his Cheerios, because he looks about ready to strangle me.

His hand moves toward the door, so I hit the door-lock button.

I will not listen to or entertain someone else's displeasure that I'm doing my damn job today. If avoiding confrontation had a definition, my picture would be right alongside it in every dictionary known to mankind.

"Open the door, Wildflower."

Fuck these cute nicknames. He doesn't get to use them when he was a dick yesterday.

"I don't think that he's going to go away, Mead," Willow whispers.

"I know that, dummy. But that doesn't mean that I'm going to let him into my car when he looks madder than a wet hen."

"You know that I can hear you, right?" Griff says.

"Yes, I know you can hear me, and no, I don't care. Buzz off, Gallagher."

"No can do. And seeing as it's almost opening time, you'll have to come out of there eventually. Come on, I just want to talk."

I glare at him and crack my window until my eyes meet his. "I don't want to talk to you."

I shoot a furtive glance toward Willow. She pulls out

her headphones and pops them in her ears. "You two go ahead. Lemme know when you're done."

Treating Willow to her addiction—Dutch Bros coffee—for the next month ought to repay the favor.

"Wildflower."

"Uh-uh." I hold up a finger. "Nicknames will get you nowhere right now, buddy, so you better knock that off."

"Can you please open the door? It looks like we're doing a shady drug deal right now, and I would prefer not to get arrested tonight."

Fuck. He has a point. It'd just cap Dad's low opinion of me lately if I got picked up by the local police for suspicious activity in a nudie joint.

Plus, I need to get in there.

"Fine. I'm coming out, but keep your hands to yourself."

Griffin's a grabby motherfucker, and I don't have the defense to go against that while talking about feelings.

I hit the unlock button and then shove the door open. Griffin barely jumps out of the way to avoid it slamming into his groin. I'm sure he doesn't want to get racked twice in one week. And maybe I opened the door too hard, but can you blame me?

His hot and cold routine is more than I have the desire to deal with today.

His jaw tics, but otherwise there's no outward signs of his irritation, which is good because if anyone gets to be irritated, it's me.

"What?" I ask flatly.

"Look. About last night."

Aaaand I'm already done with this conversation.

"Yeah, we don't need to talk about it. You made your feelings clear." I turn back to the car, but he snags my bicep and stops me.

"Hands off."

He drops his hand. "Meadow, how's a man supposed to beg for forgiveness when you won't give him a chance to get a word in edgewise?"

The hold on my patience and temper snaps. "I don't give a good goddamn about your begging, or the fact that you want forgiveness. You *hurt* me. Don't you get that? For all your words about believing in my ability to do the job and us being partners, the second that was put to the test, you failed."

"I didn't fail."

"And what do you call selling me out to my family over a tiny scratch that had nothing to do with the case?"

"Look, it's not like that." He scrubs a hand through his hair, irritation visible.

"Then, please, Your Majesty of Investigations, explain it to me. Exactly what was it like?"

"I was frustrated and scared, all right? I was frustrated that he didn't show up, that I sat there looking like a fool for over an hour when I promised you that I'd catch him. I'm frustrated that you have to go around with a gash in your head because I can't manage to track down and catch this guy. I'm out of my mind with worry for you, and I handled it badly. Okay?"

"You did handle it badly, but you're also handling it self-ishly right now. I get being worried and frustrated. How do you think I feel? I was essentially banished to 'safety' on this case, and then the second I get you to relent on that, you call my dad in when I get a bump on the head. You call my family without even talking to me about it first, right after we agreed to *talk* to each other. You may be frustrated and worried about me, but you have a shit way of dealing with it. While I understand your feelings, it's not my responsibility to manage your emotions and stress level. It's my job to manage mine, and of the two of us, I'd say I'm a sight better at it than you are if yesterday was anything to go by."

No one gets to walk all over me and blame it on being frustrated and scared.

"You're right. I'm being a selfish asshole. I'm sorry. You shouldn't be and aren't responsible for the fallout of how my feelings impact me. I just..."

"Just?"

"None of my cases have ever been personal before. And all of a sudden this one is because I care about you and I'm floundering. Only one person in my life has ever depended on me for anything, and now I have you and I...I'm scared."

I hate that I can be mad at him and want to hug him all at once. Some of my anger bleeds away. "This is different for me too."

"I'm sorry, Wildflower. I saw you get hurt and I wasn't thinking clearly."

"Let's chalk yesterday up to a bad day and forget about it, okay?"

This time when he reaches for me, I don't pull away. I let my head rest on his chest, careful of my stitches. I'm tired. It's been a long couple of days, and I'm worn out.

"No, I don't want to forget about it. That means that I don't learn from it. And I want to learn from it. To do better and be better." I tilt my head back to look at him. His nose brushes against mine, lips tentatively teasing mine.

"Okay. We've both done some stupid things over the last week and keep apologizing for it."

He tucks a strand of hair behind my ear. "I think all couples apologize a lot at the beginning of a relationship. It's part of learning how to be together."

My belly jumps at the words *couple* and *relationship*,

but before I can say anything, he continues, "I also think that we should talk about how we each define *partner*. To get on the same page. For me, that means no more trying to keep you from the case in the name of protecting you, and no more making decisions that affect you without talking to you about it first. I know that we said that before, but I actually have to do it. But you need to tell me what you're thinking too—no more going off on your own and leaving me behind."

"Hey!"

"First the country club and now this, babe. That's too close for comfort for me, and I don't want anything to happen to you. We talk to each other, okay?"

I remember the cool civility between us in the office this morning and ask, "What changed your mind?"

"Honestly? Your dad."

"What?"

"Yeah. In his office, he pointed out that you've been doing this job and that we were both letting our personal feelings for you get in the way. I started to realize that last night lying in bed, so his words just drove the point home."

"Does this mean that you're going to trust me?"

"Yeah. I'm going to trust you to do your job and I'll do mine. We'll both look out for each other. That's what partners do, right? Let's finish this case out as equals."

I smile. "I like the sound of that. I'm in."

A car door opens behind me, and Willow calls out, "Are you two done kissing and making up? It's ten after seven."

Griffin grins at me when I say, "Let's do this."

25

GRIFFIN

I can breathe again. After the lack of contact with Meadow, I was a weird mix of feelings. Like a knee-jerk reflex as soon as it started to get too real for me, I pushed her away when I should have been pulling her closer.

No more running from scary things.

After the dead-eye stare she gave me and then talking with her dad, I realized that I have to step up my game and actually walk the 'partners' talk.

If I could have kicked my own ass any harder for mishandling the situation yesterday, I would have. I've been mishandling a lot recently when it comes to Meadow, but that's what I get for falling for my neighbor.

Selfish isn't a word that I normally would have used to describe myself, but since she pointed it out, I can't deny it. Meadow's right. I was selfish by trying to protect her and assuming that my concerns and worries were bigger or more important than hers. And not talking to her first? That was another checkmark in the column of things I need to get my act together on.

Now that we're walking across the parking lot, I can't keep ignoring what Meadow looks like tonight, and I nearly swallow my tongue. A very short black miniskirt sways around her thighs, and a five-inch-wide strip of her midriff is bared in a tight crop top. My fingers twitch with the desire to touch that extra skin on display. Her makeup is heavier, darker than I've seen her wear. But the kicker is the blood-red lipstick she's painted on her mouth.

I want to kiss her until it smears, and then I want the imprint of her lipstick on my dick.

But first, I have questions.

"How'd you find out about the club?"

"Jenn remembered Martin's login information for his credit card, and there's been a charge from this club every night this week."

"Is she still logged in?" Having Martin's banking information is a huge win for us, even if it isn't exactly legal. We can keep an eye on him through the charges that he makes on the card.

He doesn't know it yet, but he's incrementally tightening the noose around his own neck.

"She is."

Meadow and Willow go ahead of me through the door of the club, and I nod to the bouncer.

Heavy bass vibrates my ear drums once we're inside the club, and the pounding beat of music is timed with the flash of strobe lights. Even though it's still early, there are bodies everywhere.

"Oh, man! Look at that." Willow points to the main stage, where one of the dancers is inverted on a pole doing a split.

"That's Alesha. She offers classes at a gym downtown if you're interested."

Willow's jaw drops and Meadow asks, "You know the dancers by name?"

"Yeah. A couple of months ago, one of the dancers had a problem with a guy and hired me to look into it. I spent a lot of time here. It's a good crew."

"Well then, where do you think we should start?"

I point toward the bar and turn to head that way.

Willow says, "You two go ahead; I'm going to look around," and melts into the crowd.

"Hey, Britt," I say when Meadow and I reach an empty space at the bar.

Brittney grins. "Hiya, handsome, what can I getcha?"

"Information. You seen this guy here recently?" I pull up Martin's mugshot on my phone and turn the device in her direction.

"Oh, that's the bottle service bastard."

"Who?" Meadow asks.

"He's in here damn near every night and requests bottle service."

"And the bastard part?" I ask.

"He doesn't tip. Mallory started adding gratuity to his bill because he stiffs the girls otherwise. He got handsy with Tanya last night too. Ended up getting thrown out, and Mark told him to watch his hands or he was going to get banned. I haven't seen him tonight, but Mark's been making the rounds if you want to check with him."

"Is he friendly with any of the girls?"

Britt nods. "Jada's his usual. She tends to give him some *extra* attention during the private dance that he pays for. She's still young and naive enough that the assholes of the world are exciting for her."

"Is she here?" Meadow asks.

"Yep. She's on stage right now."

"Could we talk to her?"

"Yeah, once she finishes her set, I'll grab her from the back. You two wanna grab some seats here or a table?"

"We're gonna look around. We'll be back though—about ten minutes?" I say.

Britt nods at my phone. "What'd he do?"

"Jumped bail."

"Figures. He looks like the type."

"Thanks, Britt. We'll be back." I drop my arm across Meadow's shoulders and steer her away.

"Where are we going?"

"To talk to the owner, Mark."

I head down a hallway toward the back of the club. It gets cooler and a little quieter the farther we go. I knock on the painted black door and wait for the "Enter!" to open it.

"Griff, how's it going?"

Mark has the build of a bouncer and the temperament of a monk. But he's also a fucking flirt, and I wish I had left Meadow at the front when his eyes practically devour her.

"It's good." I lean across the desk to shake his hand. "This is Meadow Ridley."

"Well, hello there." He practically drools while shaking her hand.

"Hands off, she's with me."

Mark smirks at me but asks Meadow, "What can I do for you, angel?"

She smiles at him, and I fight off a chuckle. It's not the smile she uses when speaking with strangers—it's her "step wrong and I will verbally eviscerate you" smile. Having been on the receiving end of it for months, I'm thrilled that she's pointing it in someone else's direction.

"You can keep your eyes above my collarbones when you tell me if you've seen this man tonight."

Her smooth delivery makes him choke on a laugh. Once he stops coughing, he looks at the same mugshot that we showed Britt. "He's a regular—a shitty one, but still a regular. Usually comes in around eight and then stays till close."

"Jada's his usual?" Meadow asks.

"Yeah. They started seeing each other outside of her working hours."

"Oh yeah, how'd you know that?"

"She was bragging about it to the other girls. He took her to a big golf thing last I heard."

"The Phoenix Open?"

Mark snaps his fingers. "That's the one."

"Thanks. We're gonna go talk to Jada, but if you see him, let me know."

"You've got it. You gonna hang around to see if he shows up tonight?"

"Yeah. We'll be around."

"Don't cause problems," he warns.

"We won't."

We head back out to the bar, but there's no sign of Jada. I glance at the stage and confirm that there are two new dancers up there.

"Britt, where's Jada?"

She shrugs. "She said she had to go to the bathroom and she'd be right back."

"Mead! Griffin!" Willow's out of breath as she maneuvers around tables to reach us.

"What's wrong?" Meadow asks her.

"I saw Martin. He was talking to one of the dancers and he left in a hurry. There were too many people, so I couldn't follow him."

Motherfucker.

"What'd the dancer look like?" Meadow asks her.

"Black, dark-brown hair, skinny, in an emerald thong."

"That's Jada," I say.

The dancer in question comes out of one of the back hallways and stops like a deer in headlights at the three of us standing here.

"Jada! Come here a minute," Britt calls out.

Reluctantly Jada starts toward us, and as soon as she's in hearing distance, I bite out, "Why'd you warn him off?"

"He's innocent. He told me so."

I roll my eyes and before I can shake some sense into the dancer, Meadow pulls out her phone.

"Does this look like he's innocent to you?" Meadow turns her phone, and I catch a glimpse of Jenn's injury pictures.

"He didn't do that. He wouldn't. He said you faked those pictures and that bitch was just trying to frame him."

Meadow snorts. "Oh, he did this. I was the one who pulled him off her and called the cops on his ass. I was the one who sat in her hospital room and the one who had to tell her mother that I didn't stop him before he shattered her cheekbone and fractured her nose." Meadow's voice is harder than I've ever heard it.

Jada visibly gulps. "You're sure?"

"Yes, I'm sure. And you just killed our chance to send him back to jail—where he belongs. When are you seeing him again?"

"I don't know. We don't have anything planned."

"How do you get hold of him?" I ask.

"I don't. He just shows up here. If we plan something, I put it in my phone and he picks me up."

"How the hell did you know we were even here for him in the first place?"

"After my set I came to grab some water from the bar, and Britt said you were looking to talk to me about him."

I glance back to Britt, who winces. "Sorry."

I wave it off and ask a few more questions before giving up. Jada doesn't have any way of getting hold of him. I trail off and Meadow passes her a card, saying, "If you see him, text or call me. But be careful when you do."

Jada heads for backstage, and I turn to Meadow. "He's not coming back here tonight."

She shakes her head. "No, he's not."

Once we're back outside I suck in a lungful of cleaner air.

Even though tonight was a bust, we have options. The transaction history of this guy's card is going to go a long way toward helping us nail him. If he tries to talk to Jada again, then she's likely going to call us.

All good things.

I open Meadow's car door, and once she's inside, I grin at her.

"What?" she asks.

I hang on the door and lean in. "We work well together."

And we do. We have for the better part of two weeks. Being in the club with her and getting the information that we needed was seamless, which is unusual because I've always worked alone. The way that she picked up when and where I needed her to makes me think that this partner thing isn't so bad.

"We do, but don't get a big head about it. Your ego doesn't need any more stroking."

"No, but I've got something you can stroke." I bobble my eyebrows.

Meadow deadpans. "That's what he said."

Before I can respond, Meadow tugs the door closed and backs out of the spot. I stand there staring until her car tail-lights disappear.

Now that we're back on safe ground, the floaty sensation in my chest is back. And the kicker is, I'm starting to like it.

———

THE NEXT AFTERNOON, I'm dressed in my nicest shirt, which isn't saying much since it's older than most toddlers. I've brushed my hair and cleaned up my beard as best I can and am clutching a unique bouquet ready to make for a proper grovel.

I had to go to every grocery store within a five-mile radius to find what I needed, but like always, I got the job done.

A grand total of seventy nut-butter cups make up a bouquet of candy. I found flavors ranging from dark chocolate to white and even some crispy chocolate cups to cover every single nut butter option I can think of.

She better like this.

I grab the bouquet and leave my apartment. "Hey Griff, how's it going?" Owen asks. He's juggling a couple bags of groceries.

"Good. How about you?"

"No complaints. The girls get out of school early, so I'm dropping some supplies off before I go pick them up."

"You need a hand?"

"Nah, I got it. Those for Meadow?" He nods at the candy in my arms.

"Yeah. I can't cook worth a damn, so I figured this is the next best thing."

He winks at me. "Good choice." And with that parting shot disappears into his place.

I stand outside Meadow's apartment and knock and wait.

Nerves tingle through my fingers, and I really hope the heat of my fingers isn't ruining this damn thing.

Why's it taking her so long to get here? I know she's somewhere in the apartment because her car is downstairs. I made sure of that, confirming with Jenn by text that they didn't have any plans tonight.

After eons the door opens, but it's not Meadow. It's Willow—wearing the formidable glare she must have perfected somewhere in preschool for its intimidation factor alone—that greets me.

"Is Meadow home?" I ask like the good boyfriend that I am.

"Why'd you want to know, dick muncher?"

I nearly lose it at the name, but I can't—not if I'm serious about this, about us.

"Uh. I wanted to talk to her." Willow was there last night when we made up. So she's fucking with me, right?

Willow opens her mouth, but Fawn shoves her to the side, eyes the peace offering in my hand, and says, "She's in the bedroom. Come in. I'll go get her."

I know that I shouldn't have favorites out of her little gang, but if I did, Fawn would be it. She's quiet, doesn't give me a ton of shit, and seems to operate with the cold hard truth of facts and logic.

Something that I'm lacking in my own convictions currently.

I stand awkwardly just inside the door, and Willow shoots another glare at me. "Just because you sweet-talked my sister into forgiving you doesn't mean I have. You better watch yourself."

Well okay then. Maybe not fucking with me. My hands are slippery with sweat. I wasn't this nervous taking Meadow to bed with me; why the hell am I nervous asking her out on a date?

Before I can think on that too long, Meadow's door opens, and she steps into the hall. Her gaze latches onto what's in my arms, and her excitement lights me up when she skips down the hall to me.

Four layers of nut butter cups sit in a cascading bouquet of popsicle sticks, glue, and fake foliage.

She smacks a kiss to my lips, grabs the vase from me, and tears into the first almond butter cup.

I knew that Meadow liked almond butter, but I don't think that I fully understood the depth of her love, because in a short succession of flying wrappers, she demolishes a quarter of the project that took me three hours and four YouTube videos to make.

A crafty man, I am not.

"Well, it's clear that you hate it. I'll just take it back." I reach a hand out but yank it back when she growls—actually growls—and slaps at my hand.

"No. Mine." The guttural statement sends the nerves firing in my brain, and my dick jumps, ready to be of assistance in any way needed.

I want her to claim me like that.

"I've got to give you credit; you know your quarry." The grudging compliment comes from Willow, and I nod.

"It wasn't hard to figure out when nine times out of ten she comes home from that big warehouse store with the mega-size pack of peanut butter and almond butter."

Meadow talks through a mouthful of chocolate. "Most

guys would have gone with Reese's. Where did you even find this thing?"

My neck heats, and I clap a hand over it as if that will stem some of the embarrassment. "I, uh, I didn't buy it. I made it."

Meadow sucks in a breath and chokes a little. Fawn hands her a water bottle, and after a few deep chugs and some throat clearing, she manages to ask, "You made that?"

"I did."

"How?" At the shock evident in her tone, the heat in my face increases until I'm sure I look sunburned.

"I looked up candy bouquets and then found the Justin's Almond Butter Cups and then went from there. I was hoping it would soften you up so you'd go to dinner with me."

"Oh." Her smile slowly dies. Did I miscalculate?

"If not, that's totally fine—"

She shoots a look over her shoulder before wincing at me. "I just—I've been gone a lot lately. Rain check?"

"Sure. That's fine. We can—"

"Uh-uh," Fawn says. "Do you think that Willow and I are incapable of hanging out with Jenn for a few hours?"

"No..." Meadow starts.

"Um. Don't I get a say in this?" Jenn asks.

"Of course," Meadow responds.

I can tell that she wasn't ready for the conversation going sideways, but I've never been happier to see her sisters gang up on her.

"Go. Stop worrying about me. I have these two fabulous bodyguards, and I know how to properly handle myself should Martin miraculously show up and get past Fawn and Willow."

"Are you sure?"

"Mead, I'm not a victim anymore. I refuse to be. Go. Eat. Drink. Get laid and be merry."

Jenn winks at me and I grin back at her. I kinda feel like I have a coconspirator in her, and I'm taking full advantage of it.

"You get ready," I tell Meadow. "I'll head back over in an hour, and we'll go out but stay close to home in case we need to rush back, okay?"

I've never seen Meadow shy before, so the small smile that curls her lips before she looks away is fucking adorable.

The romancing portion of our evening is about to begin.

And I'm fucking excited for it.

26

MEADOW

THE MAN THINKS I CAN GET READY IN AN HOUR. I don't know if he understands that I'm low maintenance or if he has no idea about what goes on in a woman's head when she's getting ready for a date.

Fawn and Jenn are digging through my closet while I take the world's fastest shower, careful not to get my hair wet. Willow ran home—luckily she only lives two blocks away—for cosmetic provisions.

I forgot how exhilarating it is to have a boyfriend, but even the ones I've had in the past aren't like Griff.

How many guys would find almond butter cups and make them into a floral arrangement? Not many. Hell, I'd have been happy with Reese's, and they'd have likely been easier to find, but no, he found enough Justin's Almond Butter Cups to make a whole-ass bouquet.

I jump out of the shower, dry off at the speed of light, and attack my hair with my brush. Which was exactly the wrong thing to do.

It poofs out, and no amount of gel is going to get it back to fighting form.

The bedroom door flies open and nearly slams into the back of the wall. Willow's arms are overflowing with her makeup bag and—God bless her—a flat iron.

Mine broke a couple of weeks back, and I haven't replaced it yet.

Jenn and Fawn are laying out two separate outfits, but I ignore them for now and all but yank Willow into the bathroom with me. She starts on my makeup while I section my hair, careful of my stitches. Our arms nearly tangle every couple of minutes. Finally, Jenn comes in and takes the iron from me, saving me from a third-degree burn on my forehead.

"I wonder where he's gonna take you," Jenn says.

I shrug. "I don't know, but he said it would be close."

"Maybe Longhorn?" The chain steak house is probably the closest thing to fine dining in our area, but we're a short hop down the freeway from a huge shopping plaza with more options.

"Maybe. Oh God. What the hell do I wear if I don't know where I'm going?"

Griffin looked good—if not a little nervous—when he brought over the bouquet. I find it fascinating that we've both defaulted to food when trying to make up for something.

"Stop. You'll look fine. Both of the outfits we picked work for casual or fancy."

In record time, my makeup is done, my hair is straightened with my bangs swept off to the side, and I'm stepping into one of the few dressy dresses that I own. A dark bluish green, it's on the shorter side and has a deep V-cut in the front, which shows off the meager amount of cleavage I can produce. Pleated fabric gathers at the side, and the material gives off a soft glowing sheen. Jenn found it for me on one of the few shopping trips she dragged me to.

Shopping is not my favorite pastime. Most of my closet is the result of my sisters' castoffs or gifts from Mom, all of which I wear until they are too threadbare to wear legally in public. Jenn managed to wheedle a single shopping excursion out of me in the last six months, and I have this dress to show for it.

Now she asks Willow to go with her, and thank God for that.

A knock sounds at the door, and I glance down at my watch. It's been nearly an exact hour, and I don't know if I should attribute that to nerves or excitement, but I'm ready to get the show on the road.

Willow swings the door open. "You'll have her home at a respectable hour?"

Griff's lip twitch. "That depends on your definition of respectable."

I stifle a laugh at that and push Willow aside, then walk out. "Don't wait up!" Once I'm clear, I shut the door on the sounds of my sisters catcalling at us.

"Sorry about that," I say, heat dancing along my cheekbones.

Griff slips his hand into mine. "It's okay. They're actually pretty funny. You look beautiful."

"Thanks. You clean up nicely yourself."

"What, this old thing?" He waves a hand at his shirt, and I really hope that I'm not overdressed. It's not a suit and tie, but it is a button-down, and that's fancy for a guy I rarely see outside of a black T-shirt.

"So, uh, where are we going?"

"You'll see. It's not far."

Once again, I rack my brain trying to figure out where

he might be taking me, but I come up short. I've lived in this area for a long time, but don't eat out much, so my knowledge of local restaurants is limited.

After a quick jaunt down the freeway, we turn onto Washington and then into one of the many parking garages. Once we park and get out of the car, Griff takes a look at my shoes and breathes a sigh of relief.

"Yeah, I'm not coordinated enough to walk in heels."

"It's not far, but I panicked a little bit there."

We walk back down Washington toward a red-and-white awning that shades an empty outdoor seating area. Bold and bright, the hand-painted sign on the whitewashed brick wall reads "The Arrogant Butcher."

My shoulders loosen a little bit when we walk inside. Griffin's spiffed-up look made me worry that he was going to take me someplace ultrafancy where I'd have stuck out like a sore thumb. The aroma of bar food in a trendy setting is reassuring as we follow the hostess to a table.

"You okay?"

"Yeah, just feeling a little overdressed, but also happy that you didn't take me out for a fine dining, multiple-course meal."

His thumb coasts along my knuckles. "For one, that's not really my style. Two, if I ever take you somewhere you're not comfortable or don't like, you just have to let me know and we'll leave. No questions asked."

"Thanks."

In the past, my relationships could be described in one way—lackluster. I didn't care enough about any of them to put in any real effort, but for some reason I am with Griff. I don't know what that means, or what it's saying, but he has a power over me that's scary.

I am seriously out of practice with this dating thing.

"So, what do you think our best bet is moving forward?"

Oh, thank God.

He wants to talk shop, and I could kiss him for it. I look over the menu briefly before deciding on what I want and setting it aside.

"We keep watching his card activity and hope Mark or Britt call us if he shows up."

"You don't think Jada will?"

"She could go either way, but I'm not putting my eggs into her basket if I don't have to."

He bobs his head. "Makes sense."

The waiter stops at our table and tells us the drink and food specials.

"The Marg for me."

Griff says, "The Rickey, please."

Once the waiter is gone again, I say, "I didn't think that it would be this hard to catch him again. It's not like he has an extensive criminal background, but the two of us can't seem to track him down."

"Fucker."

"Yep." I nod.

The waiter drops off our drinks and takes our orders.

"Meatloaf?" I ask Griff. "There were so many more interesting choices on the menu and you pick meatloaf?"

"Hey, no dissing the loaf of meat. This is one of the few places in the valley that does it almost right, and I don't get it very often. Plus, it's my favorite."

"Your favorite ever or something newly acquired?"

"It's been my favorite since I was a kid. One of the kids at school was talking about it and how it made so much food he couldn't finish it all, and that sounded great to me. So I begged my mom to make it, and it became a thing. Every birthday or special occasion, I'd have the whole pan to myself since she didn't like it."

"Your mom sounds wonderful. Does she live here?"

"Uh." His gaze cuts away. "Yeah. She's near Papago Park."

"Oh, that's not far from us at all."

He fidgets in his seat. "I actually picked my place because of how close it is to her."

Why does he look so uncomfortable? I ignore it and smile. "I bet you're a great son."

His jaw clenches, but he says, "I try to be, but the truth of it is it's hard."

"Hard?"

"She's got early onset Alzheimer's."

Oh God.

"I'm so sorry, Griff. That's..."

"Hard. I know."

"Tell me about her?" I reach over and lay my hand on top of his drumming fingers.

His chest expands on a deep breath before he quietly blows it out. "It's always been just the two of us. Then I noticed she was forgetting things. It was little stuff at first, but then it got to be bigger. When she started to have mood swings and confuse me with dead relatives, I had her get checked out. It was the scariest time of my life."

I take a sip of my drink to clear my throat, unsure what I should or shouldn't ask. I feel clumsy in the conversation because I don't want to bring up bad memories, but I want to know more.

"Does she have help?"

"Yeah. I have her in a great memory care facility, which was the reason we moved down here in the first place—"

"Wait. You're not from the valley?" How did I not know this?

"No. Ma and I lived in Flagstaff. She used to live in Phoenix, but moved right around the time she had me. I grew up there."

"Oh, wow. And you moved here six months ago?"

"Yeah. Mom took a turn for the worse, and I couldn't keep up with her even with part-time staff. Her doctor recommended the move because we didn't have the resources that she needed up there."

"Well, I was right."

"Right about what?"

"You're a great son. Not many kids would pack up their lives and move with their mother so she has the care she needs."

Griffin's cheeks tint and he changes the topic. "Tell me about your family. What were your things growing up?"

The change is abrupt, but I get it—talking about his mom can't be easy. "What do you mean 'things'? We didn't have things."

He takes a sip of his drink. "Oh, come on, everyone has things. I didn't grow up with siblings, so enlighten me how that was."

"My 'thing' was not getting lumped in with my sisters. My parents did a pretty good job of letting us form our own hobbies and interests, but now I realize that was probably complicated. My sisters are like a pack of best friends that you fight with when they get on your nerves."

"And you're the oldest?"

"By a whopping three minutes. With how serious and stern Fawn is, it's the running joke in our family that she should have been the oldest. I say she was born exactly when she was supposed to be because she's the mediator.

Willow's wild, and it takes a lot of effort to talk sense into her when she gets it in her mind that a direct course of action is the right one. I swear most of our childhood was me trying to rein her in. Fawn is great at helping me pick which battles I want to fight, while preserving the wild and carefree awesomeness of our baby sister."

Griffin seems to like hearing about my childhood, so I tell stories and keep my questions light. I want to ask more about his mother, but it's obviously a sore subject for him, and I don't want to upset him.

I tell him about cutting off all of my hair one summer because I was too irritated to deal with it while playing basketball in the driveway. And how we still love getting together for family game nights.

Griffin's visibly listening. Not just nodding along and checking scores on ESPN as I talk, but he's invested in the conversation and that makes my insides do a backflip.

He's invested in this. And me.

And I think I'm invested in him too.

27

GRIFFIN

Dinner with Meadow is both better and worse than I thought it would be. While I'm getting to know more about her, I didn't consider how reciprocal the conversation would be. For every question she answers, she wants to know the same thing about me.

And I answer. To a degree. I tell her about being a crazy kid and the trouble that I got into. I share how I hated school until starting high school and discovering girls responded to charm. But anytime the topic veers toward my mom, I clam up and shut down.

Does she really need to know more? Telling her about the Alzheimer's was hard enough, but I can't help but think that I should tell her all of it. It's not like she's not going to find out eventually. Especially if she and I continue to see each other for any length of time. I worry that if I tell her, then she's going to have questions or want to help or—God forbid—she'll pity me.

I don't think I'd be able to handle her pity.

It's bad enough when relative strangers give me sad looks and tell me how sorry they are, then treat me like blown glass—as though my emotions are too delicate to deal with the reality of the situation. Worse are the people who assume that I'll be dealing with my own diagnosis soon simply because my mother is.

I don't want to bring any of that into my relationship with Meadow.

No. Tonight I've given myself permission to live in the moment—to enjoy her and her company. I've told her enough of it. We can save the heavy topics for another day, right?

As we walk back to the car after dinner, I put my hand on Meadow's waist. My fingers rest in the curve of her lower back like that spot was made for me. The fabric of her dress is soft, her skin warm beneath it.

We're standing at a busy intersection, waiting for the crossing signal to change when I dip my mouth next to her ear and whisper, "Not a single panty line in that dress. Is my girl bare?"

Her breath hitches, but she doesn't answer before the light changes. We cross the street, each footfall heavier, tenser than the last. Meadow's breathing becomes staccato, and she rolls her hips a little more with each step.

It's twenty minutes to my apartment, but I'm not going to make it.

I drop my hand down to her ass and squeeze. I'd never move my hand from this delicious spot again if I didn't have to.

Meadow's ass in my hand bends the space-time continuum, and somehow we end up in the parking garage elevator and the doors are sliding closed when I back her into the corner.

A small "oof" leaves her lips as her shoulders connect with the steel wall, but I swallow the sound with my mouth.

With one hand on the delicate line of her jaw and the other on her hip, I yank her into me. All of her soft cushions my hard.

My tongue teases along her lips, then slips inside to dance with hers, the tart bite of tequila from her drink lingering there. I wonder if she's as addicted to my taste as I am to hers.

The elevator dings, and I draw back, clenching my molars to keep it together.

We stumble-run to the car. I drop her hand and pop the locks before flying into the driver's seat, assuming that Meadow is headed for the passenger side. But when I look over, she's standing next to the open driver's side door.

Manners, idiot. I step back out of the car and am about to skirt the hood for the passenger door so we can go already when Meadow pulls me to a stop.

"I can't wait." She kisses me and reaches for my hand, slipping it under her dress. The soft skin of her thighs begs my hand to slow down, to explore, but I continue higher until her heat and damp, plump folds tease the tips of my fingers.

"Meadow," I groan into her mouth, unable to separate from her long enough to get the words out. "Let me get you home, Wildflower."

"Nope." She breaks the kiss and tosses a devious grin and wink at me before pulling the back door open.

I slam the driver's side door and we dive into the back seat.

Thank God for cars with legroom.

Hands on Meadow's hips, I haul her into my lap. Her shoes are already gone, and she hikes her dress above her thighs.

Every glistening inch of her is on display and completely bare to me.

"Fuck. This pretty pussy needs to come, doesn't it?"

"Yes. Yes it does." She hums.

My fingers slide through the folds of her cunt, stroking, teasing, and swirling around her clit, but not making direct contact.

Meadow moans low in her throat and falls forward. My wrist is at an awkward angle, but it'll fucking fall off before I quit.

Her lips whisper against mine. "Griff, that feels so good."

I slip the shoulder of her dress down, palming her tit with my free hand. I pinch her nipple, soft at first and then harder and harder. Her hips shoot against my hand, and a new wave of wet drenches my fingers while she keens.

"That's it, Wildflower, ride my fingers as hard as you need." Her hips pick up rhythm, grinding harder.

Moving my hand, I thrust first one, then two fingers into her core while pressing my palm against her clit.

Her need is visible in the shaking arms, bunched muscles, and unsteady breaths.

Sliding my fingers out of her, I pull her back down for another kiss while my fingers find her clit, and I pinch the nubbin between my thumb and forefinger.

She goes off like a bottle rocket, the pitch of her moans guiding me through her orgasm. I work her core until she slumps against me.

My dick is a raging testament to my own need, but I hold it back, more eager to hold Meadow close.

The windows of the car are completely fogged, the two of us in our own world. A quiet world meant for sharing breaths and secrets.

I kiss Meadow before the spell cast on us can take over, before I say something permanent, something vulnerable that can't be taken back.

When we pull back from the kiss, Meadow's makeup is a little smudged, but the sated look is a good one for her.

My dick jumps against the lips of her bare pussy and a new light enters her eyes.

"You have your back seat caged in?"

I nod.

"For work?"

"What else would it be for?" I had the cage installed the last time a skip got violent with me.

"Why don't I show you?" Meadow opens her clutch and pulls out a condom. I cock a brow at her. "That's for later," she says as she scoots back and unzips my pants, careful not to strangle my dick while pulling it out.

Her hand circles me, and involuntarily I thrust into her grip.

I love to make her come, but I missed out on the action the first time around being solely focused on her pleasure.

She nudges my hip and I scoot down. Once I'm situated behind the driver's seat, she leans over and slides her mouth down my cock until her throat closes around the head.

Eyes rolling back in my head, I bury my hands in her hair and grunt.

"Fuck," I growl. "That's my girl. My good little cocksucker."

She hums around my dick, her tongue flicking the underside until I'm nearly levitating with need.

"Take me deep. All the way down, Wildflower. That's my girl."

Less than ten seconds of her mouth on me and I'm

about to blow my load in the back seat of my car in a parking garage like a high school freshman.

My fingers tighten along her scalp, and I tug lightly at her hair, directing her in speed and because I can't stop touching her.

She moans around my dick when I pull particularly hard. "Does sucking me off make you hot, Wildflower? Are you getting all nice and wet for me again?"

She nods around my dick before sliding down and swallowing around me.

"Okay, Meadow, it's later. It's definitely later." I tug her mouth off me, which may be the hardest fucking thing I've ever done in my life. I press a kiss to her lips and reach for the foil packet to quickly sheath myself.

Once I'm covered, Meadow pulls the other shoulder of her dress down and crawls back onto my lap. Her breasts on display make my mouth water for another taste of her.

I tug her close, shoving my hand into her hair again to draw her head back, which makes her chest thrust forward. My tongue flicks out, lapping at her nipple.

Taking one of her hands, I wrap it tightly around my dick. "Play with that. Make sure you get it wet with you. Then I'll fuck you with it." I let go of her hand and go back to licking, biting, and pinching her stiff nipples until she starts to squirm.

Meadow cups the lips of her pussy around my girth and rolls her hips. Soon I'm coated in her and at the limit of my control. She rises up and slides my cock down to notch the head at her entrance.

I freeze, my mouth locked on one of her nipples, and look up at her.

She leans back, a slight arch in her spine. Bringing her hands up, she locks her fingers around the grate of the cage.

With a twist of her hips, she sits down on my cock hard, taking me to the hilt.

We both cry out, breathing hard. Meadow's hair is starting to stand up because of the humidity back here.

She rolls her hips in a circle, and I cup her face for a kiss.

Thousands of tiny muscles are gripping and clasping me so fucking tight I'm about to lose my damn mind.

After a few seconds she leans back again and starts to ride—tits and ass bouncing, hips rolling, she's using my dick to get off. It's the sexiest thing I've ever seen in my life. I'm trying to stay alive and conscious to ensure I remember this for the rest of my life.

"Fuck. I'm going to come," she pants.

I drag my fingers down to her clit and ass. Using some of her moisture, I drag it back to the puckered opening of her ass and press while massaging her clit.

A quiver starts in her belly, the muscles visibly jumping, the shaking slowly spreading through her body, and then she cries out as the orgasm takes her over.

The first clasp of her climax pushes me to follow. I curl into her, hunched over as my release runs through me, my cock kicking hard, trying to fuck her deeper, longer.

Meadow and I have been a lot of things to each other in a short amount of time. We've been neighbors, enemies, colleagues, reluctant partners, friends, and now lovers. Each of those titles brought something *more* into my life. A challenge when I argued with her to remind me that I'm still living. Help as a partner with a case that holds a large part of my mom's future in the balance. A lover who sets my chest on fire with *feeling*. I'd like to know when I fell in love with Meadow Ridley, because I sure as shit don't have a clue when it happened.

But my brain is starting to catch up with my body, and I'm realizing that Meadow is a woman that you keep.

How do I make that happen?

ONCE OUR HEART rates return to normal, we both maneuver back into our clothes. Meadow has just managed to get her arms back into her dress when a very important fact comes to mind.

"We're in the back seat."

She laughs. "What was your first clue, Ace?"

I want to laugh at the nickname but I can't, because now I'm panicking. "We're in the back seat of my car."

She catches on to the distress in my tone. "What's wrong?"

I nod to the front of the car. The keys are dangling from the ignition, where I shoved them when I was in a hurry to get Meadow home.

Her eyes follow. "We can't get out, can we?"

I shake my head.

The back doors can't be opened from the inside, preventing skips from jumping out when I'm returning them to the welcoming arms of the law.

"Well, shit. Okay then." Meadow opens her purse and pulls out her phone. I snatch the device before she can unlock it.

"What the hell, Griff? We have to call someone."

"No, we don't. Let me just think."

She throws her hands up. "What do you have to think about? We're locked in the back seat of the car with no way out. We need to call one of my sisters."

"We don't need to call them."

Meadow shoots me a look that says to stop being stupid. "Would you rather one of my sisters come down here or my parents? Because those are the only people I can think to call, unless you have someone who can let us out?"

"I'll break the window." The last thing that I need is to lose all the charm points I've worked my ass off for when her sisters find out I fucked her in the back seat of the car like a savage.

"Oh my God. No. Stop. My sisters are well aware of the fact that I have sex."

I slump back against the seat, throwing an arm over my eyes. "Fine, but can you call Fawn? She's less likely to rip my trachea out for touching you."

Meadow dials, and the hyena cackling on the other end of the line means that I'm not going to get out of this without some good-natured ribbing.

Sure enough, less than twenty minutes later Willow, Fawn, and Jenn pile out of a car. Willow pops open the back door and takes a huge step back.

I climb out first and then help Meadow out, glad that we did what little we could to put ourselves back together.

Willow waves her hands around in an exaggerated manner. Fawn and Jenn are holding back giggles, and Meadow snaps, "What the hell are you doing?"

"Dispersing the sexual tension between you two."

Meadow rolls her eyes, then snaps forward and yanks Willow into a headlock, giving her a noogie.

"How's this for sexual tension, Willie?"

"Ew yrmph aww segswety."

Meadow releases her enough to ask, "What?"

Theatrically, Willow sucks in air and bellows, "You're all sex sweaty! Get off me."

Meadow clamps her arm around Willow and then rubs

her armpit along the top of her sister's head, screeching, "How's this for sweaty, huh? Huh?"

And I lose it. I start laughing my ass off, and soon Jenn and Fawn join in. Meadow giggles a couple of times before giving up the fight, letting her sister go and cracking up.

"What the fuck, Meadow? I could have died. You almost suffocated me with your pit stank." But Willow is laughing just as hard as the rest of us.

"Thanks for the save, guys," I say. "We, erm, didn't mean to—what I mean is..."

"What he means is thanks. We'll see you all at home."

Fawn says, "Before we go, Griffin, you got a visitor about two hours ago. He tried your door and when you didn't answer, he knocked on Meadow's door, asking for you. Left a card and said to call as soon as you can."

My first thought is it has something to do with Mom, but I dismiss that. The shift manager at the facility would have called my cell, not sent someone over.

"What'd he look like?" I question.

I can't think of any reason that someone would be looking for me. I keep a pretty low profile.

"About six feet, one-eighty, dark brown hair and brown eyes. Really fucking grumpy looking. I didn't see what he was driving, though I did try to peek out the window."

That doesn't ring any bells for me. "Hmm. Okay, I'll give him a call. Thanks."

The girls leave, and Meadow climbs into the passenger seat. Before I turn on the car, I say, "Back seat calamity aside, I had a really good time tonight, Wildflower."

She smiles at me. "Me too."

"Maybe next time we can do it without having to call your sisters for an SOS?"

Her grin stretches wider. "Definitely."

I drive us home on autopilot, her hand locked in mine the whole way, and let the idea of a future play out with every mile we drive.

Maybe I can make it work.

What if I got tested? What if the results came back negative, and I could finally kick away this cloud that's been looming over me for so long?

I'll call my doctor tomorrow.

What would Mom think of Meadow?

What would Meadow think of Mom?

Maybe I'll take Meadow to see Mom, assuming it's a good day.

The future's looking a little less lonely, and I'm surprisingly okay with that.

28

MEADOW

I ANTICIPATED THE INTERROGATION, SO I'M NOT surprised to be remanded to the couch by three harpies after changing into my pajamas.

"I'm really worried about your career paths," I tell them. "If you can't tell that the date was that good even after you had to save us from the back seat, then you shouldn't be investigating anything."

"Oh, hush. We don't care about the back seat," Fawn says.

"I do," Willow counters.

"I definitely care about the back seat. I want to hear all about the back seat," Jenn agrees.

I smirk. "You guys aren't going to hear anything about anything if you don't shut up."

Fawn grabs a bag of popcorn and the three of them pass it around, munching while I summarize the date.

Willow chucks a handful of kernels at me and cries, "You're censoring. Stop censoring and give us the dirty details, you hooker."

Jenn nods so hard she looks like a bobblehead in an

earthquake, and I relent. "Fine. Mostly dinner was just us talking about our family and childhoods. He told me a little bit about his mom, but kept grilling me about our family, so I didn't get to learn as much as I wanted to. I kinda get the feeling that this is a sore subject for him."

"Why'd you say that?" Fawn asks.

"Because he'd ask me something about you guys, or Mom and Dad, and then he'd hedge when I asked him the same question. I did learn that it was just him and his mom when he was growing up, and his mom is in memory care here in the valley."

Willow pulls her phone out and starts tapping. "Hang on. I don't know why we didn't do this when we first started working with him. But give me five seconds, and I'll have a full dossier on him."

"What? No, don't," I snap. They all look at me in surprise. "I don't want to run a background on him. Not for this. For one, it's illegal as hell and two, I want to find out about him *from* him. How would you like it if every time you went on a date with someone they had the ability to pry into your past?"

"I wear my crazy on my sleeve, thank you very much. That's pretty hard to keep secret."

"That's fine for you, but not everyone is like that. Not everyone just coughs out the first thought to fritter across their brain matter, Willie." I pin each of them with a glare. "We all need to respect his right to privacy. If he wants me to know more, he'll tell me."

"It could be..." Jenn begins.

"What?" I ask softly, all of the irritation in my voice gone at the emotion on Jenn's face.

She clears her throat. "It could be that he's ashamed, or doesn't want pity—and that makes it hard for him to open up. People don't only keep secrets out of selfishness or self-preservation. Sometimes it's scar tissue that splits open when it's brought up. Other times it's a bleeding gash and talking about it rubs salt in. The point is, we don't know what or if he's hiding anything." Jenn turns to my sisters. "I want to protect Mead as much as you both do, but they have to find their way on their own."

Fawn smiles at me. "I'm a fan of anyone who can make you glow so hard your hair curls after how long we spent straightening it."

"Oh yeah, glow so hard. That's what we're going with?" Willow snarks.

I laugh even though my heart is heavy. I want Griffin to be comfortable enough to talk to me. Until he does, all I can do is wait and hope for the best.

WARM ARMS WRAP AROUND ME, nestling under my boobs, and lips touch my neck. I blink my eyes open, and the amount of sunlight coming through my window causes panic to rip through me.

"Shit! What time is it! Did I miss my ride?"

Griffin lies back against my pillows, laughing at me. His damp hair is neatly combed, and he's dressed in his habitual black T-shirt and jeans.

How did I sleep so late?

A quick glance at the clock shows me that it's well past my alarm time, and then I kick myself.

I stayed up late with my sisters and Jenn and then was too busy mooning over Griffin when I went to bed last night to remember to set my alarm.

"You can still ride if you want. We've got time."

"What? Do we have plans?"

We. I love the sound of that.

"I wanted to...I might, uh, maybe I could take you to meet my mom."

His gaze is trained on his lap while he picks at the skin around his left thumb. His nervousness is really fucking cute, and I pounce. My elbow magically lands in his gut, and he twists us, landing between my thighs. My sleep shorts creep up my ass crack most mornings, and now having his groin right there. Is. Torture.

"Unngh" is the best I can come up with. I'd give up almond butter for a week to have an empty apartment right now. Well, maybe not a week. But I could totally make it a day. Maybe.

Griffin's whiskers tickle my lips and cheek when he kisses me, and I can just make out the hint of toothpaste on his breath.

"Hi, Wildflower." His smile makes the butterflies in my stomach turn into full-on floaty weightlessness, and I'm reduced to grinning back at him like a fool.

"Hi, Griffin."

"You down for meeting my mom?"

I nod. I don't trust my voice to come out normal when everything inside me is shouting *squeeeeeeee.*

He gives my ass a hard slap. "Then get up, woman. You want to get a ride in beforehand?"

"I'd like to ride something," I mumble, crawling out from under him.

"Ms. Ridley, I heard that and am thoroughly scandalized. Intrigued, but also scandalized."

Griffin watches me as I change into some workout gear and program my ride. The leaderboard looks empty without

EagleEyeBeastPI there, and I wish I would have known it was him sooner.

My quads are warming up when I notice Griffin poking around my room, peeking into the closet then disappearing into the bathroom.

"What are you doing?" I ask.

"Checking to see if you ever picked up that lube I told you about?"

I bark out a laugh, my cadence faltering and slipping below the instructor's mark.

Griffin comes to stand next to the bike, his smile brighter than the sun. "I bet you did, didn't you?"

"And if I did?" I'm breathless and not just from the bike ride.

I totally didn't, but I want to play the game. I want to see what makes him lose his cool and arouses him...other than me, that is.

"Then I'd have to wonder where the rest of your toys are because I doubt you'd buy that much lube just for your fingers."

The exercise video in front of me disappears and only muscle memory keeps my feet circling. Griffin holds all my attention.

"No...if you were going to lube anything, it'd be a toy, one that probably vibrates so hard it makes your teeth chatter. One that gets all those"—he breathes right into my ear—" sensitive places. Isn't that right, Wildflower?"

"Maybe. But you'd never prove it."

An unholy light enters his eyes, and his fingers clench on the handlebar. I'd bet every jar of almond butter in my pantry that he wants to touch me right now.

"Oh, I can prove it, Meadow. I couldn't tell you how many

nights I lay in bed, my dick in my hand, and jacked off to the sound of you fucking your tight little pussy with a vibrator. I had to bite down on my pillow to stop you from hearing me fuck my fist nearly every damn time. Then you'd get this breathy little catch in your throat—the one that I'm intimately acquainted with now and know it means you're coming—and I'd damn near break the wall down to get to you. How's that for proof?"

I hit the red knob in the center of the bike to bring myself to a complete stop. I twist one foot free and throw my body over the bike seat, unclipping my other leg.

"I heard you," I confess. "The gruff grunt you make in the back of your throat when you're about to go off has lived rent free in my head since the first time I heard it. I just told myself it was my imagination."

"We're going to be late."

"You bet your ass we are." I fist my hands in his shirt and kiss him hard enough to bruise my own lips.

We're going to be so late.

ONCE WE'RE in the car, nerves start to get the better of me. My leg is bouncing a million miles a minute, and I'm sure I chewed off the little bit of lipstick I put on before leaving the house. The scenery of Papago Park would usually be enough to pull me out of my own head. The mountain is the color of rust and contrasts with the greenery of the desert trees and cacti, and it's one of my favorite parks in the valley. But it's not enough to distract me.

What if she doesn't like me?

What if she thinks I'm not good enough for her son?

What if Griffin decides to break up with me because she hates me?

Each scenario that I cook up is more outlandish than the last. I shake my head hard and mentally get ahold of myself.

If she doesn't like me, then she doesn't like me. I might be the best thing since sliced bread, but not everyone likes bread and that's okay.

I've never met a boyfriend's family before. This is new, exciting, scary, and terrifyingly barf-inducing all at once. The single piece of almond butter toast I managed to get down with some coffee is about to make a reappearance all over Griffin's front seat.

His hand in mine is the little bit of reassurance that I need to get through this. He exits the freeway, driving a few more minutes before pulling into a gated community. This place looks swanky. Almost all of the buildings connect to one another by covered walkways, and the tall fencing fully surrounds the grounds. Precise landscaping makes the most of the desert options with a mix of gravel, rock, and drought-friendly bushes and trees.

Griff scans a key card and puts in a passcode to open the gate.

My throat is scratchy, and I wish I would have brought water.

"Wow, the security here is tight. Did you research it before she moved in?"

"Yeah," he answers as we park. His tone is tight, and my nerves ratchet up in response.

"Is everything okay?" I squeeze his hand. He squeezes back, but his expression doesn't change. "I don't have to meet her yet, if you're not ready. I know this is—"

"I'm fine. Come on, let's go." The easy affection, the laughter and happy feelings that we had this morning evaporate as he climbs out of the car.

Something is wrong, but I don't know what.

I trail behind him through a double set of automatic doors. A lady dressed in scrubs about my mom's age is standing behind a receptionist's desk. Her eyes brighten when they land on Griff.

"Hey, Griff, how's it going?"

"Hey, Amy, how's Ma?"

"So far, so good today. She had a light breakfast, and we played a couple rounds of rummy. Who's this?"

His arm comes around my middle, and I'm thankful for the brief moment of extra contact, but then he loosens his hold. "This is Meadow Ridley. She's going to visit with me today."

Amy turns her friendly smile my way and says, "Just sign in here and you're good to go."

Griffin leads me down a hallway painted bright green, then we turn down a yellow corridor. With every step we take, more of the man I know disappears, replaced by a stranger.

His easy smile, his charm, his joking, laid-back nature all dissipate until an emotionless robot walks next to me.

Griffin raises his hand to knock and pushes open the door when we hear "come in" called.

I let him go first. A knot has tied itself in my stomach.

"Hey, Mom. How's it going?"

A woman sits at the window overlooking the mountain preserve park. Weak sunlight filters through the tinted glass and warms her features as she faces us. She and Griffin look so similar, from their coloring to the shape of their mouths. Her brown hair is pulled back in a ponytail, highlighting her sharp cheekbones and making her seem somehow fragile.

"I'm sorry, who are you?" A wheezy laugh accompanies the question and Griffin freezes.

I take a step forward to introduce myself, but he speaks first.

"Sorry, ma'am. My name's Griffin Gallagher."

My stomach plummets, and I drop my hand. She doesn't recognize him.

Oh shit. This is bad.

"Oh, how wonderful! My last name is Gallagher too. I'm Celia. And who is this lovely young lady?"

He turns heartbroken eyes on me, and my sternum cracks. This is the first hint of emotion he's shown since we left the car, and it's pure sorrow.

The day started so happy. But it's not now.

Not when the guy I've gone and fallen in love with is in pain that's so sharp I feel the echoes of it in my own chest.

29

GRIFFIN

A good morning so far.

That's what Amy said. It's not even ten yet. If she was having a good morning, which her ponytail showed, then how could it have deteriorated so fast?

I know that answer. I know it, but I don't want to acknowledge it. Mom's getting worse. The hazy days are happening closer and closer together.

The woman who raised me, who taught me how to ride a bike and tie my shoes, is looking at me like I'm a stranger. She's disappearing right before my eyes, and there's nothing I can do to stop it.

Someday, this could be me.

"And who is this lovely young lady?"

I turn to Meadow. The pity on her face guts me.

My chest goes hollow at the sight, familiar loneliness rising up. I could be the last person in the world, and it would feel exactly the same as I do right now.

I thought that it could be different with her. That maybe she got me. But I was wrong. Just like my sunny optimism and plans to get tested were wrong.

I imagine years of the same look on Meadow's face.

No.

I'm better off not knowing if this future is the one I'm destined for.

I force a smile. "This is Meadow. She's my friend."

Meadow's eyes fly to mine again at the friend comment, and I ignore the lurch in my chest as I downplay what we are. What I had hoped we would be.

This is my future, and it's bleak. But it's also alone, where it can't hurt anyone else.

I'll make sure it's alone.

"It's lovely to meet you, Meadow."

Meadow and I snap out of our staring contest and she smiles. But it's fake, like the ones she used to give me when I would tease her in the hallway of our building.

Those days seem so far away when it's been less than two weeks. How in the world could I have possibly called Meadow my own for this small space of time?

Too bad that, like all good things, this too must come to an end.

"It's nice to meet you too, Celia. Aren't the mountains beautiful this morning?"

For the first time since my mom moved out of our house and into this care facility, I let someone else take the lead. They chat while Meadow serves drinks and tries to make my mom comfortable.

I should be ashamed of myself for allowing Meadow to take responsibility for entertaining my mother when they've never met before, but it's a terrible relief to have that weight lifted off my shoulders when I didn't realize it was crushing me in the first place.

After about a half hour, I wrap up their conversation by saying goodbye. Meadow and I step into the yellow hallway, but exiting the building passes in a blur. She loads me into the passenger seat of my own car and drives us home, holding my hand the entire way without saying a word. She unlocks my apartment and enters it with me.

"Griff, are you okay—wait, that's a stupid question; of course you're not okay."

A million responses fly through my head, most of them some variation of "nothing," but I don't voice a single one.

Compassionate inquiry is the only expression on her face now, but it was pity when we were in Mom's room. Pity that would worsen, that would turn into resentment once she realizes that Mom's disorder is genetic. I have no right to ask her to take on something like that, no matter that I wish otherwise. No matter that I haven't done the tests.

I'm terrified of the test results. I'd honestly rather not know. And before Meadow, that philosophy felt right. Now it feels even more painful, and yet more right than ever.

I shake my head in response to her question because I don't have words right now.

Suddenly, I'm heartsick and pissed off at the world. What right does it have to take my mom away from me? How fair is it that I'm going to lose the only family that I have left, that I can't make my own family because of the disease that looms over me?

"Is there anything that I can do for you?" Meadow's question opens the flood.

"No. But you should probably go."

"What? I'm not leaving you like this."

"Flower Power, this isn't going to work for me anymore."

She flinches, gives me a slow blink, then stutters, "Wh-what?"

"It's genetic. Mom's disease. It's genetic and I don't

know if I carry the markers for it. I've never gotten tested. I don't want to get tested. So this"—I wave a finger between us—"this was never going to work. I'm sorry I led you to believe otherwise."

"I don't understand."

"I won't have you pitying me or being burdened by me if this were to go any further than this. It's not fair to you."

"Griffin—"

I hold up a hand. "No, Mead. You deserve a bright future, not a couple of decades—at best—before being relegated to a full-time caregiver. I won't...I *can't* do that to you."

"That's not fair. You're not fighting fair, Griff."

I cup her face, and her hands lock around my forearms. I drop a kiss to her forehead. "There's no such thing as a fair fight, Wildflower."

"I don't need you to save me. What happened to partners, to being a couple? What happened to *relationship*? To not trying to protect me?" Her fingers dig into my wrists, like she's trying to hang on to this—to our connection—but like me, the happiness we found is slipping through her fingers.

"It's over, Meadow." I brush one last kiss across her lips and drop my hands.

The second my meaning penetrates is visible. Her face falls flat, and I have to fist my hands to stop myself from reaching for her. So many words and thoughts fly through my head, but I bite them back. I want to apologize, to take it all back. I want to seize a little bit of happiness for myself and damn the potential cost down the road.

"If that's what you want, Griffin."

I manage to stay silent as she leaves.

It's for the best.

In three steps and fifteen seconds, I've got a bottle of Jameson in hand. It's not the smartest choice—burying myself in work would be—but I'm entitled to a little pity party, right?

After a healthy swallow, I flop down onto the couch. Memories of the last week and a half dominate my thoughts. Obviously, I'll need to find a way to continue working with her, at least until we find Martin.

But today? Today I'm going to be raw and just simmer in my emotions. I'll be strong tomorrow.

Who would have thought that my uptight, competitive neighbor would be the woman of my dreams?

Certainly not me.

But the simple fact of the matter is that I can't give her what she deserves.

So, for the first time in my life, I concede defeat.

TIME HAPPENS—I'M not sure how much—then there's a knock at the door. I crawl off the couch and carefully set my much emptier whiskey bottle on the floor. My thoughts are still maudlin, but there's a small sliver of hope that I'll find Meadow on the other side of the door.

I shoved her out the door once, but I know I can't do it a second time.

But when I squint through my peephole because I *still* haven't put a camera in there, the only thing I see is a dude in a suit.

Oh, yeah. Fawn gave me a business card last night. I forgot about it and didn't call the number to see what was up. Maybe this has something to do with that.

Opening the door while I'm drunk probably isn't the

best idea. I turn the knob and swing it open, leaning against the frame to maintain my balance.

"Yeah?"

The guy is about my age, but dressed to the nines on a Sunday afternoon, which makes no sense at all. This dude looks wealthy. He's got the wrong place.

"Griffin Gallagher?"

"Thas me." Words are hard after half a bottle of whiskey; who knew?

He rolls his eyes. "May I come in?"

"Whatchu want?"

"It's a personal matter, best discussed in private."

This guy forms words like he's talking around hundred-dollar bills. I swing the door open wider and say, "By alls mean."

I turn and walk back to the couch. Before my ass meets the cushions, I've got the bottle in hand and take a hard swig from it. Holding it out, I ask, "You want?"

The suit looks pointedly at his watch. "No, thank you. I don't make a habit of imbibing at midday."

Eh. Fuck it. More for me.

"Well, Mr. La-Di-Da, what can I do for you?"

"My name is Gabriel Aldric. Does that name sound familiar?"

Why the hell would it? I shake my head.

Fancy Pants sighs like he's put out. "I figured. My father recently passed away."

"I'm sorry." I tip the bottle toward him before taking another swallow. The heat of the whiskey is starting to dull my senses, but I hang on to the thread of the conversation. Is this guy here for a job? If so, where'd he get my name?

"I'm not sorry. I'm here because he left a note in his will

naming you as a son from an affair—one of hundreds he had over the years."

What the fuck?

He pulls a packet of papers out of the breast pocket of his coat and hands them over. I read through the letter—with one eye closed to prevent double vision—and then a copy of the will before looking up at my unwelcome visitor again.

"There are also paternity test results and documents indicating your mother accepted a large settlement from my father for relinquishing his parental rights and her agreement to silence. I can provide a copy of those for you as well."

I hold up a hand to get the information overload to stop.

The letter in my hand explains it all. Mom had an affair with this guy, told him she was pregnant, he admitted to being married and then paid her off to keep her silent about the whole thing.

This guy's eyes look like mine. "Who the hell is your dad?"

"Was. And he was the CEO of Aldric Aerospace. Half of that is now yours as he gave you half of my inheritance."

The room is spinning. And not in a fun way. "I'll be right back. I need to throw up to process this."

I lurch to my feet and stumble down the hall. After a few minutes of praying to porcelain gods, I rinse my mouth out and brush my teeth. My head feels a little clearer.

No wonder my mother never told me a thing about my dad. If she had, she would have violated the NDA that fucker made her sign.

But where'd the money go? We were hand-to-mouth my entire childhood.

The house and land.

Mom and I lived on an acre of land. I don't remember her making a single house payment growing up, but I was a kid, and kids don't see stuff like that. When Mom got sick and we moved, we sold it, paying off the mortgage that was way smaller than I would have thought and all of her medical bills. The rest we used to cover the first few months of her memory care costs. That would explain why we weren't so tight all the time when she mostly worked part-time.

Fancy pants can keep his inheritance. I don't want any of it. I don't even care that he's a half brother of sorts. A couple of months ago I would have welcomed it, maybe gotten to know him so he could be a friend as well as family, but now? It doesn't matter. If I can't have the one that I truly want in my life, then what's the fucking point, you know?

"Griffin! Where the hell is Griffin? And what are you doing back here?" Either I'm hallucinating or not nearly as sober as I thought, because I swear I just heard Willow in my living room yelling.

What the hell?

When I make it back into the living room, Willow's standing with her taser pointed at Gabriel. She's red in the face and about two seconds away from shooting him.

"What the hell's going on?"

She turns terrified eyes in my direction. "Meadow's missing."

30

MEADOW

My pulse throbs in my gums, and the skull-splitting headache makes my eyes tear when I try to open them.

Wherever I am, it's dark. Cramped. My arms are tied behind my back.

Am I in the trunk of a car?

That *motherfucker*. Rage courses through me as my memory returns.

Heart aching, I left Griffin's place. I had just gotten into my apartment when my phone rang. It was Jada saying Martin was at the club.

I drove over there like a bat out of hell and pulled up to the back.

This fucking coward snuck up behind me to knock me out.

I should have called Mark or Britt, but instead I reacted without any planning, and now I'm paying for it. I don't know why I'm so appalled. It's not like I should have expected a fair fight from him.

There's no such thing as a fair fight, Wildflower.

Don't think about that right now. I squeeze my eyes shut.

The car drops into a pothole and my shoulder socket burns when I land on the arm under my side. If he hits another hole like that, it may dislocate my shoulder.

I feel around my bonds, trying to determine what he used to restrain me. When I discover the smooth, cool plastic under my touch, I smile.

This amateur thinks that basic-ass zip ties are going to keep me down?

Nope.

I shift and wiggle, moving my arms down my lower back, over my hips and finally to the backs of my knees, then I thread one leg back through my arms and finally the other leg.

Now my hands are in front of me.

The next part is tricky. I turn on to my back and bring my hands to my mouth.

This idiot didn't cut off the lead on the bonds. I grab the tail of the tie with my teeth and pull it tighter. Once I have it as tight as it'll go without cutting off circulation, I wrench my arms down my body. I can't get a lot of force in the confined space, but I'll make it work. The first pass doesn't break the tie, so I repeat the movement until the plastic finally breaks.

I look and feel around for the emergency opening latch, but apparently Martin isn't stupid enough to leave that. Or possibly this car was manufactured before the latches became required.

I roll over onto my stomach. Bracing my feet on one end of the trunk and my arms against the other, I lift the floor covering to reach underneath. Sure enough, there's a spare tire, but even better is the tire iron I find. I reach down with one hand and snag that before putting the flooring back in place.

Lying back, I try to calm my breathing. I could feel around the floor for a trunk release or knock out one of the brake lights, but I don't know where we are. At best, knocking out a brake light could notify another motorist that I'm trapped back here, but Martin might hear that, and he could pull over or evade whoever might call the cops to come save me.

Most likely Fawn and Willow will have noticed that I'm missing by now, and they would have gotten a notification on our family tracking app when my phone was shut off or lost signal. Griffin would have been able to tell them when I left.

I just have to keep my wits about me, get out of this skirmish, and survive to tell the tale.

No sweat.

We drive for forever. I don't have a watch, and my phone is gone, but I suspect that we've been driving for at least an hour or more, depending on how long I was unconscious.

Where the fuck is this nut taking me? There's no way that we're in the city anymore.

Pointless panic will get me nowhere, so I focus on my breathing.

The car slows to a stop.

The engine cuts off, and I take a deep breath. I put my arms behind my back and scoot as far back as I can. The tire iron in my hand is reassuring.

I close my eyes, working hard to keep the panic at bay and my breathing even.

You're only going to get one chance at this, Meadow. So make it fucking count.

The car door opens and closes, then footsteps on dirt move toward me.

I suck in a lungful of air and let it out slowly as the trunk clicks open.

Moving myself as deeply as possible into the trunk makes it harder for Martin to get me out. But most importantly, being flush against the back seat hides my weapon. I need him close for this tire iron to do any good, and I don't have a lot of room to maneuver.

Once his hand closes on my hip, I open my eyes and swing for the fences.

The iron connects with his temple, and he straightens too fast, slamming his head on the trunk lid.

I swing around to bring my feet up and kick him as hard as I can in the chest. He flies backward.

I scramble out of the trunk as fast as I can, the tire iron still clutched in my hand.

We're in the middle of fucking nowhere. This asshole brought me out to the desert.

Martin's cursing me in two languages, but I'm not hanging around. I bolt for the driver's door, hoping he left the keys in the ignition. My hand connects with the door handle just as he grabs a fistful of my hair, ripping my head back and tossing me to the side like a rag doll.

By some miracle, I hang on to the iron as I roll and come back up to my knees before climbing back to my feet. My scalp is on fire.

"You fucking bitch." Martin swipes at the blood on his temple, and I stay silent.

His head is bleeding like a stuck pig, and he's squinting his right eye shut. He pulls a knife out of a sheath on his belt.

"What the fuck, Martin? This is going to be so much worse for you now. You know that, right?"

"You should have left me alone, puta. If you kept your nose out of *my* business, then I wouldn't have to handle you."

I sneer. "Is this you handling me? Because last I checked, you're the one seriously injured."

"You're going to pay for that."

"Then let's dance, asshole."

Like an enraged boar, he shouts and drops his shoulders to charge me, swiping out with the knife as soon as he's in striking distance. I smash the tire iron down on the back of his hand, sending the knife flying, and sidestep his tackle attempt.

He changes direction on a dime and swings around with the back of his hand, catching me across the face. Stars burst in my vision, then a hard shoulder connects with my gut. I fall to the ground, Martin landing on top of me.

I buck my hips and roll before pushing back to my feet in time to see him rushing me again. Out of reflex, I swing the tire iron at his face.

Instead of the glancing hit I got in from the trunk, the dull thud rings through the afternoon. Martin topples like a tree, knocked out cold.

I sprint for the car, and sure enough, the keys are in the ignition *and* there's a cell phone in the cup holder.

Please don't be code locked, please don't be code locked.

I tap the screen and swipe up, nearly crying in relief when there's no lock and full service, but the battery is about to die.

Please don't die. Please don't die.

If the phone goes, I have to figure out another way to get help, and I'm too fucking exhausted for that.

I pull up the map and zoom out until I find the closest town to us. We're just outside of Florence—less than an hour southeast of Phoenix, in the desert that separates the two metropolitan areas.

Once I know about where I am, I dial 9-1-1, while keeping an eye on Martin's prone form. Sirens aren't too far away when the phone finally dies, and I drop it into the cup holder.

After that, it's a flurry of activity. I get a ride to the hospital in one of the ambulances, and Martin's handcuffed to his gurney in another.

The doctor checks me over, and other than some bumps and bruises, I'm just waiting on discharge when I ask a nurse to borrow her phone.

I don't have Fawn or Willow's phone numbers memorized, so I call the house landline and then the security firm's phone and leave a message letting my family know where I am. Then I use the Internet to look up Bobby's number.

"Hello?"

"Hey, Bobby, it's Meadow."

"Girl, where the hell are you? Your mom and dad are frantic."

"Don't worry, I'm fine. I'm at the hospital in Florence. I was just calling to tell you that we got Martin. He's here in the hospital, but once he wakes up, they're going to transport him back to jail."

"I don't give a single shit about him. Are you okay?"

I chuckle weakly. Fine is subjective. Now that the adrenaline dump is gone, I'm exhausted and heartbroken, but I'm not sharing that with anyone right now.

"Yeah, Bobby, I'm fine. Can you call my parents and do me a favor?"

"Anything."

He's going to regret saying that.

"Give Griff the full bounty. I don't want any of it, okay?"

The other end of the line is silent for a second. "You two together?"

"No." My voice breaks on the word.

"Bullshit, Meadow. What's going on? Do I need to break his legs? Because I'll break his legs, baby girl."

I wipe a tear off my cheek. "We were something, but I don't know if I'd say that was together. Regardless, none of that matters because he ended it today."

Mumbled curses come through the line, and I really want to curl up and sleep, so I say, "Listen, Bobby, I don't want to argue with you. Just put him down for the completed job. He could use the money, okay?"

He needs it more than I or Phoenician Investigations do, and I'll clear the change with Dad. His mother has immediate needs, and even though I'm really pissed at him right now, I'm not vindictive enough to look for revenge.

Bobby goes quiet again. "He tell you about his mom?"

"Yeah."

If I could just alleviate that one worry for him, maybe we could...

No. We can't. I know that we can't. He made it perfectly clear that he was done with me. I have to respect that.

Maybe that's just me running from confrontation, but heartsick and sore, I don't care right now.

"Okay, baby girl. Whatever you say."

"Thanks."

Discharge paperwork is finally signed, and I'm exiting

the triage area when my family swarms in. Arms wrap around me and there's hugging and crying.

I don't feel the pinch that Griffin isn't one of the sets of arms holding me. I don't feel that at all.

That's the lie I'm going to keep telling myself until it's true.

But even I know that won't be for a while.

31

GRIFFIN

"WHERE IS SHE?" WILLOW'S GOT JADA BY THE COLLAR of her shirt, and is two seconds away from losing her shit.

I don't blame her.

I sobered up real fast after she told me she got the notification from their tracking app that Meadow's phone was shut off even though there were no previous dying battery notifications.

The last known location was the strip club, so we flew over here while Jenn and Fawn stayed behind just in case Meadow reappeared. Jada was crying and holding an ice pack to her eye after we stormed in when Mark opened the door. That's as far as we got before Willow got to her.

"Where is my sister?"

"I don't know!"

"What do you mean, you don't know? You just said you're the one who called her and told her to come down here. Now you have two seconds before I call the cops."

"I don't know where he took her, okay? He called me and told me to meet him here. Once we got here, he pulled a knife on me and told me to call Meadow and have her come down here. After I did, he punched me and knocked me out. I woke up about twenty minutes ago."

Martin has her. Panic is clawing through my chest. I can't catch my breath, and my ears are ringing like church bells.

Why didn't she tell me she was coming here?

But she had no reason to tell me. Especially not after how I treated her today. We both went back on our word today; she was just doing what I did when I shoved her out the door.

"Do you have any idea where he would take her?" Willow asks. "Where he's staying?"

"His house," I say.

I don't know why I didn't think of it before.

She turns to me. "You think he'd take her there?"

"I don't know, but we have to look."

Willow and I sprint for her car. I'm in no shape to drive even though I threw up most of the alcohol and adrenaline burned off the rest. I don't trust myself to get behind the wheel right now.

We make it to Martin's house in half the time it should have taken.

I stalk straight up the front path and kick the front door in.

The smell and mess are gone. And the house is completely empty. Like moved out empty.

Fuck.

"What?" she asks.

"This place was trashed the last time I was here, and now there's nothing."

"Shit."

"Where do we—" Her ringing phone interrupts me, and she swipes to answer.

"Bobby, have you—Oh my God. You did? Where is she? Okay. We'll be right there." Willow hangs up. "She's fine. Martin's in custody and she's at the hospital in Florence for bumps and bruises. We can pick up Fawn and Jenn on the way."

I want more than anything to go with them to the hospital. To see with my own eyes that she's safe and whole.

But I can't. That wouldn't be fair to her. After the back-and-forth of the last couple weeks, I can't insert myself into her life again. Not if I want to give her a clean break.

"You go ahead." I already hurt her once today. I don't deserve to be one of the people in the ER for her.

She looks incredulous. "Are you serious right now?"

"Yeah. You go ahead. I'll catch up with you later."

She eyes me suspiciously, clearly wondering what happened to the happy couple she broke out of the back seat of my car last night.

With a narrow-eyed glare, she leaves me alone.

I dial a ride share service and check my phone every five seconds on the way home, waiting for a call that's never going to come.

I drop my keys on the side table and immediately pick them up again. The bar around the corner feels more welcoming than my apartment, and now that the Martin threat is clear, I'm free to drink myself into oblivion—at least for the rest of the day. With Meadow making this arrest, I need to get back to work since I'll likely be out the bounty fee on this case.

Other than the few jobs process serving that I managed to pick up while I was working with Meadow, I don't know if I even have enough to cover the cost of my own rent this month.

Luckily, Visa is accepted everywhere, and I'm okay going into debt for a little bit of numbing relief.

I leave my place and pause at Meadow's door.

I need to find somewhere else to live. I won't survive living close to her, knowing I can't have her.

Wait a second. I pull my phone out of my pocket and dial as I walk.

Gabriel answers on the first ring. "This is Aldric."

"Hey, it's Griffin Gallagher. Can you meet me at the bar on the corner of McDowell and Scottsdale?"

There's a pause and then he says, "I can be there in about a half hour."

"Thanks." I disconnect.

If the plan that I'm piecing together in my head works, then I'll be out of here soon.

I turn back to look at the apartment building. I don't want to move, but it doesn't make sense for me to stay here, not this close to her.

It's a quick jaunt to the bar, and I'm settling in with my first drink and some mozzarella sticks when Aldric shows up. Now that I'm not slightly drunk or emotionally compromised, I look him over. He's taller than me—something that burns my ass—and there are only a few similarities between our features.

I wish I could talk to my mom, ask her questions about who my father was. But since I can't...

I gesture to the seat next to me. Aldric's ditched the suit jacket but still looks pressed and polished to within an inch of his life.

"Get you a drink?" I ask.

"Just water for me."

I turn in my seat. "Look. I don't want any part of your

empire. I'm not here to take advantage of you. But you grew up with the guy, right? What was he like?"

Aldric takes a drink of water. Gathering his thoughts?

"He was an alcoholic asshole who emotionally abused my mother, cheated on her, and made our lives a living hell."

Well, fuck. Now the water makes sense. "And you didn't know about me until he croaked?"

"Nope. Neither my mother nor I knew a single thing. Of course, she knew about the affairs—kind of hard to miss them when he went out of his way to flaunt them. Nothing was ever good enough for him. No matter how hard Mom and I tried, he never gave a damn."

He lifts his hand and waves the bartender down. "Whiskey, neat."

I chuckle and he asks, "What?"

Tipping my glass to him, I say, "Well, at least we have similar drinking tastes."

He smirks. "If you're not here to take advantage of me then why did you call me down here?"

"Your dad was worthless. Is your mom a good person?" When he stiffens, his eyes narrow on me so I add, "It's nothing like that; calm down."

Once he relaxes, he says, "She's a great person."

"That's awesome, man. I'm happy for you. My mom is the best...but she's not doing great."

"She's sick?"

"Alzheimer's."

"Fuck."

"Yep." We both drink.

"Do you have any other family?" he asks.

"No. It's always been just me and her. Wait. Are there any more like me?"

If I was a bastard and the guy had dozens of affairs, chances are there might be more.

"Not that we know of. You're the only one that he named. I think your mom was one of his early affairs and he got smarter after that."

"Well, that's good at least."

"You were saying about your mother?"

I nod. "I have her in a memory care facility, but it's expensive as hell. I've been working my ass off to keep her there because it's what she needs."

"So you need money?"

"I do, but I don't want any of your empire. I like my job." I make a face. "Most of the time. I don't know anything about aerospace, and I don't want to know about it."

"You want me to buy you out of the company?"

I shrug. If that's the right term for it. I need to figure out what it entails, but it's probably better than the alternative of me trying to run a business in an industry that I have no clue about. Aldric, on the other hand, looks like he was bred for the role. Whether that was voluntary or not is another question, but we don't know each other well enough for me to ask.

"I can have the lawyers draft something up." He picks up and tosses back the rest of his drink. "But a word of advice. Get a lawyer to look it over on your end."

"I can do that."

"What are we going to do about this whole being-related thing?"

I can't tell the direction of his thoughts, but I go with honesty. "I've always wanted a sibling, but never the hassle of a younger brother or sister following me around."

"How old are you?"

"I'll be thirty-two next month," I reply.

"Thirty-two as of this month, so you're the younger sibling, not me."

I clap a hand on his shoulder and laugh.

"Ain't that a bitch, Gabby."

I signal the bartender for another round and think about how fucking weird the world is sometimes.

I lost Meadow and gained a brother all in a day.

Wish I could have 'em both, though.

GABRIEL and I stumble out of the elevator—well, I stumble. He just kinda leans on me while I tow him down the hall. Apparently, my brother can't hold his liquor, and he's feeling the effects of it. I don't know where he lives, so he and I are going to have our first sleepover.

This is officially the weirdest day of my life.

The elevator doors close at my back, and I try to stay as quiet as I possibly can, but Gabriel's singing "Toxic" by Britney Spears at the top of his lungs no matter how much I shush him.

My eyes are trained on the floor so I can keep track of where we're going. Suddenly, his weight gets dragged off my shoulder.

"Who the hell is this, Gallagher?"

I don't know who I expected to help me drag my semi-blackout-drunk sibling down the hall, but it sure as hell wasn't Bobby.

I was hoping that I wouldn't have to deal with the fallout of my life until tomorrow morning. You know, save the excitement for the least exciting day of the week, but I guess the universe is just shitting on me today.

We inch and lurch past Meadow's door, and when I

cast a nervous glance at it, Bobby says, "Don't worry about her. She's staying at her parents' house tonight."

And that's a topic I'd like to avoid if the censure in his voice is an indicator. I shove my left hand into my pocket and dig my keys out to unlock the door. Once we're inside, Bobby puts Gabriel on the couch, and I head into the kitchen to grab a bottle of water.

Bobby grabs a seat at the counter, and his hands form a steeple in front of his mouth.

"Son, I'm gonna need you to be real honest with me for a minute. What exactly is going on with you and Meadow?"

He knows. I assumed that I'd have to answer to Andrew, not Bobby, but then I remember the gimlet stare he hit me with in his office the day he gave us this job.

"I love her," I tell him. "I don't know how it happened. I know that it shouldn't have. But it did. You don't have to worry about it, though."

He cocks an eyebrow. "Oh, I don't?"

"No. I ended it."

"Now why the hell would you go and do somethin' stupid like that? I saw firsthand how you looked at her in my office, and I've heard plenty about you getting her goat, but as soon as it gets scary, you roll over and give up? Explain that shit to me."

"I...I can't ask her to take the risk of early onset Alzheimer's. I won't do it, Bobby."

The cowboy hat comes off and Bobby rubs a hand through his hair. "You're a damned idiot, kid."

"For not wanting to ruin her life?"

"For being a coward." The last word is all but roared. "I've got news for you, kid. It don't hurt any less if you push people who care about you away now instead of wringing every single piece of happiness out of life first. In the end, all that's left for you is pain because you don't know how to open up your knucklehead heart to anyone but your own selfish needs. Meadow deserves better than that."

He stands and throws an envelope down on the table. "Here's your pay from the job. You and I, though? We're done until you can pull your head out of your ass. You need to straighten up and talk to someone about your mom, and figure out your own mess."

Bobby stalks out of my apartment.

I eye the envelope warily. Pay usually comes by direct deposit, so Bobby bringing a check down is weird. I didn't expect to get paid, especially since I wasn't even there when Martin was turned in.

My chest hurts, but I settle into the pain. It's probably not going anywhere.

I open the envelope to look at the check.

The number is wrong. It's all wrong.

I run out the door, and luckily Bobby is still standing at the elevator bank. "Bobby, wait. This isn't right; the check isn't right. This is Meadow's."

"Meadow said it was to go to you. That you needed it more than she did."

"I can't take that."

"Well, I ain't taking it back. And if you don't cash the check, then I'll just wire the funds and block returning them. Donate it or use it to take care of your mom. I don't care."

Of course, Meadow gave me all the money. She just had to get the last word in.

Just twist the knife, why don't you, Wildflower.

32

MEADOW

THE AMOUNT OF ALMOND BUTTER I CAN COMFORT EAT in two weeks is alarming. But now? I'm totally fine. I'm going to work every day, exercising, and taking care of myself like normal.

Everything is a-okay. Nothing to see here, folks.

Except I miss Griffin. I don't know when the sneaky asshat slithered into my heart, but somewhere in the last few weeks, I fell hard for Griffin Gallagher, and I'm more than a little pissed off at him about it.

I have half a mind to go pound his door in and demand an explanation. I went from barely dating to seducing the neighbor I couldn't stand to being in love with him.

Wham-bam-thank-you-ma'am. Done.

At the start of all this I thought that Griffin wasn't going to know what hit him. Turns out he slammed into me like a ton of bricks, and I'm still reeling from the blow.

Willow, Fawn, and Jenn all know what went down. They didn't even have to ply me with alcohol. After being discharged from the hospital, the four of us went to stay with my parents for the night and camped out in the living room. Fawn asked a single, "What happened with Griff," and I lost my shit.

I told them everything. His back-and-forth between us while we working on the case. Everything that had happened, how I'd been stupid and fallen for him. Willow demanded that I knock some sense into his head. Fawn uncharacteristically agreed with Willow. But Jenn just listened until I got it out. Then she gave me a hug that prompted another slew of tears, which was when we broke out the alcohol.

The next morning? I pretended like nothing had happened. I got up, took a shower and some ibuprofen, then got to work filing the case notes on Martin and looking at my agenda for the week.

Mom and Dad urged me to take some time off, but idle time is the last thing I need right now. Dad and I cleared the air. And I understood his worry from a whole new perspective post-Griffin. Parents worry for their kids; kids worry about their parents. Meeting Celia and seeing how much it hurt Griffin made me appreciate how lucky I am to have both of my parents still. After that? My dad wanting to kick me from the case made sense, and I forgave him.

I've been more scatterbrained lately too, which is why I'm back at home in the middle of the afternoon when I normally avoid this building as much as possible.

I leave early, work long days, then tiptoe down the hall with all the ninja skills I possess. Once I'm in my apartment for the night, my ass is planted.

But I haven't seen Griffin once since he ended things.

The elevator doors open, and I step lightly into the hallway. It's been quiet in his apartment lately—not that I've been listening—but there's a racket going on right now and his door is wide open.

I reach into my purse—the one missing my freaking wallet, which is why I'm home in the middle of a workday—and pull out my taser. It's not like him to leave his door open.

With my back to the wall, I tiptoe closer to his door. Just as I'm about to reach it, two burly guys in coveralls come out carrying Griffin's dresser. The back of their uniform says, "All My Sons Moving," and I freeze in place.

Did Griffin move? Why didn't he tell me?

Why would he tell you, dummy? He's done with you.

"Uh, excuse me," I say. "Did the gentleman who lived there move?"

"Yep," the one closest to me answers before smacking and popping his gum, then they shuffle down the hallway with the dresser between them.

I unlock and let myself into my place before the first tear can fall.

This is me. Being totally fine.

And it fucking sucks.

SHOVING the hurt away is surprisingly easy when I throw myself into work. Every blistering sunrise is observed from behind my desk downtown. I've doubled up on my bike rides, and I'd be lying if I didn't check Eagle-Eye's bike activity every day hoping to catch him in a workout. I even caught up our entire office on paperwork, something that hasn't happened since I started officially working for the firm. I haven't taken any skip traces because I'm not ready to run into Griffin. I'm still perfecting and piecing together my armor, knowing it's inevitable that I'm going to run into him eventually. We work in the same line of business, and we get a lot of our work from the same clients.

Friday night, I let myself into my apartment and kick off my shoes, dropping my bag on the side table. The crinkle of paper sounds from under my foot, and I glance down. There's a white envelope on my floor.

Where the hell did that come from?

Our doors are sealed, so it's not like someone could have slipped it under the door.

I snag the small tablet that sits next to the door and open the footage from today, letting it play through.

I leave my apartment and there's nothing in the hallway aside from our neighbors coming and going until just after lunch.

Seeing Griff, even on a screen, is a punch to the gut. The camera does nothing to enhance his arresting features; if anything it washes them out and dulls him down. I'm hit with a sharp pain at the abruptness with which he pops my door open and drops the envelope.

He broke into my apartment without my alarm going off? What the actual hell? I watch as he lets himself back out and locks my door from the outside before I set the tablet down.

My name is printed in neat block letters on the front of the envelope. I eye it like I would a rattlesnake in the desert. For all I know, it's going to strike and bite me in the ass too.

I head toward the kitchen and grab a bottle of wine. I'm in the middle of uncorking it when my door opens and my sisters and Jenn walk in.

Oh, fuck. I forgot it's my turn to host Friday night dinner.

"Hey, guys."

I swivel and open the fridge. Other than half a block of

moldy cheese and some questionable Chinese leftovers, it's barren.

Pizza it is.

"Where the hell is all of your food, Mead?"

Willow's voice carries through my apartment, and I wince at the three of them standing in my kitchen. I'm about to get it.

Sure enough, all three of them crowd into the small space and fling questions at me faster than I can answer them.

"Shut up! Jesus. I just haven't gotten to the grocery store in a little bit. I'll order pizza. Chill out."

They share a look, then Jenn says, "We're worried about you, Mead. You barely come to Friday night dinners anymore. We haven't seen you outside of the office in nearly two weeks, and then we come over to find your fridge empty. Help us understand."

A stupid, traitorous tear snakes down my cheek. God, I am so done crying. I wipe it away and force a smile. "I'm fine, guys. Just a little sad, but I'll be okay. I'll do better, I promise."

"What's that?" Willow asks, pointing to the envelope on the counter.

"Griffin broke in and left that on my floor."

"On the floor? Why wouldn't he just put it on the table?" Fawn asks.

"He popped the door open, and there's only a ten-second delay before my alarm goes off. He didn't have time. It was just there when I came in."

"Have you opened it yet?" Jenn asks.

"No."

Willow rolls her eyes and snags the envelope. "This is stupid. Let's open it, then whatever it is, light it on fire."

Now it's my turn to roll my eyes, and I snatch the envelope back.

They are looking at me expectantly, so I pull the flap open and lift out the folded paper.

A cashier's check falls out, and I see red.

"That asshole!"

"What?" three voices chorus in unison.

I pick up the check and wave it in the air. "That asshole sent me the payout for Martin's case."

"Wait. Didn't you get paid for that already?"

I shake my head. "No. I told Bobby to give it to Griffin. He needs it for his mom."

Fawn pulls the check from my fingers and whistles. "That's a fuck-ton of money."

"I know. And that insufferable asshat gave it back when he's killing himself every month to pay for his mother's memory care."

"So keep it," Willow cuts in.

"I don't want to keep it. I told Bobby to give it to him for a reason, and if his pea brain can't handle that, then I'll find him and shove it down his throat." All plans to avoid Griffin for as long as possible evaporate. I'm done running from the fight.

"Find him? Where'd he go?" Jenn asks.

"There were movers at his place this morning when I came to get my wallet. He moved. I don't know where, but I'm about to find out."

"Wait!" Fawn says.

"What?"

"What does the note say?"

I swipe the paper up and unfold it. To be honest, I completely forgot about the paper because I was so mad about the check.

Griffin's handwriting is similar to the front—all caps, just on a smaller scale.

MEADOW, THANK YOU FOR THINKING OF MY MOTHER AND ME. HOWEVER, I CAN'T ACCEPT. I WISH YOU ALL THE BEST AND I'LL SEE YOU AROUND.

LOVE,

GRIFFIN

What the actual fuck is this? He can't accept? Pigheaded, pain-in-my-ass caveman.

My hands start to shake so I pass the letter off to Jenn who reads it out loud.

I get not wanting to accept help, especially when you never have before. I understand needing to stand on your own feet and figure it out. But I don't understand this. He may not want me—that's fine, I can deal with that. But why would he pass up the help he legitimately needs for his mother?

Griffin, what the hell are you thinking?

God, I miss him. I promised myself I wouldn't cry over him anymore. He made it abundantly clear that he doesn't want me, so why can't I stop thinking about him?

Why do I stalk his bike profile to see if he's logged in recently? He hasn't. Why does every single sound next door make me still and hold my breath, hoping to catch the slightest sound from him?

No. I won't let him get away with just sending this check. I can't rip it up and throw it away, because a cashier's check is guaranteed funds and he'd have no way of reclaiming the money, so I'll have to make good on my promise and find him to shove the letter down his throat.

"Meadow, you've got crazy eyes. What are you going to do?" Willow asks. She'd know crazy eyes since she has them enough.

"I'm going to trace a skip tracer, and when I find him, he will rue the day he ever crossed me."

Willow grins evilly, Jenn smirks, and Fawn laughs.

"When do we start?" Willow asks.

"Right now."

33

GRIFFIN

The midmorning sun shines into my face as the automatic doors close behind me. My sunglasses cut the glare, and through the pinprick floating lights in my eyes, I see a figure leaning against my car. I should have assumed she'd track me down here—it's not like I could move Mom when I moved too.

Even fifty feet away, I'd know it was Meadow. There's no distance between us that I'd ever mistake that wavy hair or the *fuck around and find out* expression creasing her brows.

She's a sucker punch followed by fresh air, and I'm almost used to the ache in my chest that thinking about her inspires.

It worked. It fucking worked.

My long strides eat up the pavement between us and she opens her mouth—no doubt to blast the shit out of me—when I take her mouth with mine. She tastes like almond butter and forever, and I'll be willingly addicted for the rest of my life.

There's no knee in my balls and her lips move under

mine, the anger on her face disappearing as I let my eyes shut.

I need to touch her.

I want to consume all of her. Her flaws, her attributes, the good times, the bad. I'll stand next to her through all of them and love her every day harder than the day before.

After a small nibble on her lip, I break the kiss and drop my lips to her forehead. "Wildflower, I missed you."

My nickname seems to wake her up because she shoves against my shirt and says, "You missed me? Then you have a funny fucking way of showing it, Griff." She pivots on her heel, puts her hands on her hips, and starts pacing back and forth between the car and me.

"First you break up with me because you're a fucking idiot. Then you move so I can't torture you for the rest of your life, and then—and then!—the cherry on top was you sending me this! And now you kiss me? What the fuck? Your mom needs this. You need this to take care of her." She reaches into her back pocket and pulls out the cashier's check, then lobs it at me.

"Not anymore," I say, and she looks confused.

I stride forward and tug her back into my arms. "Look, I know that you're mad at me. Seems I can't go more than a day without pissing you off and needing to apologize. But I can explain. First off, I sent you the check because I needed to talk to you, but didn't want to just show up after being an asshole. I was hoping you'd come find me, and how could I pass up the chance to needle you? Second, I was a scared asshole when I broke it off with you. I was too scared to get tested to see if there was a risk of me having Alzheimer's, I was scared to tell you about my mom at first, and I was scared of seeing pity or resentment in your eyes down the road if we took the chance. But mostly I was scared of trapping you and being a burden to you when you deserve—"

Before I can continue, she pushes me back again. "You don't get to decide what I deserve, Griffin. Who I love and choose is my decision, not yours, and you're wrong if you think otherwise. You don't get to make all the decisions for us. Love is a goddamn *partnership*, and if, *if* you got sick, then you bet your ass that I'd take care of you. If you lost your memories of us, then it's my goddamn duty to hold them close and remember for the both of us."

This woman. Every inch of her is magnificent. From the sunlight burning a halo around her head all the way down to the feet she has planted to better yell at me in a memory care facility parking lot.

Her voice quiets. "Don't you know that I'd take a second with you over a lifetime with anyone else?" She wipes at her face, cleaning the tears from her cheeks.

"I've been dealing with Mom's illness for a long time." I scrub a hand through my hair. "Always on my own. I knew that I if I could just work harder, be better, and do more, that she'd have the care she needed, and that I might be able to repay some of what she gave me growing up." I shove my hands into my pockets. "So I did that. I put in the time, I hit the pavement and accepted every job that I could to pay for her medical bills, her housing—no matter what, I didn't want to let her down."

I swallow hard before continuing. "But sometimes, I was so damn tired, so exhausted mentally and physically from holding everything together, that I couldn't help but think why me? Why did it have to be my mom that got sick? Why did I have to be the one to put in all the work? Why was I the one struggling?"

"Griff..."

I don't let her interrupt. "And I try not to let it eat at me, this resentment that sometimes crops up when I'm at the end of my leash. Then I'd feel guilty that I resented the work I needed to do and I'd pull myself back together. I know she's going to die. I know that this is temporary. But it sucks. Then there you were, so fucking beautiful and vivacious."

I grin at her. "You're fun and interesting, and the only way I'd ever blip on your radar was by driving you crazy. So that's what I did. Then we started working together, and I got to know you better, and the more that I learned, the harder I fell. You say you'd take a second with me over a lifetime with someone else, but I know that the lifetime would never be enough. I want it all, Wildflower."

"Then why the hell would you push me away?"

"Because knowing that you deserve better made me take a cold hard look in the mirror and realize that I deserve better too. No, not better than you. I deserve to be better for myself. I can't be a whole man for you if I'm only half of one for myself. So the last few weeks, I've been owning my shit and working through some stuff. I've got a long way to go and I'll never be perfect, but for you? I'll get as close as I fucking can."

"But what about getting sick? How do I know that you won't drop me like a bad habit if something happens?"

I swallow hard. "That's why I sent you the check in the first place."

"What?"

"I sent you the check back because I knew it would piss you off and I'd have my answer."

"Your answer?"

"If you didn't come find me, if you retreated like you did

the last couple of times I shoved my head up my ass, then I'd know you were done. If you came to find me…"

"That's so stupid. You drive me crazy! Why wouldn't you just come and talk to me?"

"Don't you know by now? You drive me crazy too. It's only fair to return the favor now and again."

She rolls her eyes at me. "Well, I found you. Now what?"

I pull her into my arms and ask, "Will you…will you come with me to the testing appointment?"

"Of course I will. Are you sure? We don't need to know…"

"Yeah, we do. I do. Knowing and not knowing doesn't change how in love with you I am. We both should know what we're getting into before I charm my way back into your heart."

She steps up to me and lays her lips across mine. "You never left. I love you. Please, just talk to me. Whatever it is, we can figure it out together, okay?"

"I love you too. I will. But we're going to have a serious talk about your situational awareness. Martin should have never gotten the jump on you, and I'm disappointed that you let him," I tease.

For the first time in days, the sun shines a little brighter because Meadow's smiling at me. This time it's the real deal.

"As much as I love having this conversation, I'm dying in this heat. And I have an appointment. Do you want to come with?" For the first time I look around for her car, and when I don't see it I ask, "Where'd you park?"

Meadow tucks her bangs behind her ear. "My sisters dropped me off. They assumed you wouldn't just leave me stranded here."

"They'd be right. I guess you have to come with me now. Come on." I usher her into my car.

On the way downtown, I tell her about the testing, the discussion with the doctor, and the steps that I'll be going through. Even if the tests come back normal, I'm going to get regular checkups to stay in the know. I don't tell her why I moved out, but when I pull into the parking garage at Aldric Aerospace, she gets a puzzled look on her face.

We make our way through the lobby and to the bank of elevators. I pull out a key card and swipe it for the top floor.

"Where are we going?" she asks.

"To meet more of my family."

"But I thought you said you..."

"Yeah, it was a shock to me too." I tell her about Gabriel and his dad while the elevator makes several stops to let people on and off.

Gabriel's assistant, Madeline, shows us into a conference room and offers us some water and snacks.

"How're you handling all this?"

"It was a shock at first. But the more I thought about it and hung out with Gabby—getting to know him and eventually his mom, I kinda like the idea of having a brother."

"Gabby?"

"Yeah, I figure I have about thirty years of annoying him to catch up on."

Meadow's laugh sparkles through the conference room like rainbows and sunbeams.

We don't wait more than ten minutes before Gabriel walks in with whom I'm assuming is the lawyer dealing with the whole thing and his mom. I didn't expect her to be here today, but I'm kinda glad that she is.

I stand and clap a hug around Gabriel. He's still not a

hundred percent comfortable with me yet, but we'll get there.

"This is Meadow Ridley," I say. "She's with me."

"Is this...?" Gabriel asks.

I nod. He and I have talked about Meadow and the case over the last few days.

Eleanor's face lights up. "Oh! I've heard so much about you. It's a pleasure. I'm Eleanor, Gabriel's mother."

"Should we get started?" the lawyer asks.

Meadow shoots a confused frown my way, so I explain, "I'm selling my half back to Gabriel and Eleanor, since it should have been theirs in the first place."

She rolls her lips. "Are you going to work for them or..."

I shake my head. "I was actually going to ask you if you could use me at the firm since I think that my freelance-work-until-I-collapse days are over."

"Hmm. You're an *okay* investigator. I'm sure we can find a place for you."

I lean over and lay my lips on hers before saying, "My place is always with you, Wildflower."

EPILOGUE
MEADOW

THERE ARE THREE THINGS IN THE WORLD THAT I LOVE beyond any measure. Almond butter, Griffin Gallagher, and my family. That love is why I've indulgently kept my silence while my boyfriend is about to climb the walls of this office.

Griffin's leg jiggles next to me, the light tap of his heel on the tile loud in the quiet waiting room. It's another stunner of a day, and I plan to take full advantage of it once we're done here. My boyfriend, on the other hand, looks grim as hell and I can't have that.

I set aside the magazine depicting the path to driving your man crazy in bed—thanks, but I've got it—and say, "How'd it feel to lose this morning, Gallagher?"

As expected, the taunt stops the leg shaking, and Griffin turns to me with a cocked eyebrow. "That's not how I remember it going down, Wildflower."

He's both right and wrong. I came out on top on the leaderboard, and he came out on top on the floor of our home gym after he hauled me off my bike and we had a bout of amazing sweaty sex.

Win-win, right?

"I owned your ass on the leaderboard this morning, or don't you remember?" I make like I'm reaching for my phone to remind him when he snags my hand, bringing it up to his mouth to nibble on.

"But I owned your ass afterward."

Oh boy, had he.

Since his doctor called to schedule the appointment to go over the results of the genetic testing, he's either been bouncing off the walls or staring into space with very little in between. Even during an impromptu trip to Vegas, he was distracted as hell the entire time we were there.

"You know it's going to be okay, right?" I ask.

"Griffin Gallagher?" A nurse calls from the open door, stopping him from being able to respond.

We've talked over what the results of the test are going to look like. Either way, we'll figure out a path forward, but I know that he's worried. Hell, I'm worried too, but I have faith that we can work through it together.

The last few months have been nothing less than bliss. Griffin formally interviewed with the firm, and Dad offered him a job. We start and end nearly every day together. Griffin bought a house, and even though I haven't officially moved in yet, it's inevitable when I spend every night there. I wake up with my guy, we go to work together, and then end the night with each other.

Sure, there have been some adjustments, and we're still figuring things out, but I love him and he loves me and that's all that matters to us both.

I've gone with him to visit his mother a few times, and we've managed to catch a lucky streak of clear days. My own mother has gone to visit her a few times as well, and on the good days our families are starting to blend in the best way possible.

And on the bad days? We hug each other a little tighter.

We both stand and follow the nurse to the exam room. Once inside, she goes over the basics of the appointment and leaves us to wait for the doctor to come in. Griffin takes my hand in a vise grip.

"Griff, look at me."

His brown eyes are filled with fear and apprehension.

I lean forward and brush my lips against his. "Do you want to leave? I don't care what a test says. We can walk right out that door and go back home. There's a piece of almond butter toast with our names on it."

A small smile curls his lips and he kisses me. Griffin Gallagher's kisses have ruined me, but it's a ruination I'll revel in until the end of time.

"No, Wildflower, I need to know. I'm just nervous, you know?"

"I know." And that's why I planned a middle of the week block party with the neighbors at my family's house. Most of the block took the day off from work to come together to celebrate my guy, regardless of the news he gets today.

"You know I'm so proud of you, right?"

Surprise covers his features. "What?"

"I'm proud of you. I know how hard this is for you. So you doing the testing and then coming in today for the results? You're incredibly brave."

"I'm only brave because I have you here."

I shake my head. "That's not true. Maybe my being here helps, but I believe you would have gotten the tests done anyway with or without me here."

Another of the changes that's taken place over the last

few months is Griffin's counseling. He contacted a grief counselor here in the valley and has a session every week. Sometimes he's raw after them, sometimes he's fine, sometimes I go, and sometimes I hold back, but he no longer locks away his emotions when he goes to see his mom. The days of him piling on a facade to visit are over. He's been working through his fear of the future as well, and this is just the first step to putting his mind at ease.

There's a brief knock at the door and Griffin calls out, "Come in."

I bring our clasped hands up and brush a kiss along the back of his. "We've got this."

#

I pull the car into my parents' driveway and kill the ignition. Griff hasn't said much since we left the doctor's office and frankly, I'm a little worried.

Not for us, but for him.

I don't know what he's feeling right now, but I want to.

The grills are out and adults are milling around. It's the beginning of November and cool outside, but we haven't gotten our first cold front.

"What are we doing here?" he asks.

"I planned for us to hang out with my family today. I didn't think—"

"It's okay, Mead. Come on."

We both climb out of the car and head toward where most of the camping chairs are set up. Like normal, there's a movie playing in the garage and the smell of grilled meat drifting through the air. But conversation dies down the closer we get to everyone.

Mom stands up and comes over to us, first giving me a hug and then gathering Griffin—who still looks a little shell-shocked—into her arms.

Dad follows but veers off and grabs drinks. After handing one to me and then Griffin, they exchange a handshake hug and Dad asks, "So, what's the news?"

The placid facial expressions don't fool me. The same tension that covered their faces when I wrecked the car my sisters and I shared in high school is apparent on their faces.

They're as worried about him as I am.

"I'd rather just tell everyone at once, if that's okay." His tone is deadpan and devoid of emotion.

"Of course, honey." Mom pops her fingers between her lips and lets out a shrill whistle. "Come on over, everyone. Griffin's got something to say."

Quieter to Griffin she says, "It's gonna be okay, honey. We've got you." My dad nods his agreement, and the first crack of emotion crosses Griffin's face, a small smile.

He's milking this for all he's worth. I roll my eyes.

Once the crowd of adults is close enough, he wraps his arm around my waist and says, "I got some news from the doctor today, and instead of telling it over and over I'd just like to say, the results for the APOE-4 gene came back negative in testing."

Instantly, there's a rush of excitement. Jenn whoops and Fawn laughs. The Laffertys clap and damn near everyone cheers.

His doctor explained the testing results, and the chance of his having Alzheimer's like his mother is rare, but they're still going to monitor him. While routine genetic testing isn't something they encourage, he's going to continue to see the doctors in case something changes in the future.

The relief on his face in the doctor's office isn't a memory that I'll ever forget.

If something changes down the line, then the only thing

that I can do is keep my promise to hold our memories close and love him all the same.

"Now that doesn't mean that I'm totally in the clear. The doctor explained that familial Alzheimer's is still a concern, because studies have shown that people with a direct family member with the disease are at a higher risk of being diagnosed. But I'll be working with my doctor to continue monitoring my health. But for now, we're good."

The tension that was thrumming through the group just minutes ago dissipates and now? Now the party's on.

After making the rounds for hugs and handshakes, Griffin looks around. "Is Gabe not here?"

I look around and sure enough, I can't find him. I know that I invited him, and he said he and Eleanor would be here. She's across the way talking to Mom about something in Mom's garden, and like always she's super dressed up for a basic block party, but I don't see Gabe anywhere.

"Maybe he's running late. I don't see Willow either, though."

I track down Mom and ask, "Is Willow here?"

"She said she would be late because she had a meeting this morning."

The sound of a car door slamming behind me catches my attention, and I turn to watch both Willow and Gabriel climbing out of his SUV. Willow bites something out to Gabriel, and he winces before his expression shutters.

What the hell are they doing together? The few times that we've gotten together over the last few months, they've barely interacted at all outside of arguing. We all hung out in Vegas over the weekend, but I didn't notice them spending any extra time together. Willow's chaos to Gabriel's cold aloofness was always bound to clash, but they've put aside the majority of their bickering.

Griffin calls out, "Hey big bro, did you hear the news?" Gabriel's shoulders stiffen, and he casts a glance at Willow who shakes her head.

Why the hell are they both acting so weird?

The two come over to stand by us, and my attention snags on Willow's left hand.

My sister, the chaos of our family, has an obscenely large diamond sitting on a very important finger.

I screech and reach out to grab her hand, but she whips it away and sticks it behind her back.

"What the hell is that?!" my voice booms out, and heads swivel our way.

Mom, Dad, Fawn, and Jenn all come over at the abject shock in my voice, and Griffin's staring his brother down in a glare that'd scare the fur off a tiger.

"You want to tell me what the hell is going on here?" he bites out.

Willow bites her lip, and for the first time in I don't know how long, Willow doesn't blurt out the answer to our question. My ballsy, whirlwind-personified sister stays silent. Instead, she looks to Gabriel, who's sporting a matching band on his very important finger.

"Are you...Did you two..." I can't say the words. They just won't form.

Gabriel reaches out and threads his fingers through my sister's, and just when my head is about to explode, he says, "Willow and I eloped."

"But it's for a job," my sister jumps in.

Holy shit.

EXTENDED EPILOGUE
MEADOW

"You're going down," I say. I tighten the strap of my bike shoe on my right foot and clip into the pedal before swinging my foot over to the other side and clipping in fully.

"Mm-hmm sure, Wildflower. Whatever you say."

Griffin's busy getting himself set up on his own bike when I pop my earbuds into my ears and click into the waiting room for the live class with one of my favorite instructors, Caleb. At first we had our bikes stationed next to each other for workouts, but after one too many arguments about one of us watching the other's screen, we turned them so they're back to back.

Like always, EagleEyeBeastPI is keeping me on my toes, but in the best ways possible now.

Life? Life is so good it's scary. Griffin asked me to move in shortly after we got the results of his testing back. He's kept up with his counseling and regular medical checkups. But the looming worry that something was going to go wrong has completely disappeared. Though there have been other changes in our lives, we're going with the flow, and living in the moment.

I sip my water while slowly pedaling to warm up my legs. The waiting room gives way to the start of the class just as my preworkout kicks in, the energy making my face itchy.

Every month or so, the celebrity instructor has fans ask questions on his Instagram page and then chooses questions to answer during a live ride. They're wildly popular and fun, and there's little to no competition because we all come for the antics this instructor is famous for.

Dressed in a neon tank and bright purple feathered boa, he's wearing his signature heart-shaped glasses when he mounts his own bike.

"Hey, boo..." he says and we're off.

The class itself is easy, and we're all moving at a moderate to easy pace as Caleb answers questions about life, love, sex, and everything in between. Most of the questions are tame, but the answers are anything but.

"All right, ladies and gents. Our next question is a doozy. G.G. from Phoenix, Arizona, asks, 'My girl and I have been together for seven months and I'm totally head over heels for her. Should I ask her to marry me, or is it too soon since she might not be ready for it yet?'"

Caleb takes a drink of his water and gathers his thoughts.

"I was going to say something cheesy about following your heart and gut instinct, but fuck that, boo. If you love this woman, you ask her to marry you, and if she says no? Then you keep asking her until her feelings catch up to yours. Life is short, y'all. So you listen to me, G.G. from Phoenix, Arizona—you go forth with confidence, and ask this woman to marry you."

He shakes his head, and I chuckle at the passionate snark in his voice. Caleb isn't one to mince words, and I mentally send the happy couple luck.

"I have a confession of my own to make," Caleb stage whispers into his mic. "That question didn't come from my IG post. It came from a fan who has something special planned. EagleEyeBeastPI, go get your girl!"

My left leg stops pedaling in shock, the forward momentum the only thing keeping my legs moving at all, and I gape at the leaderboard that shows Griffin's username falling farther and farther down the leaderboard.

I smack my hand down on the brake and twist off the seat.

"RollerSkatingRidley..." the rest of the instructor's words fade away as I turn around and take in Griffin down on one knee and our family standing behind him. I yank my headphones out of my ears.

"Wildflower, I love you. Will you be my wife and make a lifetime of memories with me that we'll both hold close?"

The first happy tear falls down my cheek, and I nod before croaking out, "Yes." Griffin's grin is brighter than the desert sun when he stands and swoops me into his arms.

"Considering they're both not showing up on the leaderboard, I'd say the proposal went well, y'all."

I turn around, and the instructor's voice comes from the bikes' speakers as I see high fives from other riders in the class explode across the leaderboard.

Turning back to Griffin, I kiss him, every promise, every hope, and every ounce of love I have for him evident in the lip-lock.

He pulls back and grabs my hand to slide the vintage-cut diamond and sapphire ring on my finger.

My family crowds around us, passing around hugs, handshakes, and hearty back slaps.

"How'd you pull this off?" I ask.

"I sent Caleb a message, and he said he'd be happy to

help. I figured since a large part of our relationship started with me skunking you on the leaderboard, it's only fitting that I make your dreams come true on it too."

"Make my dreams come true, huh?" I snark.

"From there, it was all just getting everything set up."

"And now? What happens next?"

"Now? Now I work on making you the happiest woman in the world, and just think, we can go pick up weird shit at Costco together now. Because all of my weird shit will be your weird shit."

I bark out a laugh and fist my hand in his shirt, hauling him in for another kiss.

This freaking man. If anyone's going to drive me crazy and compete with me for the rest of my life, I want it to be him.

To the sound of my family's happiness for me, I kiss the pain in my ass of my dreams.

I wouldn't have it any other way.

PER RIDLEY FAMILY TRADITION, a big-ass dinner was the only way to celebrate our engagement. I managed to catch a three-second shower before we were summoned downstairs with the troops.

Details flew around the table at Mach speed, but I caught a few salient details. By the time dishes are done and the house is empty, I have more than a wine buzz.

I have a love buzz.

I tuck the dishtowel around the handle of the stove and head out in search of my hubby-to-be. Mom and Dad were the last to leave, and when Griffin asked my mom to help him pick out his tux, I got all squishy emotional and beelined for the dishes.

Scrubbing grease is infinitely preferable to blubbering all over my fiancé and his forming relationship with my parents.

I climb the stairs, and at the top is a riot of wildflower petals leading to our bedroom. My heart swoons at the sight, and I carefully step around them toward the cracked open bedroom door.

Griffin's too busy to notice me watching him as he works around the room lighting candles. The soft, content look on his face is relaxed and happy all at once, and I marvel at the thought that I put that there. I make him happy enough that he wants to take the chance of forever on us.

My eyes prickle and before I get too emotional, I push the door open wider. "Griffin?"

He turns to me, and the smile on his face is enough to make my soul sigh with happiness.

"Hey there, Wildflower." He crosses the room and draws me into his arms. He pulls the stereo remote out of his pocket, and when an achingly slow ballad plays through the surround sound, he sways me to the melody of the song.

Excitement, plans, details, dates...I let all of that fall away with the press of Griffin's body against mine. His lips press to my temple and trail down my neck. The slow sweetness of the dance turns hotter when he presses his lips to mine and licks into my mouth.

I'll never get enough of the taste of him on my tongue as I kiss him back.

He slips the straps of my dress off my shoulders, and the basic sundress I threw on after my shower earlier drifts to my feet. His hands come up to cup my face and he lays his lips on mine, more gently this time.

I drag his shirt up and off and slowly work him out of his clothes, our touch lingering on each other while we kiss in the candlelight.

We make our way to the bed, and I fall lightly against the flowers he's sprinkled across the comforter. His lips work their way down my body, first at my neck, then my breasts, and across my belly before he settles himself between my legs.

The first swipe of his tongue against my core has my hips shooting up to grind against his face.

"Ah, ah. You'll get what you're looking for, but only when I'm ready." The whispered decree makes me shiver even as I reach down and lace my fingers through his. With his free hand, he dips a finger into my core, my inner muscles clamping down on the digit in an effort to keep him there.

He sucks softly at my clit, mouth and fingers slowly working me until my release unfurls through me. I pant to catch my breath as he leans over to snag a condom. Once he's covered, he lifts my legs around his waist and slides inside me. The sudden fullness is enough to steal my breath again.

Achingly slow and tender, we move against each other until the tension in my stomach tightens and I find my peak again. My toes curl, and the muscles in my belly quiver as another devastating orgasm rocks my system.

Griffin's rhythm increases, the steady cadence falling away to something faster, something more primal, and there's a split second of tension creasing his face before he finds his release, the kick and throb of his cock unmistakable. I clench my core around him to heighten his pleasure, and he chokes out a garbled version of my name.

He drops down and covers me with his body, pressing a kiss first to my forehead and then to my lips.

"I love you, Wildflower. Thank you for being mine."

"Thank you for letting me be yours. I love you too."

Thank you so much for reading All's Fair in Love and Leaderboards!

Turn the page for a sneak peek of Bridegroom and the Boardroom featuring the fiesty firebrand Willow and her hero Gabe, or as Willow likes to call him, Prissy Gabe.

SNEAK PEEK OF BRIDEGROOM AND THE BOARDROOM

WILLOW

"What do you mean, this place is closing?"

I shift my feet and my shoe chooses that moment to come unstuck from the floor with a *scriiiip*. Yellowed walls, dingy flooring that's a little sticky no matter how many times we scrub it, and temperamental flickering lights make up one of my favorite places in the world.

The Steward Center.

Sure, it's worn in, but it's clean, it's safe, and it's a haven to many.

It might not have some of the bells and whistles bigger centers do, but I've been volunteering here since I was a teenager, and it's a second home to me.

"The building's being sold. Once our lease is up, we have to be out."

Lynn Steward is family. She might not be blood, but she's another mother to me all the same. With a single look, she's able to put me in my place, and with a warm hug, she's cured all my woes. I've seen her cry one single time when her husband passed away a couple of years back. The fact there are tears in her eyes right now speaks volumes.

"What about the guests?"

"I'm reaching out to other centers to see if they have room."

"And if they don't?" The question is soft but necessary.

"I don't know."

We don't have a huge capacity, but we have about a hundred and fifty people living here now, and the shelters in the Valley are overrun as it is. We're coming up on the holiday season and it's damn near impossible to find places for people right now. We need some serious upgrades and renovations, but there's never enough money. The thought of these doors closing chokes the air from my chest.

A glance at the clock shows I'm late, but I take a second longer to hold one of Lynn's hands in mine. "Have you told them?"

"Not yet. I was trying to see if I could find them places before I break the news."

Having the information of where the residents go next would soften the blow, but that's assuming that they *have* somewhere to go next.

"Don't make any calls yet, and don't tell them. I'm going to fix this. I have to go teach this class, but we'll talk after, okay?"

"Okay." Defeat saturates her tone, and I've never seen her so worn down.

I start back toward the general purpose room. The same room that these women and children eat in. Where they come every day to work on themselves. Where they put their families first. Where they grow and heal. My heart pinches at the thought of it all not existing anymore, until I have to blink back my own tears.

No. I can fix this. I don't know how, but I know I can.

The tables have been cleared, the floors covered with thick mats to soften landings.

I started out as a gofer, going where help was needed in the center. Over the years and through training for numerous belts in martial arts, I channeled all my knowledge into something constructive. Something *useful*.

That's when I got certified and started offering self-defense classes here.

Not everyone at the shelter is a survivor of domestic violence or comes from a background of abuse, but everyone's personal safety is priceless, and if they only absorb enough from these classes to avoid a single dicey situation, it's a win in my book.

"Hey, everyone! Let's get started. Everyone square off. We're going to start with the basics. Sing to me, babes."

A practiced chorus of "Eyes, throat, nose, and groin" is called out to the kids' song "Head, Shoulders, Knees, and Toes."

I smile and clap when they're done. "A symphony to my ears. For those of you who haven't been here before, those are the soft tissue, low pain tolerance places on the body. Know them. Love them. Remember them. And if you need to, use them. I'm Willow Ridley, resident badass, and I'll be your instructor for the day. Now, if we're getting bad vibes, what's the first thing we do?"

I fall into my routine. I love teaching these classes, and energy courses through me. I walk them through the beginning stages of self-defense, which aren't actually defense but trusting your instincts and practicing target denial. If you can get away before the first blow is thrown, it's always preferable to sticking around.

There's a cadence to these classes. The beginning of the

course is the warm-up, and participants loosen up and start to have fun with it while paying close attention to the physical steps of most of the moves. Their confidence starts to build the more they do, and it's beautiful to watch. It also helps that it's a physical outlet and something they can control when control's often been absent in their lives.

My job is to empower the residents here. I love my job.

For every drill we run, we talk it through for at least double the amount of time before we practice it over and over again. Muscle memory in dangerous situations can save lives.

"Dan, you're up," I call out.

Dan Crawfield is a fresh eighteen-year-old and disinterested in just about everything. He, his mom, and six-year-old sister have been residents here for a few months. All three of them have been in my classes since they got here.

He's one of the few guys around the center, and considering he's built like a linebacker, he helps a lot of the time in class, despite being quiet and shy.

"Dan's going to grab me from behind; pay attention to what I do." I bobble my eyebrows at him and his cheeks turn red.

I turn back toward the group and let my body relax.

Dan lurches forward in a parody of attack, and I let him get his arms around me before I shift my hips and twist to throw my elbow back toward his face—stopping a millisecond before making contact with his nose. He drops his arms and takes a stuttering step back.

Murmurs of surprise run through the crowd. I toss the kid a wink and turn back to the group. "If someone grabs you from behind, stay calm; you can get out of the hold. Dan's arms were around my stomach, which left my arms unhindered and gave me the opportunity to defend myself." I pace in front of the women. "This wasn't rehearsed. Dan's reaction to my elbow nearly making contact with his oh-so-handsome mug was authentic and what you can expect from an attacker."

"What if they grab you higher?" Emily Bruce—one of the newest guests—asks.

"That's a great question. Let me show you what to do and then we'll practice it."

I walk them through the steps and stages to avoid, evade, and, if necessary, fight their way out of a confrontation. They put on threadbare protective gear to square off with partners and start to simulate the scenario using what I'm teaching to stay safe.

Dan's a good sport and some of his stiffness leaks away the more we work through the moves. At first he refused to even step foot into these classes, equating helping with them to being like his father, something that terrified him at the time. I had him sit in and worked with him a little one-on-one before he was comfortable enough with *why* we offer them to help out.

When I was seventeen, I spent the bulk of my time blowing off schoolwork and wondering if Jensen from third-period chemistry kissed as well as rumors suggested.

At the same age, Dan was hospitalized for the injuries his father inflicted when he tried to stop him from hitting his mom. She got them all out of there and we helped her to find a job. All three of them are seeing a therapist, both individually and as a family.

"Come on, cutie, let's run through it again." I blow him a kiss as we square off, and he shakes his head at me.

Should I be shamelessly flirting with an eighteen-year-old? Probably not considering I have a decade in age on him. But I do a lot of things that I shouldn't, and at least my overt flirting is harmless and puts a smile on his face.

When he first came here, he could barely make eye contact with me or any of the counselors. My heart hurts for his stolen childhood. Seeing little bits of himself he tucked away under the abusive regime of his father peek back through makes me ecstatic. The fact that he not only looks at me but also blushes and rolls his eyes at me is proof this place is fundamental for him and for the community.

We can't close.

I won't let us close.

I GUZZLE WATER AFTER CLASS. The mats are mopped and tucked away, the tables set back up in anticipation of dinner when Dan's mom, Debbie, calls my name. "Willow, a minute?"

"Sure, what's up?"

"You said that you had a friend with a job opening?"

"Cameron?"

"Yes, him. A skating rink, if I remember correctly?"

My eyes narrow in question. "Is the admin position gig not working anymore?"

"Oh no, it's working wonderfully, but Dan wants to get a job so he can pay for his community college classes, and I wondered if it might work out for him?"

"Oh! Great idea. Dan would be perfect. Let me get with Cameron and then we can set up an interview."

"And Cameron, is he..."

I catch the slightest inkling of worry from her. "Cam's a

good guy. He's one of my closest friends. He'd be a solid role model for Dan. Promise."

The pinch between her eyebrows disappears, and she blows out a breath. "Okay. I think this would be good for Dan. Do you think that would be good for him?"

"Oh, for sure."

"What'll be good for me?" the guy in question asks from behind me.

"I'll let your mom talk to you about it, big guy." I skirt around them and back to my bag. Once the strap is slung over my shoulder, I head back to the office. Lynn's door is open, and she's working on something in Excel when I drop down into the chair behind her.

"Okay. Let's see what we're dealing with. The building is being sold?"

Lynn turns from her desk and hands a stack of papers to me. It's a breakdown of the current lease terms and a notice of intent to sell the property, followed by the contact information for the real estate company handling the sale.

"Do you know if the new owners will allow you to lease the building like you have been?"

"I don't know yet. But that's cutting it close for placement at other locations if I wait to talk to the new owners of the building."

She's got a point. Usually getting placed at a shelter takes time, effort, and a shit ton of luck. The homeless population in the Valley is rampant, but when you throw in families on top of it? That's a lot of bodies to move.

"Okay. Can we buy the building? Is there enough money for us to try to swing that? Maybe the owners will give you a deal?"

There's gotta be *something* we can do.

"I don't have the funds for the purchase or even a loan,

Willie. It's way out of our budget. Even if I applied for grants, I wouldn't get them before we have to be out." She slides another paper to me, the real estate logo at the top, the same one named in the notice to sell.

The figure highlighted and underlined on the listing steals the air from my lungs, and I have to squeeze my eyes shut in hopes that when I open them it's a whole lot less than the seven-figure fiasco we're looking at.

Over two million dollars for this place. There's no way we'd be able to raise that amount of money in the three months they've given us to make a decision.

She leans back in her chair. "Yeah. I had the same reaction. This damned economy. Everything is more expensive, but very little of it needs to be. That purchase price is as is too."

"What does that mean?"

"It means that the laundry list of repairs that the landlord has been putting off would fall to the new owners to fix. The roof, the plumbing, the electrical? All of them need to be overhauled and I haven't had the money to just do it myself. We're stretched thin, being at capacity."

"And they're not going to try to fix any of that before they sell?"

"Nope."

"Fudge knuckles."

"Fudge knuckles?" she asks.

"I'm trying to curb my swearing. Megan's daughter said 'shit' after class last week and I got 'the look.'"

Mom looks are real, they're scary, and I will do just about everything in my power to avoid them. Why buck authority when you can avoid the long arm of the mom law?

Lynn laughs and my mission is accomplished.

"Can we raise the funds for the purchase?" I ask. Maybe she has some ideas.

My caseload is light right now, so I have the time to help more than I normally would. I'm here three days a week, on top of my regular workload at Phoenician Investigations. I could swing by at least another day or two. If I tapped Cam, he'd be able to help with some of the repairs that need to be made around here, plus my family would help if I asked them. But that doesn't even address the humongous price tag this place comes with, not to mention the operating and upkeep expenses. Lynn already squeezes every penny she spends.

Talk about a molehill problem turning into a mountain.

"We'd have to hustle our asses off—and again, it's cutting it really close for these families. I was looking at other properties—"

I wave that away. Buying another place would be just as expensive and then we'd have to figure out how to outfit it. Plus, this place is home. We can't move. "Let me talk to my family. Let's see what we can do."

Lynn smiles sadly. "Unless you guys suddenly became millionaires, I don't think there are a lot of options here."

Wait a second. Wait a fucking second.

We didn't become millionaires recently, but someone close to us did.

I'd bet my ass that same someone is going to propose to my sister or I'll eat my shorts. So that makes him almost family—like very nearly family.

You can ask family for help, right?

"Can you give me a week?"

"Sure, I don't know what good it'll do, though."

Asking my sister's boyfriend to purchase a commercial

property to save my favorite women's shelter isn't too much to ask, is it?

For good or ill, I'm about to find out.

WANT MORE? Snag Bridegroom and the Boardroom on all retailers now!

WANT ALL THE NEWS?

Sign up for my newsletter to stay up to date on the latest book news, receive exclusive content and be entered for giveaways.

Not a fan of newsletters?

Join my reader group! The Happily Ever After Addicts on Facebook has all the teasers, excerpts, random pickup lines my husband hits me with and bookish news you'll need from me!

ALSO BY ALINA LANE

The HeartFelt Series

Reclaimed Love

Love Reimagined

Uncovered Love

Phoenician Heat

All's Fair in Love and Leaderboards

Bridegroom and the Boardroom

ACKNOWLEDGMENTS

First off, thank YOU reader. I don't have the words to express my joy and gratitude that you took a chance on my book. I hope you loved this story as much as I loved writing it.

Nick - You're always my number one fan. Thank you for pushing me to be better, do better and reach for my dreams. I couldn't do this without your support and love.

C & B - Do I even really need to say all the things you do for me or how much you both mean to me? Thanks for being in my corner and having my back. Sorry I'm a nutcase, but you're stuck with me now!

Jenn, Sax, Mel & Kan - I love you all to pieces and am so thankful for you in my life.

Jess - Thank you for forcing me out of my comfort zone, for being there when I hit a wall and helping me do the damn thing. I wouldn't be where I am without your guidance, support and encouragement.

Happily Editing Anns - Woofty. This story was a mess amiright?! Thank you for your keen eyes, diligent edits and thorough knowledge of the rules to the English language —

which I've apparently completely forgotten since high school.

Members of RWR and The HEA Club - I'm so lucky that I'm part of not one, but two amazing groups that support my career and me as a person. Thanks for being awesome!

Because I always feel like I forget someone - This thank you is for *YOU*. Thank you for helping me to create and craft beautiful stories.

ABOUT THE AUTHOR

A pocket-sized powerhouse, Alina lives with her personal Hunky Hero and two children in Arizona. Slathering on sunscreen and living life to its fullest she enjoys hiking, camping, fishing and rock climbing in her desert backyard.

When not hard at work on your next literary escape, you can find Alina embracing her bad-assery on Call of Duty, binge reading or baking her heart out.

Sign up for her newsletter to stay up to date on the latest Alina news.

You can follow Alina on:

Reader Group: Happily Ever After Addicts

Website: AlinaLane.com

Facebook: AlinaLaneAuthor

Instagram: AlinaLaneAuthor

39807768R00187